# IMPROBABLE
# MAGIC
## *for*
# CYNICAL
# WITCHES

## ALSO BY KATE SCELSA

*Fans of the Impossible Life*

# IMPROBABLE MAGIC for CYNICAL WITCHES

## KATE SCELSA

BALZER + BRAY

*An Imprint of HarperCollinsPublishers*

Balzer + Bray is an imprint of HarperCollins Publishers.

Improbable Magic for Cynical Witches
Copyright © 2022 by Kate Scelsa
Tarot cards by Wonder-studio / Shutterstock
All rights reserved. Printed in Lithuania.
No part of this book may be used or reproduced in any manner whatsoever without
written permission except in the case of brief quotations embodied in critical
articles and reviews. For information address HarperCollins Children's Books, a
division of HarperCollins Publishers, 195 Broadway, New York, NY 10007.
www.epicreads.com

Library of Congress Control Number: 2021950862
ISBN 978-0-06-246503-0

Typography by Jenna Stempel-Lobell
22 23 24 25 26   SB   10 9 8 7 6 5 4 3 2 1
❖

First Edition

For Mom

# IMPROBABLE
# MAGIC
### *for*
# CYNICAL
# WITCHES

# THE FOOL

Hello and welcome, human seeker.

If you have found this book, it means that it has found you.

Just a warning: you may find after picking up this book that magic begins to enter your life unexpectedly. Please proceed accordingly.

The journey that you are about to embark on is the journey that we all must take. It is the life journey. The hero's journey. The human journey.

Start at the beginning.

With the Fool.

Dear Fool. Foolish Fool.

Look at you. A cheerful blond dude with a feather in your cap and a flower in your hand, standing at the edge of a cliff, staring out at the vista. Not a care in the world. You probably took a long hike to get up here. *Why not?* you thought. *It's a nice day.* You've got your little dog at your side, your essential possessions tied up to carry on your shoulder. The sun is shining. The bell sleeves of your Ren faire tunic are blowing delicately in the wind. And you have absolutely no idea what's coming.

The soul's journey begins here. So what must you start now, even if you are not ready, you can't be ready, you wouldn't even know how to be ready? What is going to begin whether you are ready or not?

Something's coming, friend. Watch for it. Keep an eye out along that vista. It'll be here before you know it.

The mail being delivered to the Salem Gift Emporium on Essex Street in Salem, Massachusetts, on a quiet September afternoon is not normally a remarkable occasion. It's our regular drop of pre-Halloween-season deliveries, which mostly consists of box after box of witch-themed crap—black capes and black cat figurines and mugs with Samantha from *Bewitched* on them.

This non-momentous occasion has interrupted my non-momentous activity of sitting behind the counter at the Salem Gift Emporium bored out of my mind, watching the slow September foot traffic move past the window. Susan doesn't allow phones at work. She says I "don't look ready to help the customers" if I'm staring at a screen. So instead I mostly do nothing.

I have found that the key to fighting boredom is to tell yourself that you are not really bored. You are actually quite interested in the minutia of daily life. That tree across the street. The cars going by. That guy who likes to protest in front of the store sometimes, brandishing his *Witchcraft Is Evil* sign like it's his last hope on earth. At least he has a hobby.

I did not choose to work here at the Salem Gift Emporium. Just as I did not choose to live in Witch City, USA. My mother barely even chose to live here. And yet here I am, surrounded by pink T-shirts that say *I'm 100% THAT witch* and plastic broomstick key chains. This is the tackiest of Salem, Massachusetts. And it is where I work six days a week.

When you are unimaginably bored, there are two things that you definitely do not want to do. The first is to let yourself start thinking about anything other than what is right in front of you: the tree, the traffic, the guy with his protest sign—they are all that can exist for you right now. Anything else needs to be pushed aside—dreams, plans, memories—those things will rush right into the void that is boredom and cause you only pain.

The second thing you do not want to do is think about the fact that not thinking would be much easier if you were high right now.

*I cannot be high at work. I cannot be high at work. I cannot be high at work.*

This is what I repeat to myself as I stare at the tree across the street and wonder when the leaves will start to change and when the damp, horrible chill will enter the air and enter my bones and bring everything that comes with it.

October was always a terrible month in Salem. Now it is the worst.

But with the delivery of the mail comes at least a temporary

4

break in boredom. There are boxes to be opened and invoices to be sorted. There is something to do other than sit here and feel sorry for myself, which sometimes feels like my actual full-time job.

Susan comes out of her office in the back of the store when she hears Tim the postman come in.

"Big order today, huh?" Tim says as he stacks up the boxes of deliveries.

"October waits for no woman," Susan says, already examining the shipping labels.

Tim hands me a pile of mail.

"How about you? You ready for witch season?" he asks, winking at me.

"I tend to think of it more as 'drunken jerks in mass-produced plastic costumes that will soon end up in a landfill' season," I say, going through the stack of mail.

"Where are the kids' witch hats?" Susan asks, shoving boxes aside. "They're still not here. They should have gotten here yesterday."

Tim gives me a "good luck" look and heads out.

"Which hats?" I ask Susan.

"Exactly!" she says. I can't tell if this is an intentional joke on my unintentional pun or not, because she is already heading back into her office.

I resume sorting the mail, which is mostly bills and special offers coming up for our town's big month of notoriety. But at the bottom of the stack, there is a larger silver envelope addressed to the store without a return address on it.

Susan comes out of the back room with a box of T-shirts and the phone attached to her ear.

"Why yes, I do happen to know that witches are really popular right now, Alex. I run a witch-themed gift shop. And no matter how popular witches are, that does not change the fact that you promised me that my regular Halloween order would be in by now. One hundred pointy black hats are not going to do me a lot of good come November first."

Susan starts stacking shirts on the shelf. She looks over at me and rolls her eyes. I look down at the silver envelope in my hand, turn it over, and see a purple ink stamp of a familiar image. Two crescent moons facing away from each other with a circle in the middle. The triple goddess. It's a witch thing. There's no getting away from witch things in this town.

"Susan?" I say.

She holds up a finger to indicate that she needs a minute.

"Yeah, sure," she says into the phone. "You go talk to your supervisor and get back to me. Bye-bye now." She hangs up and angrily tosses the phone into the box of shirts. "It's like he doesn't understand that we bring in ninety percent of our income in one month."

"He doesn't know Salem," I say.

"I mean, look around." Susan gestures dramatically around at the empty store. "No customers. Three weeks from now?"

This is a familiar rant. I know my part.

"Customers," I say in a monotone.

"That's right, Eleanor. October means customers. And customers mean I can pay the rent. And paying the rent means I can pay you."

"And paying me means Mom and I can eat," I say. This is meant to be a funny continuation of the regular script, but of course it is not funny at all, and I regret it as soon as I say it. Susan stops stacking T-shirts.

"How is your mom today?" she asks, suddenly serious.

I shrug. "The same as when you saw her two days ago."

"Did she hear back from that new doctor yet?"

I don't want to tell Susan that she shouldn't get her hopes up. Mom has been to so many "new doctors" with "new approaches" that I lost count a while ago. But if I say this, Susan will get upset, and I just need this day to ride out calmly until I can get to the parking lot of the convenience store at the end of the street and smoke half the joint that is waiting in my bag.

"I don't know," I say.

Susan raises an eyebrow. "You don't know?"

"You should ask her yourself," I say.

Susan does not like this answer, but she accepts it and resumes stacking. "Well, I can come over tonight with some soup I made. It's really good. Creamy celery."

"You don't have to do that."

"It's no bother."

We each pretend to be absorbed in our tasks now, because there is nothing else to say about this.

I finish sorting the mail, putting the bills in Susan's in-box and tossing out the pile of Halloween propaganda. The silver envelope is still sitting on the counter.

I hold it up.

"Do you know what this is?" I ask Susan.

"No, what is it?"

"I mean that I don't know."

"Open it."

I rip open the back of the envelope, tearing the moon symbol in half, and pull out a small book, photocopied on thin paper and stapled together. The title is written out in flowery cursive.

"It says, 'The Major Arcana, A Magical Guide to the Story Cards of the Smith Rider Waite Tarot Deck.'"

I open the book to the first page. There is a picture of a figure looking up at the sky with handwritten text under it.

*Hello and welcome, human seeker.*

"Maybe it's a sample?" Susan says. "Is there an order form with it?"

"No," I say. "And it looks homemade."

"You can just toss it," Susan says. She finishes stacking the T-shirts.

"We carry that tarot deck, don't we?" I ask.

Susan pulls a small box off the shelf and hands it to me.

"You going to learn how to tell the future?"

"I don't think I want to know the future," I say, trying to make another joke that I realize once again isn't funny.

"You never know," she says.

"If the past is any indication, I can tell you that none of it's good," I say, digging in further. I silently make a vow to stop talking for the rest of my life.

Susan ignores this. It is often best to ignore the things that I say. I open the box and take out the stack of cards.

"Hey, did you process those returns I asked you to do?" Susan asks me.

I put the cards down.

"If you asked me to do it, then I did it," I say, annoyed.

"Um, okay," Susan says, giving me a look.

"I mean, who buys thirty ceramic cups in the shape of a pumpkin just to return them all?"

"Evelyn Rosco does that, after she decides to switch the theme of her fortieth birthday party from 'autumn' to 'puppies.'"

"Evelyn Rosco is an idiot," I say, grumbling.

"Eleanor, honestly. What is wrong with you today?"

Poor Susan. She is not my mother, but her proximity to my mother makes me treat her like my mother sometimes. Especially when I feel like I must at least make an attempt to be pleasant around my mother, who has her hands full dealing with her own problems. So then Susan gets monster me. Grumpy me. The Real Me.

In pictures of them together from college, my mom and Susan look like twins, or as close to twins as my white mom could look to her Korean best friend. They had the same layered haircut, same overdrawn eyeliner and semi-ironic accessories. But these days Susan looks healthy and content, and my mom looks like someone who is very sick. Because she is.

"Sorry," I say. "Nothing's wrong. I'm fine."

"Well, maybe I can interest you . . . in some vagina vases?"

This is one of Susan's favorite jokes. The feminist collective store down the street, the polar opposite on the witch spectrum from Susan's store, once had a sign in the window that declared, *We Have Vagina Vases!*

This always makes me laugh, and I am grateful to Susan for the one millionth time for putting up with me and letting all my terrible moods fade away as quickly as they roll in.

She picks up the empty T-shirt box.

"I'll be in the back screaming at some more suppliers. If you hear shattering glass, do *not* call the police."

"Understood."

Susan goes back to her office, and I look at the two objects on the counter in front of me. The stapled booklet and the tarot deck. I turn the book over to see if there's anything on the back that might offer some clue about its origins.

*A short history*, it says.

The Smith Rider Waite deck is over a century old, although copies of it continue to be made that eliminate the name "Smith" from the title, which arguably eliminates the most important person from receiving credit for our magical tool. Waite was just a dude with an interest in the occult. Rider was his publisher. While the PERSON WHO DID THE WORK and created these iconic illustrations was named Pamela Colman Smith. The true mama of the tarot. Mystic. Suffragette. She could see sound. She liked to paint pictures of naked blue cat women. Her nickname was Pixie.

This is for Pixie.

As easily the least witchy person in Salem, I am not normally one to indulge a mysterious book that arrives in the mail. As far as I'm concerned, the only remarkable thing about this town is that it has managed to turn a gruesome historical tragedy into its own personal theme park. It's a place where the actually morbid is transformed into a parody of itself, a plastic fiction, a buyable commodity.

But there is something about how bored I am, how I have nothing better to do than flip through our display deck of the (Smith) Rider-Waite to find the Fool card, that keeps me engaged in this mystery for just a little longer.

There he is—a jaunty guy with a little dog, looking like he's ready to fall off that cliff. I rest my head on the counter and prop the card on the box in front of my face.

*Something's coming.*

I'm staring at the Fool when the bell on the shop door rings and two girls who I don't recognize come in. A girl with a blond buzz cut wearing a floral floor-length dress that would not look out of place on an Amish farm woman, and a taller, dark-haired girl wearing a bright blue silk robe over a black dress, her hair up in braids entwined with flowers.

"Did we wake you?" the blue-robe girl says to me with a smirk as I sit up and attempt to look helpful. Before I can respond, she begins flipping through a "history of Salem" book that she has taken off the shelf.

We don't get a lot of people my age in the store. The kids from Salem High actively stay away, a nice by-product of their ongoing mission to avoid any contact with me at all costs. The feeling is mutual. And although unusual outfits are not uncommon in this town, these two extravagantly dressed girls entering the store feels like an event. I suddenly feel very underdressed in my dirty black jeans and slightly-less-dirty black T-shirt.

I don't realize that I am staring at the flower-dress girl until she looks over at me and catches my eye. I quickly look down and pretend to be deeply engaged in reading the little tarot book.

"I think we should go to the library," blue-robe girl says to flower-dress girl.

"We'll go to the library next," flower-dress girl says.

"Can I help you find something?" I ask.

Blue-robe girl approaches the counter. "I'm looking for a map of the witch trial locations. Like a walking tour map."

"Walking tours leave from the kiosk down the street three times a day," I say. "Five times a day in October."

The girl shakes her head. "I obviously have been to all the locations already," she says, somehow annoyed with me.

Her friend is standing behind her, looking around the store as if there's anything special to be found here, rather than a bunch of tacky junk.

"I need the physical object of the map," blue-robe girl continues. "The commodified, capitalist, fetishized, mass-produced *thing* that attempts to profit off the deaths of perse-cuted women."

This is a slightly more interesting request than the usual "Do you have a beer cozy with a witch on it?" questions we usually get in here.

"We don't have a map," I say. "We've got a lot of other crap that fits that description, though. Take your pick."

This makes flower-dress girl laugh. I am not sure if she is laughing at me or with me. But it is when she laughs that I happen to notice that this girl is very, very cute. Like, uncomfortably cute.

Her friend is less amused. She sighs in a way that implies that I have exhausted her and goes back to browsing the shelves. I sneak another look at her friend, who is now looking at the deck of tarot cards in my hand.

"Do you read?" she asks me.

"No. Just looking at the pictures."

"Reading is just looking at the pictures very, very closely," she says. She comes over to the counter and takes the Fool out of my hand. "My favorite card."

"Why?" The closer she gets to me, the more the fact of her cuteness becomes difficult to ignore.

"He's the sign of new beginnings. Of allowing yourself to dream. Nothing happens without the Fool."

"Yeah, but he's not called 'intelligent dreamer' or 'starting-over guy,'" I say. "He's called the 'Fool.' And he looks like he's about to fall off that cliff."

The girl smiles and hands the card back to me. The tip of her finger brushes my hand, and I feel the sensation traveling up my arm until it gets to my face, where I am pretty sure I am turning bright red.

"No way," she says. "He's just getting a good look at things before he sets off on his journey. If it ended now, then there would be no story to tell. And the story is the whole point."

"Pix, I'm going to that T-shirt store on the corner," blue-robe girl says, the bell ringing as she goes out the door.

"Be right there," the flower-dress girl calls back.

"Your name is Pix?" I ask.

She smiles. I notice that her eyes close a little when she smiles, as if she is on the verge of laughing, as if she is savoring the joy. "Penny, officially," she says. "But she started calling me that when I cut my hair short. When Ofira gives you a nickname, it tends to stick. So I'm Pixie now."

Something inside me does a double backflip when she says this.

"That's so funny," I say. "I was just reading about the woman who drew these pictures. . . ."

"Pix!" The other girl has stuck her head back in the door, evidently deciding that Pix is taking too long to follow her.

"I'm Eleanor," I say, desperate to say something else to this girl before she leaves. "No nickname."

"Well," Pix says. "We'll have to do something about that."

*Triple backflip.*

She smiles and turns toward the door.

"What does she need the map for?" I ask before she can go, stalling to find some way to keep her from leaving me alone with my thoughts.

Pix seems to think about it for a moment before answering.

Then she says, "Just some witchcraft," and goes out the door.

I watch her walk down the block through the window— going after her best friend? Girlfriend?

*No, no, no. No good can come of this line of thinking.*

To distract myself, I open up "The Major Arcana, A Magical Guide to the Story Cards of the Smith Rider Waite Tarot Deck" again.

*Something's coming, friend. Watch for it. Keep an eye out along that vista. It'll be here before you know it.*

I turn the page.

# THE MAGICIAN

Oh, Magician. You really seem to think a lot of yourself for someone standing in such close proximity to a guy named "the Fool." You know that you're just one step away from court jester, right? Conjuring visions, making a big show of presenting mystical truths in front of our eyes, telling us that magic is real. You claim to be someone who can translate spiritual wisdom into something we can understand here on earth. When what we know is that you're really just a guy who figured out how to pull a rabbit out of a hat.

The truth is that you do have some inside info. One arm pointing up, the other pointing down, you are here to tell us, "As above, so below." The heavens reflect the earth. The world outside us reflects the world inside us. The brain reflects the heart.

On the table in front of you are the tools of the tarot. Pentacles, cups, swords, and wands. These represent the suits of the other cards, the minor arcana. You've got it all at your disposal to put on a good show for us. Some flashy lights and maybe a sequined cape and a top hat wouldn't hurt. Sometimes we need a little sugar to help the medicine go down.

We see you and ask ourselves—what is my song and dance? How do I make it through my days transforming difficult truths into a good show? How do I play the game that must be played, entertain the people who must be entertained, pull my rabbit out of my hat?

And how do I disappear into a puff of smoke?

Puffs of smoke happen to be my specialty.

I didn't mean to become someone who smokes pot every day. Sometimes these kinds of things just happen—when you can't stand the taste of alcohol and everyone around you is wasted every Saturday night. When the stoner kids at the party are much calmer than the drunk people you're with. When you start buying from the most notorious stoner in school, first just enough to get you through Saturday nights, then entire weekends, and finally the whole week. When somehow everything that's wrong feels just less wrong enough to become bearable when you blow a hazy layer of smoke over your own existence.

I look at the Magician card just before I leave the store for the day. He's wearing white and red robes with flowers growing above and below him. Is that a magic wand in his hand?

*Alakazam! Your life is no longer terrible!*

That seems like too big a magic trick to ask for, so how about something neutral, like a calm day? Wave a joint over me and turn me into someone who can successfully walk the ten blocks home without having a panic attack. Who can calmly climb the stairs up to our third-floor attic apartment. Who can be a kind and agreeable daughter. Transform me, oh Magician, not into a rabbit or a bouquet of flowers, but into a human who can make it through another day.

"Sanderson, you're late!"

Simon is waiting on our usual corner, ready to walk me part of the way home, as he does every Thursday. He's replaced the "white stoner boy" beanie that is the uniform of his friend group with a Red Sox baseball cap that he thinks helps him look more like a respectable preppy jock for when he is making his "deliveries." But because everyone knows everyone in this town, I have a feeling that all it accomplishes is alerting people that he's open for business.

My last name is actually Anderson, not Sanderson. This is Simon invoking the witch sisters from the movie *Hocus Pocus*, which was filmed all over this town. This is what passes for humor in Salem.

"Give me a break. It's only two minutes after five," I say, walking past him. Let him catch up.

He jogs after me. "What's wrong with you, grumpy?"

"Don't ask questions you don't want the answer to," I say. "Especially when you're talking to the town pariah."

He grabs my hand and makes me slow down. "I wish you would learn to look on the bright side of things," he says.

He likes to hold hands while we walk, which makes it easier to slip the bag of pot to me. He thinks it's funny that someone might think we're holding hands because we actually want to. At one point maybe I thought it was funny too, but I don't now. Now that no one in this town would think that Simon would have any reason to talk to me other than to sell me pot.

"Oh, please remind me exactly what the bright side of things is," I say.

"You're missing the hell of senior year, for one."

"Lucky me. Little Miss GED. Hope I get voted prom queen of Nowhere High."

Suddenly a loud clap of a backfiring engine breaks the relative peace of the afternoon and I jump about three feet, pulling my hand away from Simon and nearly throwing myself around the corner. Simon stares at me as the offending motor-cycle speeds off past us.

"A little on edge there?"

I can feel my heart thumping in my chest.

*Deep breaths, Eleanor. You're okay.*

"I'm fine," I say.

Simon grabs my hand again and swings my arm like we're about to start skipping down the sidewalk together. We keep walking.

"For real, though, the workload is already killing me and we're only two weeks in," he says. "*And* I'm supposed to know where I want to apply to college already. *And* I'm supposed to have already been working on my college essay for, like, five years. *And* I'm supposed to know what I'm going to do with the rest of my life."

"But you're already a successful businessman," I say, not

even attempting to hide my sarcasm. "What else is there to figure out?"

"It is true that I will clean up at college. That's really the main reason to go."

"They won't need you there. Over twenty-one, they can buy their own at the corner store. Welcome to Massachusetts."

"I better apply out of state, then. Follow the demand to the less enlightened territories."

He lets go of my hand and moves to my other side. When he grabs my right hand, the bag of pot is in it. I put it in my pocket. It is my favorite magic trick of all. Soon it'll disappear into a puff of smoke. Magic!

"What about you?" Simon asks.

"What about me, what?"

"Where are you applying? UMass?"

Simon has let go of my hand for good now. He will leave me at the end of this block.

I shake my head. Of the many topics I am not interested in discussing, this is in my top five.

"Nowhere," I say. "My mom needs me. And a high school dropout is not getting into UMass."

He shakes his head. "You're way too negative, you know that, Sanderson?" He steps off the sidewalk to cross the street away from me. "You've got to have a little faith," he calls back.

This comment would annoy me if I wasn't so happy that I am now three minutes away from being stoned enough to forget how much everything annoys me. All I have to do is duck into the alley behind the convenience store on the corner of our block. If the owner comes out and sees me, I just share my joint with him. There are not many bonuses to small-town life, but knowing who the other stoners are is one of them.

I sit down next to the dumpster and take out my rolling papers, roll a small joint, and light it. I feel my heart rate finally returning to normal even just from the prospect of this relief. I'll smoke half now and half later. I am regulating. Only what is needed.

Our apartment is in the attic of an old Victorian house at the end of this block. An elderly woman named Enid lives alone downstairs and gives us cheap rent in exchange for taking out her trash and making sure she's still alive. Susan arranged it for us when we moved to town two years ago, when we left Mystic because Mom couldn't really work anymore.

How my mom ended up with Lyme and not me, I will never be able to understand. We only lived half an hour from Lyme, Connecticut, the namesake of the disease caused by the tiny parasitic deer ticks that are nearly impossible to spot and can screw up your entire life within a matter of minutes. But I was the one who spent my childhood running through the reeds on the beaches, sitting in the grass of any yard I could find, climbing up trees and refusing to come down. I never checked myself once for the raised black mole of a bloodsucker or the telltale bull's-eye that lets you know you have been targeted for slow disintegration. Nature's revenge on humans. Take us down one by one.

We don't know when Mom got the tick bite that started it, which means that she probably had it for a long time before we figured out that there was something wrong. She just started getting very tired. First she was falling asleep on the couch as soon as she got home from work. Then she started falling asleep at her desk during the day, and when she woke up she would seem confused and disoriented.

For a while she thought it might be stress, but her job as a teacher at the Mystic Aquarium was not exactly high stakes. Her biggest concern was usually making sure a kid didn't fall in the eel tank.

Once the joint pain started, from the autoimmune arthritis that can kick in when Lyme goes untreated for too long, we knew it was a bigger problem. When she finally got a diagnosis, it was mostly too late. She tried rounds of megadoses of antibiotics, which just made her feel sicker. She went to every doctor she could find. Nothing helped.

The only thing I could think to do was throw myself completely into my schoolwork and the various academic clubs I had joined. If I kept busy, she wouldn't have to worry about me on top of everything else. I was already an overachieving honor roll student with the nerdiest roster of extracurriculars available—mock trial, math team, Model UN. I just went into overdrive on achievement.

I realize now that doing well in school felt like something I could accomplish, that I could actually do right, when I knew there wasn't much that I could do to help my mom. It was the only thing I could control.

Meanwhile our extended family in Mystic all felt the need to constantly weigh in on Mom's illness. My grandparents, aunts, and uncles offered endless opinions and comments and no real help.

"Bonnie's grandnephew saw a specialist who said that Lyme is a myth and it's all psychological."

In general our family seemed mystified by my mom's life choices. She had raised me alone, calling me her miracle baby, when really I was her "unexpected baby" from an old boyfriend who possibly lives in Iceland now. Or is it Norway? We had always been a self-sufficient, independent team, me and my mom.

Susan was calling every night at that point to check on Mom. I don't know when they made the decision that we would follow Susan to her hometown of Salem, but one night I heard them video chatting when Mom thought I was in my room.

"I know that they think because I couldn't keep a guy that I'm going to lose my kid," she said, followed by a long silence.

I would miss the aquarium, where I spent the majority of my childhood tagging along with Mom's classes and helping to feed the fish when they would let me, but there was something exciting to me about the idea of moving to Salem. Even though I didn't care about witchy stuff, Salem had a mythic vibe to it that I could appreciate. It felt like a place where I could reinvent myself as someone cooler, more self-assured. Someone who did things besides homework and Model UN.

It is not lost on me that we traded one place with magical connotations for another—Mystic to Salem. The Northeast loves magic. Rip Van Winkle, the Headless Horseman, the witch trials. It all makes for excellent tourist attractions.

Once we got to Salem, it made all the difference that we had Susan around to help us. She arranged for our apartment, hired a cleaning service, ordered groceries to be delivered, and hired us both to work at her store. Most nights she brought over a home-cooked meal. I was relieved to no longer be the only source of support for Mom. Susan would be the grown-up for all of us. And I was free to go live that new reinvented life for myself.

Walking down the block now to the house where we have lived in the apartment above Enid for the past two years, I am trying to maintain the floaty high that I know will keep me agreeable and calm at least for a few hours, until Susan closes up the store and comes over with soup and I can turn Mom over to her best friend for comfort.

I wave to Enid, who is sitting in her spot in the bay window on the first floor as I step onto the big covered front porch. She points to the bags of trash that she has placed next to the door, and I give her a thumbs-up.

*Yes, of course I will take the trash, Enid. Don't I always take the trash?*

I let myself in the side door that leads to our private stairs and start the long trek up to the attic. We have a kitchen, a living room, two small bedrooms, and a bathroom with an ancient tub that Mom soaks in every night. You have to duck in most corners of our apartment to avoid hitting your head on the slanted ceilings. When we first moved in, I managed to convince myself that it was charming, a kind of magical tree house to fit this life in our new magical town. I imagined someone climbing up the tree outside my window to tap on the glass and be let into my tiny bedroom. This felt romantic and secret and like an actual possibility. I do not imagine this anymore.

"Hey, honey." Mom can hear me coming from a floor away. I have to stop on the landing to catch my breath.

"Hey," I call back.

"You okay?"

I am so out of breath that it takes me a minute to call back, "Fine!"

If pot is my magic and all magic costs something, then mine takes my breath away.

*At least I'm not smoking cigarettes*, I think as I am stopped on this landing. An impressive magic trick is making a seventeen-year-old girl feel like she's about ninety. Enid should be taking out the garbage for me.

I make the trek up the final flight of stairs to find Mom wrapped in a blanket on the couch in front of the TV. She looks the way she always looks. Pale and tired.

"Hey," I say.

"Enid called up to tell me to remind you that it's garbage night," Mom says.

I go in my room to dump my bag and jacket and slip the tiny bag of pot into my underwear drawer.

"Can I suggest a hobby for Enid?" I say. "Maybe get her a cat?"

"I think she's just lonely, honey."

I go into the living room and sit down in a chair across from Mom.

"Why don't you go hang out with her?" I say.

Mom gives me a look.

"What?" I say, teasing. "You're both home all day."

"I do not need to listen to Enid's tirade against the community planning board for the four thousandth time," Mom says.

"Are you hungry?" I ask, getting up. "Susan's coming over later with some soup."

Mom shakes her head, and I go into the kitchen to make a snack. After a minute, Mom appears in the kitchen doorway, the blanket wrapped around her shoulders.

"I'm thinking I might take a shift back from you at the store later this week," she says.

Ah, I said the wrong thing, pointing out that she is home all day, instead of working at the store with Susan.

"Sure," I say, trying not to give this word any extra meaning.

She is quiet for a minute. I put two slices of bread in the toaster. Watch the toast toast. I feel like we are both watching paint dry.

"It would give you a little break," Mom says. "You could stay home and look at college stuff."

"Oh," I say. "Yeah."

*Why does everyone want to talk about college today?*

"I can help you with applications if you want."

"That's okay," I say.

"But we should talk about it. I think most kids start around now."

I feel myself getting red, a hot buildup in my head that is pushing through the pleasant haze of my magic smoke spell.

*I really do not want to talk about this.*

"I'm good," I say. I push past her, down the hallway, into my room. I know better than to slam the door. I can at least keep myself from that level of bratty display.

"Eleanor?" Mom calls from the hallway. "You want your toast?"

Mom leaves me alone until Susan arrives with the soup. I am lying in bed, silently screaming at myself for not being able to be calm, be kind. She was only trying to help me. I can't be mad at her for that. And then here come the other thoughts. All the thoughts.

*You mess up everything.*

Susan arriving offers a restart. Do-over. Magic! We eat her soup at the kitchen table, and she complains about her day of supplier problems and undelivered goods. Mom listens happily, offering advice and consolation. After we're done, Susan pulls a bottle of wine out of her bag and demands that she and Mom drink it on the front porch, where they can enjoy the night air. I grab two glasses for them and head down while Susan helps Mom down the stairs. Her pain has been mostly in her legs recently, so it takes them a long time to get down. I take Enid's trash to the curb and come back, set up two chairs for Susan and Mom where they can look out over the twilit street.

Settled in their chairs, Susan pours Mom a glass of wine and I sit on the steps while they start one of their Deep Gossip Sessions. This is when Mom really perks up. Not even the usual brain fog of her day will stop her from going over which of their college buddies announced a divorce online with a post about "conscious uncoupling." Who will get the money, the house, the kids? Susan seems to take a particular delight in humiliating divorce stories. It makes her feel better about her own.

"I'm going for a walk," I say. I will not be missed. I have nothing to contribute to the Deep Gossip. I am much more likely to be the subject of someone's Deep Gossip.

"Okay, honey," Mom says.

I walk down the block, their happy witchy cackles fading behind me. Back to the convenience store parking lot. I will finish the joint from earlier, then help Mom upstairs and pass out. That will be the day.

*Abracadabra. I made another day of my life disappear.*

I take my place in my usual behind-the-dumpster spot and light the remaining half of the joint. But before I can get stoned enough to fully reenter my preferred state of haziness, my mind wanders back to the exact place I am trying to keep it from wandering—the two girls from the store. They must be witchy tourists, making a pilgrimage to Salem. I know all the teenagers in town by sight, mostly as a protective measure. If I recognize them, they sure as hell know who I am. And that means Stay Away.

The thought occurs to me that Pix might have been making fun of me, the employee in the cheesy witch store, while those two must believe themselves to be true witches. I am the girl in all black—black jeans, black T-shirt, black sneakers—who wouldn't be caught dead in a cape and pointy hat.

I can't help but picture Pix now—not a witch in all black at all, but radiant in many colors. Her floor-length dress was green with bright flowers and puffed sleeves, like in *Anne of Green Gables*, one of my favorite books when I was little. My mom read the whole series to me. All Anne (with an *e*) ever wanted was a dress with puffed sleeves.

And what does it mean that I had just been reading about Pamela "Pixie" Colman Smith when they came into the store? If I was a different kind of person, I would see this as a sign. That Pix and I were meant to be in each other's lives. That the touch of her fingers against my hand when she gave me back the Fool card was only the first of many touches. That seeing her smile with her eyes half-closed again was my destiny. That something about this little tarot book was leading me to her.

But that is not how the biggest cynic in Salem thinks. Instead I tell myself that if I never saw her before today, I'll never see her again. It's that simple.

I exhale a large puff of smoke and feel everything in my body relax. Even if I see her again, what good would it do? I am not made for human interaction. So, just stop thinking about it.

I try to turn my thoughts instead to the tarot book, which I have shoved in my back pocket. Why send a witchy thing to a witch store if you aren't trying to sell something? No one gives magic away for free in this town.

I am about to take the book out and read about the next card when a car pulls into the convenience store parking lot and two people get out. I can't see them, but as soon as they start yelling jovial insults at each other, I recognize their voices all too well. My stomach sinks.

"You're fucking gay, man. You're gonna die a virgin."

Harrison.

*Shit shit shit.*

I toss my joint without thinking; my first instinct is to run before he sees me. But then I realize that he has to walk past the dumpster to get into the store from where he has parked. I am trapped.

The voice that responds to him is higher pitched. The voice of a born sidekick. Harrison's best friend, Tyler.

"Yeah, how about you? Gonna go look for a girlfriend in the graveyard? I heard you love it there."

"Shut the fuck up!"

"You know having sex with dead bodies is illegal, right?" Tyler says. "But you do you, man."

Harrison yells in fake rage and attacks Tyler. Tyler wrestles back. My heart is racing. I am holding as still as I can, pushed up against the brick wall, hoping that neither of them notice my sneakers under the dumpster. A few feet away from me, my hastily tossed joint has extinguished itself in a puddle of unidentifiable liquid.

I listen for them to enter the convenience store, the bell ringing and door shutting behind them, and I book it out of the parking lot, running against every instinct my poor old-before-its-time body has. I run until I am home again with Mom and Susan, safe at least from this, from him.

So much for magic.

At least I know how to make myself disappear.

# THE HIGH PRIESTESS

We are certainly glad to see you, High Priestess. You are here to tell us that there are certain important truths that can be learned in meditation at a mountain temple, sequestered away from humanity. If we are willing to take the time to listen, the universe will welcome us into these new realms of understanding.

You have the moon at your feet, the book of sacred and mysterious law in your hand. On either side of you—a black and a white column. Flanked by the letters *B* and *J*. Get your mind out of the gutter, High Priestess! These are simply a reference to the columns at the entrance to King Solomon's temple, named Jachin and Boaz. I don't know why columns have names, but you must know why, HP, because you know everything.

There's a lot you can tell us if we're ready. So how can we prove to you that we are worthy of your wisdom? What sacrifices must we make? What fears must we overcome in order to be invited to sit next to you on your temple throne and have you whisper the wonderments of the cosmos into our ears?

If we listen to you, HP, we will trust our deepest and most mysterious, intuitive thoughts. And we will learn to follow a wise woman wherever she may lead us.

I am looking at the High Priestess card when Susan comes into the store around noon. Starting this month, I open for her most mornings and she works nights, capitalizing on the tipsy tourists who will start to wander the cobblestoned streets after dark. It's amazing what people will buy when they are convinced that they are enjoying themselves.

"Playing with the cards again, are we?" Susan says.

"I just like the drawings," I say, not sure if that's exactly true. I like that this deck of cards feels like something legitimately old in a town that just pretends to have a relationship with history, while most of the original locations of the witch trials are long gone. All the old prisons, courthouses, and churches were torn down. No one back then knew that they were sitting on a budding industry of morbid attractions.

What I really don't want to admit is that the High Priestess reminds me of a girl in a long floral dress with puffed sleeves who I will most likely never see again.

"The High Priestess." Susan takes the card from me.

"I guess she's like a wise goddess," I say.

Susan raises an eyebrow. "You really are going full vagina vase on me, aren't you?"

"I'm not!" I say, grabbing the card back.

Susan is nearly as cynical as I am, a nonbeliever raised in the Vatican of witch belief. The difference between the two of us is that she likes the pretend part of it. She enjoys the kids who come into the store looking for broomsticks and plastic cauldrons. While for me that stuff just reinforces how fake it all is.

"But I don't pay you to play with cards," Susan says, putting on her "boss" voice. "I pay you to do inventory."

She pushes a clipboard at me.

"This really is becoming a hostile work environment," I say, obediently heading over to the shelves.

"Please see our HR department with your complaints. Oh, wait, I *am* the HR department." Susan laughs hysterically at her own non-joke. She heads into the back room, and I am left counting out necklaces with crystals embedded in the arms of pewter fairies.

A middle-aged couple comes into the store. Tourists. The woman starts looking through the T-shirts, methodically ruining my perfect folding technique, as she seems to hold literally every single one of them up to her body.

"Do you have a dressing room?" she asks me.

"No, sorry," I say. "But there's a mirror in the back."

"What good does a mirror do me if I can't try it on?"

*I cannot be high at work. I cannot be high at work.*

"You could try it on over the shirt you're already wearing, and then look in the mirror and make a guess at what it might look like if you weren't wearing two shirts."

The woman looks at me like I am either the biggest idiot she has ever met or someone to be deeply pitied. Either way, she is not having it.

"Come on, Fred," she says to her obedient husband, tossing the shirts back onto the shelf. The stack balances on the edge of the shelf long enough for Fred and Wife to make it out the door, and then it predictably topples to the floor.

I pick up the shirts and bring them over to the counter to refold them.

"Someone else asking for a changing room," I call back to Susan. She sticks her head out from her office.

"If you would help me clean out this closet back here, we could have one."

"You know, I would," I say. "I'm just really mobbed out here."

And that's when Pix comes in.

And suddenly I believe in the High Priestess.

Today she is wearing a plaid vintage coat over another long house dress, her short blond hair like peach fuzz on her head. She looks like she has come from another season in another place and time, as if she should have a light dusting of snow on her.

"Oh, wow," I say. Instead of "Hi" or "Hello" or another normal greeting.

Susan takes one look at the stupid grin on my face and disappears back into her office.

"Hey," Pix says.

"Did you, uh . . . find your map? I mean, did your friend?"

Pix smiles. "Ofira? Yeah. She found a map."

"Great."

I am out of things to say, because this moment was not supposed to happen. Pix looks around the store, taking in the entire scope of the room, just as she did the first time she was here. I suddenly wish that something about this place was actually mysterious, that there was some unknown shelf where truly magical objects lay in wait. I wish that I wasn't the biggest cynic in Salem, working in a store owned by the second-biggest cynic in Salem.

I am conscious of the fact that she has not smiled yet. What can I say that would make that smile come back? The silence is torture. I am racking my brain for some kind of normal question to ask her when she says, "Are you busy tonight?"

"No," I say, too quickly. "I don't think so. Why?"

She reaches into her pocket and takes out a piece of paper. She hands it to me. There's an address written on it.

"Eight p.m.," she says. "Come alone."

How to say yes without revealing that I am desperate to say yes? How to not act like this is the only nice thing that has happened to me in over a year?

"You're not going to kidnap me, are you?" I say. I am hoping that this comes off as charming.

She smiles. There it is.

"You'll have to come find out."

If Pix could vanish in a puff of smoke, I think that she

would. Instead she leaves the way she came, through the door that everyone uses—stupid, normal mortal humans. Again I wish I had something better to offer her. A secret passageway. A magic portal.

Susan is in my face so quickly that she startles me. "Who was that?"

"Susan! Honestly!"

"Well?"

"Nobody!"

"Didn't look like nobody."

"Just, like, a friendly person." This sounds idiotic and I know it.

"Friendly person is good. You could make a friend." She says this like she is informing me that it is possible: *You are capable of such an act.* I have my doubts.

Susan looks at the piece of paper on the counter. "She invited you to a party?"

"She invited me to a thing. I don't know what it is."

"Do you feel up for going to a thing?"

I shrug.

"I can hang with your mom tonight," Susan says.

"You can't take care of her every night."

"I can watch TV alone, or I can watch TV with your mom. These are my options." She slaps me on the back. "Go to the cute girl's party!"

I hold up a *Witch, Please* T-shirt as a shield against her.

"Yes! Witch, please!" she says. "Go have some fun tonight!"

I don't say that I don't know what that means anymore. I

gave up any idea of fun a long time ago. "Fun" is people acting like idiots, getting fucked up because they're bored, hooking up because they're bored. Getting in trouble, getting hurt, and hurting other people because they don't have anything better to do. I have tried "fun," and it has not ended well.

"We'll see," I say.

*And we will learn to follow a wise woman wherever she may lead us*, I think.

I almost give up on the whole idea of following Pix's mysterious bread-crumb-trail invite when I realize where it has led me. The address on the paper is the location of the Salem Yacht Club, a fancy country club where rich people dock their boats. I stop across the street from this hub of Salem's most elite boat owners and look at it. The thought occurs to me that this all might be some very elaborate prank, designed to lure me into yet more humiliation. But then I realize I would need to have some dignity left to lose in order for anyone to bother humiliating me.

It's a little before eight, and I decide to finish the half joint in my pocket before giving up on this fruitless adventure. I light it and inhale deeply, taking a deep breath of sea air as a chaser.

I always forget about the water. The whole town has that weather-beaten seaside smell, and the buildings closer to the ocean are faded from the salty air. But when was the last time that I actually saw the water? It's only a fifteen-minute walk to the harbor from the store, but we may as well be landlocked in the middle of the country for all I care about the ocean these days.

"The salt energizes the air," Mom likes to say. "Negative ions." She would tell me this when I was little on the beach in Mystic, back when she and I would build giant castles and take turns burying each other in the sand on weekends when she wasn't at the aquarium. For years I thought she was saying "negative irons," and I imagined grumpy irons surfing the waves on ironing boards.

But now the water is just a place of more unpleasant memories. And under no circumstances am I going out on a boat.

I am about to turn around and head back to the house to join my mom and Susan in watching a nineties rom-com on the couch when I see two figures moving down the dock together. They are in floor-length black dresses, and although they are far away, I can see that they are holding hands. They walk almost to the end of the dock, where they stop at a boat with a lit paper lantern flickering at the top of its mast. I watch as they seem to disappear into the darkness of the boat. Somewhere far away a foghorn sounds. And against all my better judgment, I start to walk toward them.

But to get to that lantern, I need to make it past Harrison's family's boat. I don't remember the name of it until suddenly I am passing by it, halfway down the dock. The *Well Appointed.* Of course. Harrison is the best appointed of them all, set up with everything anyone could ever want in life, and he still thinks he deserves more. I stop at the boat and decide it will give me pleasure to put my joint out on it. Toss the butt onto the deck. Maybe his dad will think it's his. Perfect little Harrison? Oh no. Not the golden boy who could slip out of any situation unscathed. Who would ever think he could do anything wrong?

My extinguished joint leaves an ash mark on the side of the perfect white hull of the *Well Appointed*, and I am plunged into a memory as if it is cold water, like the waves rising with the tide against the side of the boat. It's a little over a year ago, and I'm holding Chloe's long hair back from her increasingly green face. Harrison and his friends are laughing and passing a bottle of vodka between them. Harrison is at the steering wheel, kicking the motor into high gear, riding the waves like this is some kind of demonic video game.

"Harrison, for fuck's sake!" I yell at him.

This only seems to add to his pleasure. He laughs harder, a dangerous flash of something vengeful and violent in his eyes. It occurs to me that he is actually trying to throw me off this boat, that Chloe is the innocent bystander in a war that Harrison is fighting with me, for what? His dignity? His ego? I wanted to tell him that day, *You already won, dude. Total victory. Just let those who have surrendered go on with their lives.*

It was already too late when I realized just how far Harrison would go to prove his dominance over everything and everyone around him.

"Maybe 'Ellie' is good?" a voice says behind me, snapping me back to the present. "Or just 'Elle'?"

I turn around. It's Pix. She gives me a different smile now, delicate and almost tentative. Her dress reaches down to the dock. Around the bottom of it there is a damp ring of water and sand, as if she has emerged from under the dock, from the very water that, a moment ago, was threatening to overtake my memories.

"Trying out nicknames for you," she says. "I think we can do better, though."

"Oh," I say. I am blushing, I know. Is this flirting?

"The problem is that Eleanor really suits you," she says.

She seems to study me for a moment, and I try to arrange my face into an expression that a normal person might have—a person who lives in the present and is not paralyzed by the fear of being sucked into the past at any moment.

Then she says, "Don't worry. You're in the right place."

I don't know what she means, but it is what I need to hear. She holds out her hand. I take it. Her grip is strong and reassuring, and she leads me down the dock, toward the boat with the flickering lantern.

I am not normally touched by other people, and a girl taking my hand like this makes me soar, turns me into a bird, a plane, Superwoman. I have not been touched by a person other than my mother and Susan, and by Simon's stupid hand holding mine, in over a year. And I barely let my mom and Susan get a hug in.

But none of those people are a girl with a kind smile who is leading me somewhere. I think of the Fool standing at the edge of that cliff. Her favorite card. Why? Because she does this to people? Starts their journey for them, whether they want it or not?

It only takes about fifty feet of walking down that dock for me to start to like it too much, this hand in mine. I let the specter of the lantern boat take me away in all the ways from the *Well Appointed*. I am literally walking toward the light.

"So what exactly are we doing out here?" I finally allow myself to say, although I find even the sound of my voice to be an unwelcome intruder in this moment. I want to exist outside my body and self and just watch. I don't want the responsibility of not messing up this perfect scene. I don't want the freedom to make a mistake.

We are at the boat now. The deck is lined in candles.

"It belongs to Ofira's mom," Pix says to me. "We're allowed to use it."

In those words I catch a glimpse of something about this person. A rule follower? A worrier? A caretaker?

"Are you going out in it?" I ask. "On the water?"

Pix shakes her head. "We'll stay docked," she says. "You okay with boats?"

There is no simple answer to this question, so I decide to just say yes, and Pix leads me on board.

I know I have made a mistake when we enter the small, low-ceilinged cabin and see Ofira. She is glorious, outrageous. Intricately embroidered robes cover her body to the floor, and her dark hair is entwined in a crown of gold flowers and what look like tiny animals. A South Asian girl with dyed bright red hair that hangs to her shoulders is applying makeup to Ofira's face, putting blue and yellow streaks of eye shadow over Ofira's eyes. The red-haired girl finishes and steps back.

43

"Thank you, Anita," Ofira says.

On Ofira's hands are rings of silver snakes, seeming to writhe their way down her fingers.

She is like no witch I have ever seen before.

Pix releases my hand and goes over to Ofira and kisses her once on each cheek. Ofira holds Pix's face tenderly for a moment and then releases her.

*Of course.*

A secret cabal of queer teenage girls hiding out in my town? Of course they are already paired off, unavailable. Of course I am a third wheel before I even begin. Third wheel is my destiny; why would this situation be any different?

I attempt to keep my face impassive, hoping I am successfully hiding my disappointment. But then Pix returns to me, takes my hand again in what now feels like a pity grip, like a manipulation. If she wasn't flirting with me, then what am I doing here?

Susan's voice now in my head: *You could make a friend.*

I try to remember what it meant when I thought I had friends. When I first came to Salem and suddenly my mostly solitary existence in Mystic as the nerdy kid who joined every club was successfully transformed into "cool new girl." I was someone to break up the monotony for a group of kids who had known each other too long, traveling through the ranks of small-town public school together since kindergarten. Yes, in my first year in Salem, I had friends.

Ofira gives me a solemn nod as a greeting, and Pix leads me to a spot in the small circle of girls who are now sitting on the floor. There are three girls I am seeing for the first time tonight. Anita, the girl with the bright red hair who was doing Ofira's makeup, sits down next to a Black girl with long braids. I realize that they are the two who I saw holding hands on the dock. Their matching floor-length black dresses are perfectly tailored to their bodies. On the other side of me, a white girl with a head full of long blond ringlet curls who is wearing an elaborate black corset takes her place. She looks like something straight out of a Renaissance faire.

"Anita, Ivy, and Tatiana," Pix whispers in my ear, pointing out each of the girls.

I feel grateful at least that my regular all-black uniform allows me to look like I might belong here.

Ofira looks down upon us. She is a witch from some other version of nature. Not the stingy salt of the sea but a lush forest. One with rainbows and prancing animals and abundant fruits. Not even my cynical brain can deny that there is an aura of energy emitting from her, radiating light in the darkness of the cabin. She is somehow both glorious and terrifying, and I feel a twinge of panic in my stomach. I wonder if it is true that we really have permission to be on this boat.

"We are met," Ofira says. From somewhere under her robes she pulls out a bundle of herbs and lights it. I'm expecting sage, the cliché new age air purifier appropriated from Native American rituals, but this smells like one hundred different smells—lavender and rosemary and something minty that cuts through the air into my nose and swirls around in my head.

"We ask permission from the local spirits to sit in ceremony tonight," Ofira begins. "On the full moon we release what is no longer necessary, and tonight we have much to release."

I look out a little window in the cabin. The moon is definitely full, reflecting back to itself in the water. When I look back at the circle, Tatiana, the girl next to me with the ringlets and the Ren faire corset, is standing and Ofira is swirling the smoke from the herb bundle around her body. When she is done, she passes the bundle to Tatiana, who looks at me expectantly. Pix nudges me to stand, and I stay very still as Tatiana starts at my feet, makes her way up to my head. I look down and notice that she's wearing an actual petticoat under her long black skirt. She motions for me to turn around.

I don't know what I am supposed to feel as she does this. Safe? Purified? It's going to take more than some lavender smoke to do that. But something happens when she hands me the herb bundle and Pix stands in front of me, her smile urging me on. I mimic what I have seen the others do, and instead of being worried about getting it wrong, I feel that some part of me inherently knows what this is. It's like a wish.

*Be safe. Be happy.*

And I am surprised to find that, although I may no longer believe in hope, or the future, I still seem to be able to make a wish.

I hand the bundle to Pix, and Ivy stands, her perfect black dress cascading down around her legs. The herb bundle makes its way around the circle until everyone has had a turn, now to Anita, then finally back to Ofira, and the air is thick with the smell of the smoke.

"The circle is cast," Ofira says. "We call in the four elements. Earth, air, fire, and water. Tatiana? Will you light the candles?"

Tatiana gets up and lights four candles in the middle of the circle. She pushes her long ringlets back over her shoulder to keep them out of the path of the flames.

"We call in the energy of the god and the goddess," Ofira says, "the twin flames that keep balance in the universe, to help us with our spell of protection."

She pulls a folded piece of paper out of her pocket.

"And now," she says, "time to save the soul of this town."

She unfolds the paper. It is the map of the tourist attractions of the witch trials.

"Between the years 1692 and 1693, more than two hundred people were accused of collaborating with forces of evil in Salem," Ofira says. "Twenty people were executed. Seven died in prison."

Ofira passes the map to Anita, and she presses the paper to her heart, closes her eyes, then passes it to Ivy.

"The witch trials claimed to be a fight against forces of evil that were coming to corrupt and sabotage humanity," Ofira says, her face lit up by the candlelight. "And in those years, evil did exist in this town. But it was not the evil of the supernatural. Evil existed in how humans treated other humans, in the ways in which the accusers projected the fear of their own internal mystical power onto the marginalized members of their community. Because they could not believe in their own magic, they imagined that others must have something that they could not understand, and that it must be evil. They blamed others for wickedness that they knew they possessed in their own hearts. The accused were simply those who did not think to point a finger fast enough."

The map makes its way to me, and again I mimic what I have seen the other girls do. The thought crosses my mind that I would make a great cult member. Just let me sit next to a cute girl who's nice to me and it seems I will agree to do pretty much anything.

"This map is a map of places, but it is also a map of mis-understanding," Ofira continues. "It is a record of the ways in which we allow false stories to dominate our narratives for centuries. The ways in which control of the narrative is stolen from the victims who do not survive to write their own history books."

My stomach churns a little when she says this, and I look at the map in my hand to steady myself. False stories continue to be a specialty in this town. Or stories that we desperately wish were false. Pix looks at me, and I quickly hand the map on to Tatiana.

"Tonight, we reclaim this history for the victims." Ofira motions to Ivy, who stands and holds out her hands. The rest of the circle does the same, taking each other's hands. I follow their lead. Ofira stands in the middle of the circle. She is hold-ing the map over what looks to be a tiny cauldron.

"In destroying this map," Ivy says, "we reject the violence that the humans of this town perpetuated upon one another."

I can feel my hand getting sweaty holding Pixie's and Tati-ana's hands.

"We call now for Salem to live in accordance with the true power of magic, in which all people are cared for and accepted, and no violence or unkind action is tolerated."

Ofira dips the map in one of the candles, and it catches fire. The twinge of panic in my stomach from earlier seems to light into flame too. This is maybe where my ability to join a cult ends—I can suddenly envision this cabin on fire, the second time in my life that I am convinced that I am about to die on a boat. But Ofira drops the burning map into the little cauldron, where the flames die down into a manageable smolder. I take a deep breath to try to slow my heart rate back down to normal.

"She changes everything she touches, and everything she touches changes," Ivy says. The circle repeats this in unison. Again. And then again. I whisper along with them at first, but then they get louder, and I find myself saying the words louder along with them. I close my eyes. It must be the heat radiating off the fire, but I feel a rising energy in the room, and then my hands begin to rise as Pix and Tatiana raise our clasped hands above our heads. It's like we are whipping up the flames, bidding them to take away all the terrible secret pain of this town.

Suddenly the chant stops, and I open my eyes to see everyone in the circle standing, clasped hands over heads, looking at each other.

"So mote it be," Ofira says. "So it is."

The girls release their clasped hands, and some of them laugh, and they hug. Tatiana hugs me and whispers "Welcome!" into my ear. I am starting to wonder how exactly I got here when Pix hugs me tightly, and then I remember exactly what misguided instinct has brought me to this strange moment.

We move outside and watch as Ofira finishes the ceremony by tossing what is left of the map off the side of the boat and into the dark water. A small cloud of ash puffs up into the wind for a moment before floating down into the waves.

I move away from the group and sit and watch the moon as Ofira finishes. I am separate, a bad participant. I have taken myself out once again.

"So it is," Ofira says to the water.

Abundant amounts of food emerge from somewhere. The girls set it all up on a small table on the deck. There are cupcakes and cookies and bowls of figs and fruit. It is noisy and boisterous now in contrast to the quiet reverence of the ceremony. They pour bottles of sparkling liquid into champagne glasses, and I assume that this is about to turn into some kind of witch rager.

Which is my cue to go.

I am trying to figure out how to leave without being rude when the girl with the long braids, Ivy, comes over to me with a plate of cookies.

"It's Eleanor, right?"

"Yeah," I say.

"I'm Ivy. Resident kitchen witch. Ginger cookie?"

She holds out the plate of beautifully decorated cookies. I take one, mostly because I'm not sure what else to do.

"Sorry," I say, "kitchen witch?"

"A witch whose magic mostly focuses on the kitchen,

literally," she explains. "I make tinctures, work with herbs, grow my own veggies. Recipes are spells, you know?"

I do not know, but I nod, and Ivy moves on to offer cookies to the other girls.

Pix sits down next to me with a plate piled high with decadent treats.

"Ivy's ginger cookies are amazing," she says, seeing me holding the cookie. "Anita decorates them with a protective sigil, so they're really good for you too. That's Anita." She indicates the girl with the bright red dyed hair. "She's kind of the official coven artist and Ivy's girlfriend. She makes all of Ofira's outfits. And her and Ivy's dresses. Which is why they match so well."

"I didn't know a kitchen witch was a real thing," I say.

Pix nods. "It is. She made me this amazing flower essence for my birthday that's good for lucid dreaming."

"What's lucid dreaming?" I ask. Although I am starting to feel like I have too many questions to seem like I belong here.

"Dreams where you know that you're dreaming and you can make decisions and control what happens to you." She holds her plate up. "Fig?"

"No, thanks," I say. We are quiet for a moment, watching the other girls laughing.

"Is this, like, a regular thing that you all do?" I ask.

"Every full moon since Ofira moved to Salem in the spring. She used to live by me in Marblehead."

"That's how you met?"

Pix takes a bite of a ginger cookie and shakes her head. "Ofira's my cousin," she says.

That stupid Fool part of me allows itself to light up again with this information. Cousins! But this means that Pix is someone who kisses her platonic loves on the cheek, who allows them to hold her face lovingly. Which also means that she is probably the kind of person who would hold hands with someone she feels sorry for.

"She was always witchy," Pix says, "but it wasn't until she got to Salem that she decided to start her own coven. We're all from Marblehead," she says.

Right. Of course me being here tonight is only possible because none of these girls are from Salem. If they were, they would know better than to invite me.

I decide that I need to leave now.

*Just say thank you, Eleanor. "Thank you for inviting me to your very nice boat witch party that didn't trigger me at all."*

Instead I say, "Why did you invite me here?"

Pix looks at me. I am worried by her expression that I have offended her.

"I follow my intuition," she says finally. "And my intuition told me that you needed to come here tonight."

"But you don't know me," I say. I mean this as a question, but I forget to say it that way.

"Those kinds of things don't really matter to intuition," she says.

Tatiana makes a show of popping the cork off another bottle and messily pouring it around to the girls' glasses.

"Looks like you're in for a fun night," I say, getting up. "Thanks for having me."

Pix is studying me again. I do not like it when she does this. I realize that it must be something about her face, an affectation that she has learned how to exploit. She gets people to trust her by making this concerned, interested face.

"Why are you really going?" she asks me.

I feel my skin go cold. I suddenly wish I was wearing a sweatshirt, a jacket, something to fortify me against this chilling September air. I shove my hands into my pockets. What is the simplest answer to this question?

"I actually just don't like boats," I say. My voice cracking a little betrays my desire to sound casual about this.

"Oh."

"Yeah, sorry."

"That's okay," Pix says, and I can't tell which one of us she's trying to convince.

"I'll see you around," I say, because I am a monster and I have ruined this and I have to get out of here immediately.

I walk off the boat, not looking back, but feeling the eyes of an entire coven on me.

*What will happen, Eleanor, now that you have offended a whole boat full of witches?*

Walking back past the *Well Appointed*, I know that there is very little that any magic could do for or against me anymore. In order to burn the map of evil in my life, you would need to burn this entire town down.

# THE EMPRESS

Empress! It's you! What a relief! That High Priestess was wise and holy and all, but boy, she is not a ton of fun. But you? You are a party! You are Elizabeth Taylor in a caftan, sipping champagne and getting fanned by attendants. "Bring me more peeled grapes!" you cry out, and then laugh, and your attendants laugh, and they bring you more peeled grapes and you share them with everyone and everyone puts on glorious caftans and falls into a cuddle pile.

Quick question, Empress—what is it with peeled grapes? Is that really a thing? You can tell us later.

Of course we know any binary is bullshit, Empress, so to call you a "she" and to ascribe "feminine" energy to you is just a lazy shortcut to indicate these are things that we have associated with "womanhood" but exist to different degrees in all people—kindness, gentleness, beauty, receptivity, nurturing, empathy. At your feet, a heart, like a Valentine's Day box of candy that each of us might give to ourselves.

Can we find a place in our hearts to accept this abundance

and affection? Can we trust this deep inner wisdom that asks us to love both self and other? To allow the endless joys of life to fill our hearts with the knowledge that abundance is here for us, and fulfillment is just around the corner? Can we come to know how glorious our bodies and hearts truly are?

Pleasure is sacred, dear Empress.

Pleasure is our birthright.

3

It was a long time before I understood what everyone was talking about when they talked about love. And sex. And desire. I would say I was a late bloomer, but it's clear to me now that I just didn't know what I was looking for. Or I didn't know that I was supposed to take the initiative to look. I would just let things happen to me, watching curiously as if outside my own body when a boy would kiss me under a tree in summer camp. When another (obviously embarrassed) boy was forced into a closet with me at a middle school party where "seven minutes in heaven" seemed like a good way to pass the time. Feeling his tongue in my mouth meant no more or less to me than a science experiment with the hypothesis of "I believe sharing germs with this other person is a vaguely disgusting idea."

It's not exactly true that I only started to understand love when I met Chloe, but it's a little true. It wasn't even when I first met her. We were friends for almost five months before I fully understood that my desire to be around her every minute of the day, to talk to her on the phone every night for hours while we did our homework, to plan my weekends and school breaks around her and what she wanted to do, was not just "best friend" behavior. I had never had a best friend before—I thought maybe this was just what best friendship felt like.

All I knew in the beginning was that Chloe was the antidote to my social anxiety. I had spent the months leading up to my first day at Salem High compulsively overthinking my every move. If Salem represented a new start for me and Mom, I needed to make it the best new start it could be. I would wear the right clothes, do the right activities, and talk to the right people. I was going to be a Normal Teenager, with friends, and a social life, and someone to talk to besides her mother.

If I believed in psychic communication, I would think that the first day I walked into Salem High I was projecting these thoughts in such a way that they appeared like a sign over my head declaring, *This girl needs a friend!!!*

Somehow it was Chloe who received the message.

"Oh my god, hilarious."

I was sitting down in an empty desk in first-period homeroom when the girl next to me, a white girl with a perfectly messy brown ponytail, pointed at my T-shirt, a drawing of Tweety Bird saying *I Tawt I Taw a Puddy Tat!* It was from Goodwill, and I was praying that it came off as a cool vintage purchase rather than a clueless hand-me-down.

It took me a moment to realize she was talking to me.

"Oh." I looked down at my shirt.

"I am going to tell you something, and you need to promise that you won't think that I'm super weird," the girl said, leaning in. She had perfectly applied liquid eyeliner around her eyes, and she smelled like baby powder and vanilla, sweet and comforting.

"Okay," I said.

"I had a crush on Bugs Bunny from, like, ages four to seven."

She looked so serious when she said this, I wasn't sure how to react. But then she started laughing, and I started laughing, and a warm sensation spread through my body, a feeling of being chosen. Was this manifestation? I had asked for a friend, and here she was, ready to transform my life into something new and sparkly and full of possibility. I had only been in the building for twenty minutes and my fate was already decided.

Chloe didn't need another friend, which made me even more grateful that she wanted me around. She was one of those girls who couldn't walk down the hallway without twenty people saying hi to her. She played the right sports (lacrosse and softball), went to the right parties, and looked the right way. If a new trend was going to find its way to Salem High, it would start with Chloe.

But what she didn't have was a sidekick. A devoted follower. A person who would not leave her side. I came to wonder if any of the people who emulated her every move even liked her very much, or just put on a show of it. She needed a secure line of constant devotion. And somehow she knew that I would be the one to provide it.

When I picture her now, I think of someone crackling with energy, a star wishing it was a comet, not remembering that comets are just angry, temporary fireballs streaking gloriously toward their own ends. She wanted more of everything. And for a while I believed that she wanted me too.

It took those first five months for me to understand that my level of devotion was about more than just gratitude for Chloe ushering me into this new life of social currency.

But she was the one who kissed me.

The first time Chloe kissed me was the first weekend in February of our sophomore year. Tyler was having a party at his house, and everyone was going to be there. Chloe had been talking about it nonstop for a week, and it took me a stupidly long time to realize that she was planning her move with Harrison for that night.

Harrison was an expected choice for Chloe. Handsome, athletic, with a last name that tied him to the oldest of the old New England money. Plus Chloe's dad worked for Harrison's dad. In the hierarchy of class and status, Chloe had everything to gain from an association with Harrison. But all of this made me doubt her sincerity when she would talk about liking him. It felt like a thought exercise. "Wouldn't it be outrageous if . . . ?"

The part that's hardest for me to admit is that, when my late-night phone calls with Chloe would turn to the subject of hooking up with Harrison, it seemed impossibly romantic, as if it was just an excuse for us to talk about something intimate.

"Do you think he's had sex with, like, everyone he's ever dated?" Chloe asked me on the phone one night a couple of weeks before Tyler's party. I was sitting on my bed pretending to care about my French homework, whispering into the phone so I wouldn't bother Mom, who was already asleep in her room.

"Probably," I said. "I mean, maybe not if he dated them in, like, middle school."

"I bet I could find out if Tanya slept with him. She's still totally in love with him."

"Isn't she with Adam now?"

"Yeah, but I don't think you get over Harrison."

A pause.

"Do you think it means anything that he's never asked me out?" Chloe asked me.

"Like, means what?"

"That he's not interested? Maybe he thinks I'm too inexperienced. I've only dated, like, two people. Honestly, it's embarrassing."

"That's not embarrassing," I said, thinking of the exactly zero people I had dated.

"But, I mean, it does kind of seem like he likes me."

Another pause. More pretending to work.

Then she asked, "Would you date him?"

"Harrison?"

"Yeah. Like, if he asked you out."

There seemed to be some sort of test hidden in the question. I did not want to get it wrong.

"I guess."

"But do you think he's cute enough that even if he wasn't making a move that maybe you would try to make a move?"

What I didn't say: *Who am "I" in this scenario, Chloe? Am I*

*you? Am I you who must pretend to like Harrison? Who needs me to*
*help you perpetuate this fiction in your own mind?*

What I said instead: "Harrison's totally cute."

The night of Tyler's party, I went over to Chloe's house
as usual to get ready. This was an elaborate process that I had
come to understand to take a minimum of two hours. It was
why I agreed to any of this—to go a party I didn't want to go
to, to wearing makeup I didn't want to put on, clothes I didn't
want to wear. I would let Chloe dress me up like a doll with
things from her own closet, turning me into a mini version of
herself, a living tribute to her choices.

I should have known that it meant something that I enjoyed
the attention so much. She would instruct me to strip down to
my bra and underwear and put on something that had recently
hugged her own skin. I should have understood that my face
turning red whenever she held my chin and carefully applied
lipstick to my lips was not a normal reaction to being touched
by "just a friend."

"You definitely don't need any blush," she would say, my
cheeks already a bright pink.

I should have recognized desire when I felt it. Maybe I
could have controlled it if I had understood what it was. All I
knew was that I would do anything for those two hours alone
with her.

"Oh my god, Eleanor, we are already going to be so late to
this party."

Tyler's party had officially started an hour before, and I
was still struggling with the liquid eyeliner that Chloe had

shown me how to use about fifty times. It took me no less than four tries to look like I had done anything other than take a Sharpie to my eyelids.

"Should we even go?" Chloe asked.

I grabbed yet another makeup wipe to try to minimize the damage of what I had just done to my face. "This party is all that you've been talking about all week," I said.

Chloe looked at herself in the mirror, gave a practiced toss of her long hair over her shoulder.

"Yeah, but we look so good," she said. "Maybe we should just stay here and stare at our own beauty."

I looked at my mangled eye makeup in the mirror.

"I'm staring at my what now?" I said, trying to be funny.

Chloe turned to me.

"I hate when you do that."

"What?"

"You're being self-deprecating."

"I'm not."

She pointed at the mirror.

"Look at yourself, Eleanor."

I looked at my reflection.

"You. Are. Beautiful."

She pointed with each word to give them emphasis.

"I hate that you don't see that," she said.

I wanted to say that the person I saw in the mirror in that moment wasn't me. It was someone wearing a copy of the mask that Chloe had chosen for herself.

What I said instead: "I see it."

Chloe picked up the glass that she had filled with a generous pour of vodka from her dad's liquor cabinet and took a long contemplative sip while looking at herself in the mirror.

"I mean, I would fuck me," she said. It was meant to sound confident and boasting, but it already betrayed the coming of the question that was to follow it. "Wouldn't you?"

I looked at her reflection.

"Would I fuck myself?" I said. The word sounded strange in my mouth. Had I ever used the word *fuck* to mean what it really means? Chloe and I talked about making out with people, about hooking up. Had we ever actually talked about having sex before?

"No," she said. "I mean would you fuck me?"

Oh, the nervous laughter, meant to cover up awkwardness when it of course only makes things more awkward. It has always been my specialty.

"I mean, you look great," I said, trying to recover.

She put down the glass and turned to me. I thought at first that her expression was a joke. It was such forced seriousness, as if she was about to tell me that she was dying from some horrible disease.

"What?" I said.

Then, suddenly, a smile. She took my face in her hands, and I thought I was about to get part two of the lecture about how I didn't know my own beauty, when she put her lips on mine.

I froze, not expecting this, not knowing what I might betray by the wrong reaction. Was this a chaste, friendly gesture?

Was it supposed to prove my own desirability to me? Or was this practice? Was I one step up from a childhood stuffed animal drafted into illicit adolescent make-out sessions?

The kiss ended as little more than a peck on the lips, but Chloe kept holding my face. It felt like something that I had seen in a movie, as if she were admiring an unusual object.

I didn't move. I couldn't breathe. But suddenly everything in my body was more alive than it had ever been before.

*Please.* I nearly said the word out loud. *Please do it again.*

Maybe she heard my psychic plea, or maybe she just hadn't gotten what she wanted yet, because her lips met mine again, and this time I allowed this new aliveness of my body to guide me. This was everything that every other kiss had not been. I wanted to hold back nothing, to give her my mouth, my entire face. I wanted to say every unsaid word directly into her mouth. I wanted to communicate every uncomfortable thought, every half-formed idea that I had about desire. I wanted this kiss to be a high five. This kiss should say, *We did it! We figured it out! That the best thing to do in the whole entire world would be to kiss each other!*

Or I assumed that this was the best thing in the world, until her hand left my face and was suddenly traveling down my back, flirting with the waistband of my pants and then landing in my back pocket, pulling me closer to her until our hips touched.

*This* was the best possible thing in the world that we could do.

Chloe broke off from the kiss and looked at me, that

serious face again, and then her expression broke suddenly into a laugh.

"Haven't you always wanted to do that?" she asked.

I took a deep breath, felt the relief of air rushing into my lungs.

"Yes," I said, marveling at this moment of revelation for us both and grateful for her boldness in making it happen. My entire world had just changed in fifteen seconds.

She took her hand out of my back pocket, put the inches of air back between her body and mine.

"You've never done it?" she asked. She went back to the mirror, inspecting her mascara as if the world had not just imploded and then regenerated itself as a brand-new place, one where I understood desire.

"Done it?"

"Kissed a girl," Chloe said.

*No, I always wanted to kiss you, Chloe. I know that now.*

"Yeah," I said.

Chloe picked up the tube of lipstick and began reapplying to replace what she had left on me.

"It was hot," she said, as if that needed to be explained to me.

She handed me the lipstick and I reapplied, and we stood looking at ourselves in the mirror, a person and a copy of a person. A person and a vibrating mass of desire in the shape of a person.

It takes me a shameful three days to fully come to terms with the fact that I was a total jerk to Pix on the boat. You have to understand that when you are a person who lives with the constant sensation that something is wrong, that you have done so many things wrong that can never be made right, it can be difficult to parse out the different strains of panic and self-loathing that you are feeling in any given moment.

I felt horrible as soon as I left Pix on the boat, but I thought that I was mad at myself for trying and failing to be a part of something. It's not until I'm unpacking a box of T-shirts at the store that I start to realize that I am obsessing about that night, going over and over the details of it in my mind. What if I had just stayed? Why can't I trust that someone is just being nice to me?

I hold up a T-shirt from the box in front of me. It's purple and has the words *Worship the Goddess* on it in sequins.

"What is this order?" I call to Susan.

"One sec," she calls from her office. "I'm trying to get the stupid website to work."

Susan has been trying to make a website for the store for the past six months, and pretty much all that has come from it is the information that Susan has no idea how to build a website.

"Stupid internet," I hear her mutter.

She sticks her head out from the back, sees the shirt I'm holding, and laughs.

"Turn it around!" she says, delighted.

On the back the shirt says: *I am the goddess!*

"Okay, that is a new level of tacky," I say.

"I thought it was cute!" Susan says.

"No you didn't," I say.

"Besides, I thought you would like it, Miss Vagina Vases!"

"Why am I Miss Vagina Vases?"

"I don't know," Susan says, with a raised eyebrow. "Why don't you ask your cute friend?"

I turn back to the box.

"I don't know what you're talking about," I grumble.

Susan comes out of the back and comes over to me. She grabs the shirt out of my hand.

"Hey!"

She holds the T-shirt up as if she's playing a game of keep-away.

"What's going on with the cute girl?" she asks. "Spill."

"Nothing," I mutter.

"If you don't tell me"—Susan hands the T-shirt back to me—"then you are going to have to wear this shirt for the rest of the day."

"What? No!"

"New employee uniform!" Susan declares, obviously very proud of herself.

I refold the shirt and put the pile on the shelf.

"Nothing's going on," I say. "I went to her thing. It was like a witch thing."

Susan deadpans, "Were you the human sacrifice?"

"No, they were nice witches," I say.

"So?"

I turn away from the shelf to look directly at Susan. Why is it so hard for me to just talk to her about the way I'm feeling?

I already think I'm a horrible person; what could she say that would make me feel any worse?

"So I bolted."

"What does that mean?"

"I got freaked out. We were on a boat and there were candles and they were, like, drinking champagne." I feel like a complete prude saying this. Why am I tattling on the witches?

"Were they drunk?" Susan asks.

"No. They seemed to care more about the snacks, really," I admit. "I think maybe I overreacted. I just didn't understand what that girl Pix wanted from me."

Susan raises an eyebrow again.

"Maybe she wants to make a new friend."

"Yeah, but she's got plenty of friends."

"Maybe she *likes* you," Susan says.

I shake my head. "I don't think I want to be liked."

Susan goes behind the counter and sits on my stool that I have stashed back there. She's settling in for the long haul on this conversation.

"You can't always assume the worst about people," she says. "Even if you've gotten hurt before," she adds gently. "If this girl hasn't used you as a human sacrifice yet, you're probably in the clear."

I suddenly feel so embarrassed. How can I possibly explain my reaction when it has so little to do with reality?

"Do you like this girl?" Susan asks. "Like even as a friend?"

I think of Pix's hand in mine as we stood in the circle, our

68

arms rising up above our heads. If magic existed, it was there in that moment.

"Yes," I admit.

"So," Susan says, "fix it."

Susan is exasperatingly practical.

"Fix it how?"

"Tell her you're sorry."

"I don't even know how to find her," I say. "I don't know her last name. She doesn't even live here."

Susan rests her head in her hands and sighs with a dreamy look on her face.

"It's so romantic," she says.

I stick out my tongue at her.

"Watch it!" She points at me. "I still have the power to make you wear one of those shirts!"

I roll my eyes and return to my actual job of stocking the shelves instead of indulging Susan's rom-com fantasies.

And then something occurs to me.

"Ofira goes to Salem High," I say, mostly to myself.

"Who?"

"I could probably find her."

Susan stands up.

"I don't know what's happening, but I like it!" she declares.

I feel a surge of determination as this ridiculous plan starts to take shape in my brain. I look at the time. School gets out in twenty minutes.

"If I go now, I might catch her," I say.

"Wait a second." Susan look at me suspiciously. "Is this all a ruse to get me to let you leave early today?"

I run into the back of the store and grab my sweatshirt and backpack.

"Forty minutes!" I say, already heading out the front door.

"Make it thirty!" Susan calls after me.

Walking as quickly as I can, I make it to Salem High in fifteen minutes. My old school looks as much like a prison as the next modern high school. Squat, with orange brick and strangely placed turrets, it takes an entire block to house all the people who hate me. It is only after I have arrived breathless in front of this cursed building that I realize how truly stupid this plan is. No one here is going to be happy to see me, including Ofira. Looking around, the only cover is two large bushes that flank the entrance. I duck into one of them and try to take deep breaths. This plan is not going to work if I am in the middle of having a panic attack.

The final bell rings, and a minute later the first liberated students make it out into the sunny September afternoon. I try to remind myself to breathe as I scan the crowd, hoping to see only one familiar face and no others.

I retreat farther into the bush when I see Harrison and Tyler come down the steps. Some girl I don't recognize is hanging off Harrison, and he is laughing that perfect, untouchable laugh.

*Yup. This was a bad idea.*

There's a joint in my bag that I had rolled for the end of the day, and I desperately need to smoke it immediately. I am wondering if there's enough of a breeze to carry the smell away from this bush when I see Ofira walking down the steps alone. She is dressed only slightly less outrageously than she was that night on the boat. A long robe over an elaborately embroidered housedress, her hair braided up with ribbons that fall down her back.

"Ofira!" I yell, not remembering if I had decided to back out of this incredibly stupid plan or not.

She stops and looks around.

"In . . . uh, in here!" I say, feeling the stupidest I have ever felt in my entire life.

Ofira looks over at the bush, walks up to it.

"Hello?" she says.

"It's Eleanor," I say, "from the store. The souvenir store. And, uh, the boat."

"What are you doing in there?"

"I need to talk to you."

"Okay," she says.

"Um, not here," I say, suddenly feeling a mounting paranoia that someone else has heard my voice and is going to come over. I leave the safety of the bush, put my head down, and start walking.

"Am I supposed to follow you?" Ofira calls after me.

"Yes!" I yell back.

I don't stop until we make it around the corner, away from the football field to the place where the Salem Country Club golf course takes over with its small curated hills and impossibly green grass carpet.

Ofira stops a few feet away from me and puts her hands on her hips.

"I have other things to do today, Eleanor," she says.

"I just wanted to say I'm sorry," I say. "To you. And to Pix. She invited me to your witch thing, and I just got kind of freaked out and ran off and that wasn't nice of me."

Ofira's face softens a little.

"Okay," she says again.

"I didn't know how to find you guys, so I had to just show up like this."

I take my backpack off my back and get the joint and lighter out of the front pocket. Normally I would wait until I was alone to smoke, but being that close to Salem High qualifies as a state of emergency.

"Why were you hiding in a bush?" she asks.

"I am not exactly welcome there. It's a long story," I say, hoping that there will be no follow-up questions.

I light the joint and inhale. *Okay, I can handle this.* I offer the joint to Ofira as a courtesy.

"No, thank you," she says. Her face is unmoving. She's not giving me much to work with here.

"Anyway, I'm really sorry," I say, now worrying whether I have made another faux pas. "And I'm sure I'm not invited back or anything. But I was hoping you could tell Pix that it was really nice of her to invite me."

"Maybe magic work just isn't your thing," Ofira says. "It's not for everyone."

I shake my head. "It wasn't the magic thing. I guess it was, um, the drinking actually." This is the simplest explanation I can come up with for the approximately one hundred reasons why I was unable to act like a normal human being that night.

"Drinking?"

"I don't like to be around people drinking," I say. "It makes me nervous."

"I don't drink," Ofira says. "Certainly not during or after ceremony. The energy is far too intense to be destabilized in that way."

"You guys were pouring champagne," I say.

"That was sparkling cider."

"Oh."

*Of course. Of course I totally made up a story in my head that had nothing to do with reality.*

She looks at the joint in my hand. "Would it have been okay with you if we were getting high?"

"Yeah. Actually. High people are too relaxed to make trouble."

Ofira steps closer to me. "The only kind of trouble I make," she says, "is for those who deserve it."

Then she turns and walks back toward the school.

"Pixie's last name is Ollendorff," she says, not turning around. "She's Penny Ollendorff on social media. Tell her yourself."

"Oh, okay," I call after her. "Thank you!"

I finish the rest of the joint and start to walk back to the store.

*Penny Ollendorff, Penny Ollendorff, Penny Ollendorff.*

For the first time in a long time, there is something that I can actually do to try to make something right. A tiny flame of hope flickers in me.

I have to find Penny Ollendorff and explain that I am ready for more magic.

# THE EMPEROR

Oh, hey, dude. Thanks for coming, but, uh, it wouldn't hurt you to chill out a little bit. The Empress threw such great parties and now you come in and you're all, "Clean up this mess! There are rules!" Okay, so maybe you're not the funnest guy on the block, but you have your place. Structure, strength, conviction. Sometimes we need things organized from the outside, someone to tell us what to do. Or we need to tell ourselves that there is order to the universe. Again with that silly old binary—you are only "male" in that we associate you with old-school ideas about "manliness"—aggression, authority, power. You're ready for battle in those armor pants hiding under that pretty skirt of yours (don't think we didn't see). But power can corrupt, Emperor. Be sure to always use yours wisely.

Penny Ollendorff does not have much of a social media presence, which makes me like her even more, but she is not difficult to find. There's an unmistakable profile picture, a simple snapshot of her smiling under a cherry blossom tree—her short hair slightly longer than her current buzz cut, her face flushed pink from the sun.

I deleted all my accounts last year, so I have to ask my mom if I can use her account in order to find Pix. I realize that messaging her through my mom's account might be a semi-creepy way to try to repair whatever relationship I have already ruined, but I don't have much of a choice. There will be no reviving of dead accounts for Eleanor Anderson.

I scroll through Pix's limited inventory of pictures and videos. There are a couple pictures of her and Ofira, her and her parents, her as a little kid that another family member has posted, a tiny, long-haired version of Pixie. But even as I am focused on Pix's account, working up the bravery to compose a message to her, I know that the pull of other pages will be too strong for me to resist. I would say that I am possessed by a demon when I type Harrison Turner into the search box, but since I don't believe in the supernatural, I have only my own relentless hunger for self-destruction to blame.

There he is. At the helm of the *Well Appointed*, now posing with the rest of the lacrosse team (a truly impressive sea of white boys); now sweetly visiting his grandmother, no doubt to kiss her ring and make sure his trust fund stays securely in place. There he is with his infamous group of buddies on Halloween, a half-assed mishmash of Joker, vampire, and Freddy Krueger costumes, the worst of the Salem bro contingent. As I scroll further into my own personal hell, I marvel at what is left out of this picture of the perfect grandson. Where is the binge drinking? The drunk driving? The cheating on multiple girlfriends? Where are the demonstrations of power, of status, of the ability to bend information to his own will?

And then I get to it, the thing I didn't know I was looking for, that I wish I could blame that nonexistent demon for finding—Harrison and Chloe's prom photo. That quintessential American picture that could be taken at AnyProm in Anywhere, USA. He's in a well-tailored suit; she's in a shimmery silver dress that I helped her pick out. I remember seeing this picture for the first time and realizing that the dress looked white under the glare of the flash, turning Chloe into an overeager bride.

My eyes scan down to the comments below that picture, posted many months later: "Hope you're doing okay, buddy." "I'm praying for you and Chloe." "Hang in there, man."

There was my life before this picture, and my life after this picture. Before I saw this picture I had somehow deluded myself into thinking that there was still a chance that I could win. As if Harrison and I were knights, ready to be put through a series of tests of strength in order to prove our worthiness. I was ready to joust. To slay the dragon. To hack my way through the impenetrable forest. Because I thought that in saving what Chloe and I had, I was defending something precious from the outside world. This seemed like such a noble fight—the defense of our love.

And yeah, it was love, Harrison, you fucking prick.

Because there was a secret that only Chloe and I knew. And it was simply this: she loved me. I would not be reduced to the delusional best friend, chasing after something I couldn't have, putting myself through torturous years of unrequited love. I had Chloe long before Harrison did.

Chloe did make her first move on Harrison the night of Tyler's party, the first night that she kissed me. And it took her making a move for Harrison to pay attention to her. I always wondered if that was part of my mistake. I had been too easy to get, too receptive and eager. Maybe Chloe liked a challenge. Harrison's level of disinterest existed in direct correlation to his social status. He was hard to get because he was worth it.

Once he gave in, though, he was not shy about showing off this new pairing. Only seventeen minutes passed between us arriving at Tyler's party, Chloe whispering in my ear, "Let's go see Harrison," her pulling me over to the couch where Harrison and Tyler were holding court, and the quick physical escalation of Chloe somehow ending up in Harrison's lap. I found a nonhuman chair for myself and watched as a laugh I had never heard before emanated from Chloe, stopped only by Harrison's mouth on hers, where it stayed for pretty much the next two hours.

I didn't know it was possible for a heart to break once and then somehow continue to break more every second for minutes on end. I wished more than anything that this was an attempt on Chloe's part to make me jealous, but I knew the truth was that she had forgotten that I existed. Watching her kiss Harrison was like accidentally watching the wrong movie. I'd bought a ticket for a romantic comedy and ended up with horror.

The drinking that night was even heavier than usual. Boxes of wine and jugs of hard liquor were being emptied like this was our last night on Earth. Even back then there was something about alcohol that bothered me. Maybe it was the excuse it seemed to give everyone, as if alcohol was Salem Halloween in a glass, a container for everyone's bad behavior. There was a hidden aggression behind the personas that everyone adopted under its influence that I blamed on the drinking, not on who these people actually were. Back then I still saw Salem as a positive place, a small town where we looked out for each other and had each other's best interests at heart. I hadn't yet seen what evil looks like.

It's not a woman in black riding a broomstick, dropping eye of newt into a cauldron to summon the devil, by the way. It looks a lot like a boy with strong arms holding on to a girl in his lap a little too tightly, not giving her time to come up for air. It looks very much like drowning on dry land.

I stayed by Chloe for longer than I should have that night, forcing myself to not run from the train wreck that was continuing to happen over and over in front of me. I didn't remove myself from the situation until one of Tyler's friends knocked a glass vase off the mantel, causing it to shatter on the floor, which set off Tyler, who seemed destined to turn the whole night into some kind of brawl.

I checked to make sure Chloe was not disturbed from her position locked on to Harrison's face (she was not) and took myself for a walk, pushing through the different cliques to get to the back door.

It's impossible to picture now, but because my social status had been bestowed upon me by Chloe, I was welcome everywhere. Everyone was happy to see me. I wonder if the fact that I fell so hard from this great height is proof of what a lie it all was in the first place. I know now that people resented Chloe adopting me that first day of sophomore year the way that she did. I was the new girl in a Tweety Bird shirt with no outward redeeming qualities. Why should I receive such riches? Why else would they eventually celebrate my downfall if they didn't believe that I had it coming all along?

I found the stoners when I finally made my way outside through the back door and out onto the porch. Simon was lying in a hammock, while his sometimes-girlfriend Gillian, a Black girl whose multiple ear and nose piercings seemed to identify her as more goth than stoner, was pushing him back and forth so that he was being rocked like a baby in a cradle. Everyone on the porch seemed to be deeply amused by this. The stoner chuckle was a welcome antidote to the drunken yelling and vodka-fueled make-outs going on inside.

"Sanderson!" Simon called out to me, seeing me pause among their ranks. "What brings you to the cold outdoors?"

"Looking for some fresh air," I said.

"I don't know about that," Simon said. "We've got another kind of air, though."

Gillian passed a lit joint to me, and I took it. I had smoked pot before, but it never seemed to have much of an effect on me. I was convinced I was just one of those people who weren't built for it. I took a hit anyway, quickly letting the billow of smoke back out of my mouth.

"Uh-uh," Gillian said. "You gotta hold it in."

I looked at the diminishing joint and tried again, this time holding the smoke in my lungs for as long as I could stand it, then erupting into a terrible coughing fit that marked me even further as an amateur.

Simon reached up out of the hammock and took the joint from me.

"How's that for fresh air, Sanderson?" he said, smiling.

So the first night that Chloe kissed me was the first night that Chloe kissed Harrison which was the first night that I got high and the first night I figured out how to be at a school party and watch Chloe be with Harrison and not start screaming or set the house on fire.

Hours later, in the car of an obviously drunk stranger who

offered to give us a ride to Chloe's house, I forgot to panic, forgot to remember that this was wrong and dangerous and I had to protect Chloe and protect us and get us out of there NOW. While this kid was swerving down the dark suburban streets, Chloe laughed and took my hand, and I told myself that I had won the night. I was with her, here in this death trap of a car. I would stay over at her house that night. I would wear her pajamas and get in her bed and stay up too late whispering. I would win this war.

I really believed that.

And now?

Staring at my mom's computer screen, I absent-mindedly run the cursor over Harrison and Chloe's prom picture so that her tag comes up. It would be so easy to click on it. I'm already in so deep. What's a little more pain? An extra pinch of salt in the wound?

But then I remember why I'm here.

Go to messages.

Compose a new message.

*Hey, Pix—this is actually Eleanor. I'm on my mom's account. Sorry, I know it's weird. But I would really like to see you, if you feel up for it. I think I have some explaining to do.*

# THE HIEROPHANT

Hi, Hi. May I call you Hi? Because your full name is kind of hard to say, and I can never get a straight answer about whether it's High-row-fant or Hee-row-font and I would rather not embarrass myself by saying it wrong in front of you. Because you, Hi, know everything! If the Emperor and the Empress are the popular couple, you and the High Priestess are the cool but nerdy duo, ready to teach everyone about the secrets of the universe. You want us to learn and then to teach, to find in ourselves what needs to be taught. You want to whisper some advice in the Emperor's ear, get him to stop fighting his angry wars and enforcing his arbitrary rules.

"There's so much more here," you tell him, "if you're ready to listen."

# 5

It's a full twenty-four hours before I get a response from Pix, and by this time I have basically given up all hope. My daily boredom at the store has been replaced with a new level of obsessive thinking that impresses even me. I tell myself that if she doesn't respond, that's it. That's the end of it. There's no going back to Ofira and begging her to redeliver the message. There's no waiting by the dock, hoping that the coven will return on the next full moon. It's over. There's nothing you can do about it.

*Isn't there something you can do about it?*

There is nothing you can do about it.

At home that night, Mom somehow waits hours to deliver the most important news possible: "Hey, honey, I think you got a message on my account."

I go into the living room, where she is sitting on the couch with her laptop.

"You're just telling me this now?"

"When was I supposed to tell you? I just signed in."

"Don't you have notifications on?"

"What?" My mother looks at me like I have just said something to her in German.

"Okay, can I just see it, please?"

Mom pauses for a moment.

"Is everything okay?" she asks me.

My arm is still outstretched to grab the laptop.

"What?"

"This is the girl you met at the store? You went to her party on a boat?"

*Susan, why do you tell all of my business?*

"Yes," I say, trying so hard not to sound annoyed and failing so badly. "I forgot to get her number, so this was the only way I could find her."

"She doesn't live in Salem?"

I know what Mom's doing. It's the third degree a year and a half too late. I disappeared into Chloe's life, and she let me go without any questions. And then she blamed herself for not keeping an eye on me. As if I would have done anything differently. As if she could have stopped me.

"She lives in Marblehead. Her cousin lives in Salem. They are witches, and I have agreed to be their human sacrifice. Can I please have the laptop?"

Mom eyes me for a moment, weighing her options, and finally hands it over.

"Thank you," I manage to mutter as I head to my room.

"I didn't read it," Mom calls after me.

"I wasn't . . . it's not . . ." My sputtering attempts to make it seem like I don't care about this are abandoned as soon as I open the message.

*Meet me at the Witch House at 5 p.m. tomorrow*, it says.

Only in Salem would this be a completely normal message to receive. And only because it is from Pix does this combination of words make my heart soar.

Here's the thing about Salem tourist attractions. They're all basically fake. Which I guess is appropriate for a town that's famous for a holiday where people pretend to be things that they are not. None of the original locations from the witch trials still exist in Salem. The place where most of the accused were hanged is now a chain pharmacy parking lot. The old jail where they were held is a Realtor's office. And the victims are buried in scattered locations around the outskirts of town. The most authentic memorials aren't even in Salem but next door in Danvers, which used to be a part of Salem back in the day but defected when the rural farmers who lived there got sick of putting up with the delinquent behavior of the seafaring merchants who made up one of Massachusetts' biggest ports.

So every attraction in Salem has a different kind of relationship to "the truth." At our end of Essex Street, where the store is, you get the most straightforward version of fantasy Salem. Here is where you will find the "Haunted Neighborhood" and the Salem pedestrian mall, featuring old-timey photo places that charge thirty dollars for a picture of you in a pointy black hat riding a broomstick past the moon. Here is the Salem Wax Museum, filled with decaying forty-year-old wax figures in front of peeling painted backdrops. Here are the seasonal haunted houses, the Witch Museum (more dusty wax figures), the statue of Elizabeth Montgomery as Samantha Stevens on the TV show *Bewitched*. Here are the dude-bro horror paraphernalia stores. Here is the detritus of capitalism's idea of magic, of witchery, of objects you can pay to see or be or own. Susan's store is just another cog in the wheel of Salem consumerism. The real magic spell of Salem is that no one gets out of here without buying a whole bunch of stuff they don't need.

Then there are the Salem attractions that attempt to claim some kind of authenticity, a connection to the actual history of this place beyond wishful thinking and cliché. There's the underwhelming memorial to the victims of the witch trials, a series of low stone ledges set between a parking lot and the Burying Point, the town cemetery, as if these ghosts might like a place to sit in between hauntings. There's the allegedly haunted Hawthorne Hotel built near the location of the apple orchard of Bridget Bishop, the first woman executed in the witch trials (of course she's coming back for her apples! Ghosts love apples!). And the crème de la crème of locations grasping at any kind of actual historical relationship to the witch trials—the Witch House.

The Witch House is a black, three-gabled, much-photographed building at the other end of Essex Street from Susan's store. People who have primarily seen it on social media as a perfectly framed backdrop are always surprised to see how unexceptional it feels in person, sandwiched tightly between the church next door and a busy intersection. Across the way, Salem Antiques hawks creepy old dolls (demon possession included!) and old wooden furniture salvaged from houses long gone.

The only remarkable thing about the Witch House is that it still exists. It was originally the home of Jonathan Corwin, one of the judges on the witch trials, and it used to just be called the Jonathan Corwin House, until the developing market for all things witch in Salem dictated that if you paint something black and slap the word *witch* on it, the tourists will come.

Although the iconic influencer view is of the front of the house, the actual entrance to the Witch House is in the back of the building, through the gift shop. Because of course it is.

It's five p.m. and I am waiting outside the door in the parking lot, chastising myself for not better clarifying if I am supposed to meet Pix out here or inside. I still don't have her phone number, and I don't know my mom's password even if I wanted to sign into her account to send another message. This is what I have been reduced to—needing my mother's password to try to make friends.

A few people exit the gift shop, and I catch a glimpse of the person sitting at the ticket counter inside. It's not Pix but Ofira, with tiny fake black birds poking out of the bird's nest of her hair. I go inside. She's counting the money in the cash box.

"The Witch House is closed for the day," she says without looking up.

"Hey," I say.

She looks up.

"Ah," she says. She points to a bookshelf in the corner. "There's your tour guide."

Pix is browsing the shelf, her back turned to us.

"Pix, you've got a guest."

Pix turns around, and my pulse starts racing like I have run a very long distance to get here. This girl makes me nervous.

"Hi," I say.

"Hi," she says.

"You work here?" I ask.

She clasps her hands in front of her and entwines her fingers like she is about to lead us in prayer.

"Ofira does. I just like to visit. Have you seen it?"

I shake my head. I have never had a reason to before.

"So. Let's go."

"Isn't it closed?"

Pix smiles. "Not to witches."

Pix leads me around the first floor of the Witch House. We are the only people here, and this place is not totally without a creepy vibe, even if its historical connection to the trials is minimal. There is some spare furniture, some seventeenth-century clothing displayed on mannequins, some wall cards grasping at the house's historical relevance.

"How long has Ofira worked here?" I ask Pix as I pretend to look at the displays.

"She got the job at the beginning of the summer, right after she moved to town. She's really serious about this whole 'saving the soul of Salem' thing."

"But this place barely has anything to do with the trials."

Pix looks at me.

"Someone knows their Salem history," she says.

"I have a lot of time on my hands," I say. "And I don't like the internet. So I have read every travel book in Susan's store approximately twenty times."

"You don't like the internet?"

"Nope."

"That's a big thing not to like."

"I manage it," I say, hoping that I am being clever. I can't confirm or deny if I am because Pix moves into the next room. I follow her into the kitchen, where iron utensils hang around a huge open stone fireplace that served as the house's only oven. No wonder these people believed in demon possession. They were basically living in the Middle Ages.

"Ofira thinks the house has enough of a connection to the town's history to be a place that she wants to protect," Pix says. "And I think the misuse of 'witch' just makes it all the more important to her. It's always been a word that was used as a weapon against the woman who lived on the edge of town who maybe looked different and had a relationship with animals and knew how to make herbal remedies and plan things according to the phases of the moon. That was scary to these people."

"And now it's used to sell T-shirts," I say.

Pix nods. "That's why it's important to us to remember the original intentions of the word. If we can reclaim it, we can help heal some of the energy around it."

"And what exactly is Ofira doing for this place?" I ask.

"She's been doing energy work on the house on the days when she's in the gift shop, after she closes up. I come by sometimes to help."

I want to ask what this means, but I'm worried that I won't be able to hide my skepticism if Pix explains it to me. "Energy work" is the kind of phrase that gets thrown around a lot in the more new age pockets of Salem capitalism. It usually comes with a hefty price tag and instructions to solve all your problems through positive thinking. So I don't think much of "energy work." But this is not the moment to tell Pix that.

"I just wanted to say thanks for meeting me," I say instead, trying to remember exactly how I was planning to fix things between us.

Pix turns to me expectantly, and I find myself frozen in the face of her seriousness. How to explain literally everything? I am embarrassingly silent.

"No problem," she says. "Here, let's go upstairs." She leads me up a narrow staircase to the second floor of the house, where the windows get smaller and a thick layer of dust has settled on a four-poster bed and a nightgowned mannequin.

"When do you think the last time someone updated this place was?" Pix asks me, looking around the room.

"Maybe the seventies?" I guess.

"Yeah, but which seventies?"

She smiles at me, not her biggest eyes-closing smile, but one that makes me feel like we are both in on a private joke.

*Oh, Eleanor. You're in so much trouble—you're already cataloging this girl's smiles.*

"I was really glad you invited me to the boat thing," I say, needing to start talking about this immediately before I lose the nerve to talk about it at all.

"Okay," Pix says. She clasps her hands together in that prayer-like gesture again, and I wonder if this is what she does when she's nervous.

*Is Pix nervous?*

"It seems like a really cool group," I say, "and I don't usually go for that kind of stuff."

"You work in a witch store," Pix points out.

"Yeah, but you've seen it," I say. "It's witch by association only. Susan barely even knew we had tarot cards."

Pix goes over to the nightgown and examines it. It would fit perfectly in her outfit rotation, floor-length ghost-woman chic.

"How's the Fool?" she asks without looking at me.

"The tarot card?"

"Yeah."

"I'm on to the Hierophant, actually," I say. "I've kind of been taking them one by one."

She turns now and looks at me.

"And what does the Hierophant have to say?"

I take a deep breath. I have the sudden sensation that it is important that I answer this question correctly.

"I guess what he has to say is that sometimes the truth is complicated."

"I think he says that the truth is knowable," she says. "And explainable."

Right. Explainable.

*Say some words now, Eleanor.*

"I've had a pretty bad year," I finally manage to say. "Some things happened that have made me kind of . . . jumpy."

"And now you don't like boats," she offers.

"I'm not crazy about boats. But it's the drinking really. Being in groups of people drinking makes me nervous."

"Drinking sparkling cider," she says.

"Ofira told me. I just reacted quickly and didn't think. And even if you guys were drinking, it's not my business, and I shouldn't have left like that without explaining myself, and, uh . . ." I take in a deep breath and say, "I wish that I had stayed."

"You're allowed to leave a situation that makes you uncomfortable."

"Yeah, but I didn't want you to think that I didn't like hanging out with you. Because I did. I mean, I do."

Pix looks at me for a moment, then says, "Let's sit," as if this will help things. She sits down on the floor, crossing her legs under her long skirt. I sit down, feeling the layer of dust under me, picturing it coating the back of my black jeans. I feel like a little kid waiting to hear a story.

"When Ofira really started with all of this witch stuff a couple years ago," Pix says, "she went on a big research kick to figure out what kind of witch she wanted to be. Her dad's family is Italian and Mexican, so she read about witches of Sicily and Day of the Dead practices in Mexico to try to figure out her ancestral relationship to magic. Our moms' side of the family is Welsh, so we did a bunch of research on Celtic paganism. I would help her find whatever she needed for the perfect spell, or to source the perfect crystal, and then plan the perfect astrological moment to use it all. And in the end it was exciting to learn about these ancestral traditions, but it became clear that anything that we did was actually just about intention. And intention is about energy. That's all that magic is."

I look around the room from our floor vantage point. We have time traveled to become seventeenth-century children playing in our bedroom, watching the light fade from the corners as the sun sets.

"If something feels wrong to you, it's probably because something about the energy is wrong," Pix says. "And because you are a sensitive person, you need to pay attention to what that means for you."

I want to tell Pix that "sensitive" doesn't even begin to explain what is wrong with me. She is a "sensitive" person in the good way. The way that pays attention to the people around her and tries to help them. I am the bad kind of sensitive. The kind where I have no defenses against the seemingly never-ending punches that life continues to throw at me.

"I don't think it's a good idea to be this sensitive of a person," I say, not quite sure of my own words. It comes out as almost a whisper. The darkening room has made me feel like someone is listening. Maybe this place is haunted after all.

"Being so sensitive is how we know we are witches," Pix says. "We're already in conversation with everything around us whether we want to be or not—people, places, animals, the time of year, time of day, the phase of the moon. We may as well figure out what to do with all of that information. Otherwise it'll just overwhelm us."

I say this next thing without knowing exactly how it's going to sound.

"I don't want to be like this anymore."

Pix leans back and seems to examine me, as if she is scanning me to find out exactly what's wrong.

"Like what?" she asks.

"I don't want the shitty things that have happened to prevent me from living my life anymore."

I realize that I haven't had a reason to want my life back until now.

I wait for her to ask me, "What shitty things happened?" She doesn't.

She leans forward now, rests her elbows on her knees and her head in her hands.

"I like hanging out with you," she says. It is matter-of-fact. An unremarkable statement. It is only in my mind that fireworks are now being set off in an elaborate, many-colored display.

"You don't have to say that," I say.

Old habits die hard. This self-deprecation will need more than a cute girl being nice to me to get drummed out of my system.

"I don't say things that I don't mean," she says.

I raise an eyebrow. "You like hanging out with me even though you know I'm a mess who can't be trusted to not bolt from a witch boat party?"

"Our ceremonial circles are usually held on dry land. No more boats for a while."

"Does that mean I'm invited back?"

Pix lets an uncomfortably long pause go by. I wonder what it really means for her to read people's energy. I look at her and feel a churning in my stomach as I realize that I want nothing more than to tell absolutely everything about this past year of my life to this person who I barely know. But I stop myself, because the only thing better than talking to someone about this year would be talking to someone who has no idea what has happened to me in the past year.

The now-familiar smell of smoke from one of Ofira's herb bundles comes wafting up the stairs.

"She's starting," Pix says. "Should we go help?"

And then I, Eleanor (S)Anderson, Salem's biggest skeptic and non-witchy person, say the following words: "Sure, let's go help Ofira do energy work on the Witch House."

# THE LOVERS

Our first little scene involving a few players! There's the two of you, Lovers, and wait, who's that? What kind of threesome is this? Oh no, that's just a benevolent angel come to bless this Adam-and-Eve-style union. The world begins when two halves become a whole! Balance! Communion! Creation! The heavens look fondly upon such things.

It's cute that you guys are nudists. I guess when you're really ready to see each other, you've got nothing to hide. In love we will find acceptance of all the parts of us! We will find majesty in our flaws! What are flaws anyway? Humanity is beautiful!

One thing, Lovers—there is a balance of energies to be sought in our own bodies, a partnership to be made within ourselves. Love Self in the most compassionate way. Love Self as you would love the other in the garden with you, standing naked and happy under that shining sun.

A word of advice to our gal on the right—watch out for

that serpent in the tree behind you. He might start asking tough questions like: Do you want bliss, or do you want the truth? Choose wisely.

# 6

Once you think you understand what love is, you're in a whole lot of trouble. Because you think that this is a new feeling that you and this other person have invented. No one has ever felt like this, and no one will ever feel like this again. And part of what you invented is a new psychic ability—one where two people don't have to say much, because they both simply understand.

But no one gets held to promises that were only agreed to in dreams.

Chloe never promised me anything. And the promises that I made were only made in my mind.

*I will stay by your side.*

*I will protect you.*

*I will go along with your crazy plans.*

What I said out loud:

"I love you."

What she said out loud:

"I love you."

So. There's that.

The first four times Chloe told me that she loved me, she meant it as a friend. The fact that I remember every one of them tells you how far gone I was.

The first one was at the end of a phone call, and could have been a mistake, an involuntary reflex.

"Okay, love you!"

I stumbled over the word *goodbye*, as if I was trying to correct her, but she had already hung up.

The second time was when I agreed to help her with a history paper.

"Oh my god, I love you so much right now."

The third was during a hug accompanied by a shriek into my ear on the day when she heard that she got into a month-long summer program at the Fashion Institute of Technology in New York City.

"Ahhhhhh, I love you!"

We jumped up and down, holding each other and shrieking. My sad heart that had been so against her leaving me for the summer was temporarily appeased by the fact that somehow the good fortune of the moment had turned favorably on me.

The last time she said it and meant it only as a friend was when her grandmother died. She went to California with her parents and sister for the funeral and called me when they got back to their hotel that night. The time difference meant I had to whisper into the phone as our coast reached midnight and my mom tried to sleep in the next room.

"Just tell me something stupid," she said. I could hear the day's tears in her voice.

I spent the next hour whispering about nothing—school gossip, made-up gossip, what someone we hated had posted on social media that day. What someone we liked had posted. I kept wondering if I should pause and see if she was actually still on the other end, but then I would say something that made her laugh and I knew the connection was unbroken.

"I love you, Eleanor," she said before finally hanging up. This one deliberate, not a reflex. It was a plea from someone who had visited the edge of the underworld that day and was having trouble reporting back. This one meant, "I'm going to tell people this now, while I can."

I should say that there were more friend "I love yous" than there were more-than-friend "I love yous," which should have told me something at the time, but I kept thinking that there were more coming. We had a future of "I love yous" ahead of us, didn't we? All the "I love yous" a person could say or hear or accept or believe. I thought the story was far from over.

But there were only two real ones.

The first time she said it for real was a few weeks after the party at Tyler's. Harrison seemed to be playing off his and Chloe's marathon make-out session at Tyler's party as just drunken antics. I assumed that Chloe felt the same way, because the party was not mentioned again, and normally we would have spent days analyzing every moment of it. I thought this was because something more important had happened that day. Our kiss.

I knew it was important because it kept happening.

We would always sit on the floor of her room to do our homework—now she would sit right next to me, our thighs touching. The end of math homework was celebrated with her turning my face to hers and kissing me. Two weeks of this. Like an experiment.

There's another way this story could have gone. With Chloe insisting that she wasn't attracted to girls, that our intimacy was just practice, just a way to gain experience. Except it wasn't like that at all.

Because of that "I love you."

It was a Friday afternoon in early April, and we were lying in her bed next to each other, talking about nothing. Harrison had offhandedly invited Chloe to a group movie outing that night, and the fact that she had said no only to stay home and do nothing with me was making me giddy with victory.

*This is real*, I thought, lying next to her, talking about everything and nothing. *This is real, this is real, this is real.*

If spells do exist, that must have been one, because Chloe rolled over suddenly to face me. She looked confused, or like she was in pain. Maybe both.

"What?" I said.

"I love you," she said, seemingly surprised by her own words. She looked away from me after she said it, as if she needed some privacy to think about what had just come out of her mouth.

"Oh," I said. "I love you too." Each word sounded like its own sentence, as if the words themselves wanted to stay separate just to hedge their bets.

Her eyes came back to mine, and she got on top of me. It

felt playful, like she was going to start tickling me. But then we were kissing. And then we were finding out what it meant to touch every part of each other.

This went on nearly every day for two months after school and on weekends in Chloe's room. I barely saw my mother. I missed shifts at the store. I got Cs in my best subjects. This was the only thing I cared about. I couldn't imagine anyone wanting to do anything other than this.

Harrison's name lost all meaning in those months. He was just another person at the long lunch table where Chloe liked for us to sit, a part of a crowd that loosely included us. He was never spoken of with any importance. Because nothing was important anymore except for us.

And then came prom.

One afternoon in early June, Chloe offered to walk me to the store from school for my late-afternoon shift. This was a little strange. Usually she took the bus home and I would just head over to her house after I finished work. But I didn't think much of it. Spending time together was what we did. In public, in private. And wasn't it fine that the public didn't know yet about the private? I never reached to hold her hand when we were out. Never showed her affection in public. I seemed to be waiting for some kind of go-ahead that I was sure would eventually come. These things are delicate.

*Be patient, Eleanor.*

If she wasn't ready for the world to see us as a couple, I would understand. My queerness was something that I found comfort in. It fit me well, like a pair of supportive shoes. And Mom had said to me about a thousand times throughout my childhood, "You know it's okay to be in love with someone of any gender, right?" to the point where it had started to annoy me by the time I actually hit puberty and realized that I was not attracted to boys at all.

I had a feeling that Chloe's mother had not given her the same speech that I had gotten. So I had expected to wait, secure in the knowledge of what we meant to each other.

On this day we made our way up the hill from the school. Spring in Salem is everything you could want from spring—trees in full bloom and gardens magically revived from their hibernation. New England spring is glorious because it is fleeting. So you take it in while you can.

Talk of an overly complicated essay question on an English test took an abrupt shift when we turned the corner onto Essex Street.

"Prom is in a couple weeks," Chloe said.

Something in me fluttered.

"Oh yeah," I said.

"I know that's so not your thing."

"It's not?"

"You don't like to do things. Like 'do' do things."

I didn't know what this meant. I had done pretty much everything Chloe had done for the past nine months.

"I guess I don't really care that much about prom," I said. "Why?"

"Harrison asked me to go with him."

Her attempt to say this in a casual way was such a failure that I nearly laughed out loud. I looked at her. She would not look at me.

"And?" I said.

What stage of the war were we in? What maneuver had the enemy troops just dared to make? And just when things had been so peaceful.

"It feels like it would be rude to say no," she said.

A red flame was crawling up the inside of my head. I knew it was my turn to say something, but it felt like if I opened my mouth I was going to spit fire.

Chloe stopped walking and turned to me.

"Don't make this into a thing. This doesn't have to be a thing."

"It doesn't?"

"No."

I pursed my lips and said nothing. Any admission in this moment would feel like weakness. Any attempt to get her to reconsider, to beg her to either take me or to not go at all. I had to be the one who was so secure in our love that even this betrayal couldn't rock me.

"Do what you want to do," I said.

"You sure?"

If Chloe was flattered by the status that a prom date like Harrison would bring her, so be it. I couldn't give her that. Any status that I had at Salem High was a result of my connection to her. But she loved me. And that was all that mattered. So it had to be okay.

My instinct was to kiss her as a response. A kiss that would say, *Who cares what you do with Harrison, because I get to do this,* but I knew it would only complicate this moment.

"Yeah," I said, doing my best impression of a person who

was not currently imploding at one million angry thoughts per second. "You can do whatever you want."

We walked the rest of the way to the store in silence, each offering a curt "bye" upon arrival at our destination. But that night when I showed up at her house, it was as if the conversation had never happened. We were back in our old world again. That's when the second real "I love you" happened. It was a reward for my easygoing nature. I took it, happily.

And then she had sex with Harrison after the prom.

She wasn't even drunk. She had decided not to drink that night, a possibly calculated move to make sure she was fully managing her impression in the eyes of others. Sloppy girl on the arm of the most popular boy was not a cute look.

She was supposed to text me after the dance with the location of the inevitable after party and I would meet her there. But she never did. Instead she went to the party with Harrison and had sex with him in Adam Walker's parents' king-sized bed.

She waited two days to tell me. But she did tell me. We were at my house. Her suggestion. I realized later that she knew I would have to stay calm in our small apartment with my mom home. As if I would ever show her my anger. As if I could.

Mom was delighted to have us both there for dinner that night. She was doing well that spring. Her doctor had put her on a new round of antibiotics that seemed to actually make her feel a little better without taking away her energy. She was still working at the store then, but Susan had us on opposite schedules, so we rarely saw each other there, and I was usually at Chloe's after work every night. Mom had started making comments about never seeing me, but I could tell that she didn't want to interfere with whatever seemed to be making me happy. And up until that point, it was Chloe who made me happy.

In my room after dinner, Chloe and I sat on the floor scrolling through social media feeds, pausing only to show each other something. We hadn't touched each other since she'd gone to prom, and I didn't know what to make of this.

"Did you see the prom pictures?" she asked me after a little while.

Of course I had. They had shown up on social media the day after the dance like an infestation, tags blazing.

"Yeah," I said. "Your dress looked really pretty."

I was supposed to say something else now. Something like, "Did you have fun?" But I didn't.

She was supposed to say something like, "I'm sorry I didn't text you after." But she didn't.

Instead she said, "The after party was kind of wild."

"Oh yeah?" I said. Casual. So casual.

*Keep scrolling. Keep scrolling. Eyes on your screen.*

"Yeah, I had sex with Harrison."

She said it like it was just more gossip. Like she was talking about someone else. Like she had really convinced herself that this wasn't going to devastate me.

The pictures on my phone blurred. I realized I was scrolling so fast that it had become a wheel on a slot machine, spinning wildly. It mirrored the way my stomach felt in that moment. A chaotic attempt to process too much information.

"I mean, it was my first time, and I just kind of wanted to do it," she said.

"It wasn't your first time," I said before I could stop myself.

She started to protest and then stopped. Were we really going to have a conversation about the semantics of the word *sex* right now? Was she really going to sit there and tell me I didn't even rate enough to register on her personal sexual history?

"So what does this mean?" I asked. My voice shook, unable to hide my anger. Or was it fear? Was she going away from me now? Was I being left?

"I mean, it was prom. It's just what you do."

"Are you serious?" I finally turned to look her in the eyes, and I saw her flinch. Which of the five hundred things that I was feeling in this moment could she see in my eyes? Pick any one of them, Chloe.

"It's not a big deal, E," Chloe said. She leaned over and took my hand. "Come on. Are you really upset?"

I didn't answer. So she kissed me. Her best weapon. And my stupid heart leapt up like a dog being offered a treat. It didn't care about my anger or my fear or my stupid pride. All it wanted was for Chloe to keep kissing me.

"It doesn't change anything," she said, sitting back but still holding my hand.

Did she really believe that? It didn't matter. Because in

that moment I wanted to believe it. So I let myself believe. When nothing had ever been more untrue.

Ok my mother bought the whole family tickets to a ballet or something on the next full moon and how am I going to explain to her that witchcraft is more important than men in tights? Pix texts me.

>**Me:** I mean, men in tights are important.
>**Pix:** LOL but Ofira will kill me if I miss a circle.
>**Me:** Can you get excommunicated from being a witch?
>**Pix:** If it's possible, she will be the one to figure out how.
>**Me:** Can I vouch for you? Say you're a good witch and not a bad witch?
>**Pix:** What makes you so sure I'm not a bad witch? ☺

When Pix starts texting me daily, I am worried for a number of reasons:

1. I don't know if she likes me as more than a friend, and I am not very good at figuring these things out.
2. I still don't know if Pix even dates girls.
3. Her texts are clever and flirty and I am neither of those things and so I feel a deep inadequacy every time she writes and I spend about fifteen minutes trying to compose the perfect text back and each time I think she has probably lost interest by the time I respond and normal people can just send a text like "LOL" or a funny GIF or "whut's up" but none of those things feel good enough for Pix because Pix is magic and Pix is

a beautiful mystery and fuck I have an overwhelming and horrifying crush on Pix.

4. If I have an overwhelming and horrifying crush on Pix, that means that I have not trained my brain out of the capacity for love, which is what I had promised myself I would do.

5. If I have not trained my brain out of the capacity for love, then I have not protected myself and/or others.

6. Also I am afraid of Ofira, and I don't really understand yet how to make sure that I don't get on her bad side.

But since my assistance with the energy clearing of the Witch House, I seem to be back in Ofira's good graces at least enough to be invited to the next new moon circle, which unfortunately happens to coincide with October first, which unfortunately is the date of the yearly Haunted Happenings Parade, the official opening of Salem for October business.

Ofira wants to go to the parade after our circle, Pix texts.

This response I do not have to take time to consider: Has she ever been to the Haunted Happenings Parade?

No, but she figures as a true Salemite now she's obligated to go.

Can she be talked out of it? I respond.

Y? Is it bad?

I picture the throngs of drunken assholes made bolder by being able to hide their identities behind costumes. It's a practice round for the night of Halloween, when all bets are completely off.

By the time of the Haunted Happenings Parade last year, Chloe was no longer speaking to me. I assume she went to the parade with Harrison, hung off Harrison's arm, played the part of perfect half of a perfect couple. I assume that they held hands and kissed and put on a whole show. That she laughed at his jokes and made him feel like he was special, as if Harrison needed to feel any more special. Maybe she told him that she loved him that night. Made him feel like he had earned that coveted place in her heart.

Even though she didn't love him.

I know that she didn't.

I spent that night last year as I spent most of last October—relatively safe within the confines of the store. Everything was fine as long as I never left the store. If only I had been smart enough to stay in there forever.

It's not exactly that it's bad, I text Pix. It's just kind of A LOT. Like, too much.

That won't convince O not to go, she writes back. She tends to like too much.

Yeah, I noticed, I write, thinking of Ofira's bird's nest hair and layered robes. It just can get kind of rowdy. Big crowds.

If you're with us you can keep us safe, Pix responds.

I stare at that for a while. *Keep us safe.*

It was the wrong thing to say.

I am doing exactly the opposite of keeping anyone safe by allowing any of this to continue.

Sure, I write back. We'll go to the parade.

# THE CHARIOT

Time to go full steam ahead! We've heard from some wise folks, conjured up some magic, and indulged with the best of the pleasure-seekers, and now nothing can stop us! You know where you're going, Chariot, and you know you've got to get there ASAP! This is the moment! Seize it before it slips through your fingers! Let those wise sphinxes carry you away from the known territory of the village behind you, out into a brave new world of possibility!

But just remember, Chariot, charge too quickly and you might not see the hazards of the road before they trip up your cart and send you flying. Bend your knees as you accelerate. Find your place of balance. Don't let focusing too intensely on a single goal be your downfall. Don't force the world to comply with your wishes just because you feel they are RIGHT. Let the road meet you halfway, Chariot. And always keep your eyes open for what's coming.

It turns out that Ofira's goals for the night of October first are far more ambitious than just going to the Haunted Happenings Parade. The coven is instructed to meet at the most famous parking lot of the most nondescript pharmacy in the state of Massachusetts. A place that has the unfortunate historical notoriety of being built on the land where the victims of the witch trials were hanged.

As with most places in this town, once the local business owners figured out that they were sitting on a gold mine of marginalized American history, it was too late to save the most compelling locations of the trials. The pharmacy parking lot had already been paved. There was no rescuing this notorious plot of land from its destiny as a bland suburban monument to practicality that could exist in any town, in any state. It's not like it's unusual for atrocities to be paved over in this country. It's just that most places don't change their minds a couple hundred years later.

In a recent scramble to provide something to look at for

those curious enough to track down this spot, a low stone wall was assembled at what is now called Proctor's Ledge, with the names of the victims inscribed in it. A tree with big ambitions but not much to show for itself stands in the middle of the area, already shedding its leaves.

When Pix tells me that we will meet at Proctor's Ledge, I don't have the heart to warn her that they will probably not be the only coven there. Just as weekends in October bring in throngs of partiers, they also bring out the warring sects of witches in this town. As the owner of a shop that doesn't even make an attempt to seem authentically witchy, Susan manages to mostly stay out of the witch politics, but for those who consider Salem to be a witch mecca, there are several ongoing turf wars. There are those who see themselves as members of a religion with rules and traditions that need to be protected, those who seem to be in it for the glory (there is such a thing as a celebrity witch in this town), and those who are eager to cash in on the witch trend in whatever way they can, even if it means masquerading as someone who actually cares about this stuff. Salem politics looks pretty much like the petty squabbles of any small town—there's just a lot more black clothing and cats involved. Sometimes hexes.

I get to Proctor's Ledge at six, as instructed by Pix, and as I expected, there are about fifteen other people there who are not part of our group. They are lighting candles and jockeying for spots around the place at the base of the tree where the words *We Remember* have been pressed into the concrete. This crowd will grow by the week into a few hundred people on Halloween night.

I spot Ofira and Pix with the rest of the girls on the other side of the parking lot. Pix waves to me, and I go over to them.

"I meant to warn you," I said, "it's kind of hard to have places to yourself this time of year."

"We're not going over there," Ofira says. "We're going inside."

With that she leads the five of us down the sidewalk to the front of the pharmacy, where she marches confidently through the sliding automatic doors, as if she has opened them with the power of her mind.

Inside, the store is brightly lit with fluorescent lights and radiating the smell of whatever they spray to cover up the scent of industrial cleaner. Halloween doesn't just get an aisle in here, it takes up the entire front area of the store, complete with life-sized talking figurines and enough candy to keep the whole town on a sugar high all month.

We gather around Ofira, and she reaches into the bag slung on her shoulder and hands us each a small silver spray bottle.

"Smokeless purifier," she says. "So as to not set off the fire alarms."

I take the bottle that Ofira hands to me.

"This store provides a meditative labyrinth for us to walk," she announces. "As you spray the aisles, banish the curse of mediocrity that has been placed upon this hallowed land."

And since that seems to be enough explanation for the other girls, they head off, each to a different part of the store. I am standing at the entrance holding a tiny spray bottle and wondering what exactly "smokeless purifier" is.

"What am I supposed to do?" I ask Tatiana, who has started with the closest candy aisle.

"Just spray, baby!" she says gleefully. "Like this." She heads down the aisle, happily misting the air around her. "Don't overthink it!" she calls back to me.

*Right. Like that's a possibility for me.*

I head to another aisle farther into the store. Cat food and bleach. I am not totally sure what I am banishing here. If we are anti-commercialism, I don't have much of a moral upper hand as someone who survives off a salary at a souvenir store. But I have only just made my way back into the coven, and I don't want to screw this up. So I start spraying.

The mist that comes out of the little bottle smells clean and fresh. It could easily have come from one of the bottles of cleaning products I am walking past. I guess sometimes mystical and practical cleansing can be the same thing.

I take a right into the next aisle and nearly bump into Pix. She laughs and steps aside.

"Doing okay?" she asks.

"Oh yeah." I shrug. "Just a normal Friday!"

She smiles and keeps moving. I do the same. This aisle— toilet paper and magazines. Spray. Spray. Spray. Now Pix is moving down the aisle across from me, and I let out a particularly vigorous spray. Against my better judgment, I start laughing. I don't want her to think that I am not taking this seriously, but this is truly the most absurd thing that I have ever done. My laughing makes Pix start laughing, and then suddenly we are uncontrollably giggling. I take the opportunity to join her in her aisle, and we pass Ofira to make it to the final aisle of the store—beverages and frozen food.

Over the sound of the ubiquitous Halloween soundtrack ("Thriller," "Monster Mash," and "Time Warp" will be played several hundred thousand times within Salem city limits by the time this month is over), I can hear a concerned manager: "What are those kids doing?" I look at Pix, and we head to the end of the aisle to try to see the other girls. Ofira is zigzagging and spraying proudly, humming to herself. The manager walks up to her.

"Kid, what the hell are you doing?"

Ofira stops spraying.

"Purifying your psychic air, sir."

"All right, the psychic air is pure enough now, thank you."

I turn around quickly to say something to Pix, and she is closer than I thought, our faces suddenly inches apart. Her eyes are wide, and I'm not sure if it's watching Ofira getting caught or our closeness that is causing this.

I could kiss her right here and now in the last aisle of this brightly lit suburban chain pharmacy. Our first kiss could be right next to the tubs of cheddar popcorn. Cheddar popcorn would never be the same again.

But I will not do this. Because I should not do this. Because if I desire something, it probably means it is very bad for everyone involved. And then suddenly the other girls are running from all sides of the store toward the exit, and Pix takes my hand and we are running after them, leaving the manager in our wake, looking annoyed but unfazed by more unexplainable Salem behavior.

We all run laughing down Boston Street, six girls in black spraying the air around them as they go. And I am one of them.

It is only when we reach Essex that the scale of the Haunted Happenings extravaganza becomes apparent. The parade turns the corner here, onto Washington at Lappin Park, and the zombie brigade has just made it to where we stand—hundreds of people dressed in various zombie getups, moaning and stumbling. The sides of the road are packed with families. Children screaming with joy or crying in fear, or maybe doing a little of both.

"This is it," I say. "The Haunted Happenings Parade."

Ofira looks with a determined face at the crowded sidewalk. I can tell she wants in on this chaos, but walking through it now would require pushing against the stream of the parade. My heart starts fluttering just thinking about the number of people, about getting trapped, about having to push our way out.

"If you all want to go down the street to watch, that's okay," I say. "I think I might head home anyway."

Pix looks at me, and I wonder if she is doing her energy-reading thing, because she says to the other girls, "It looks pretty crowded; maybe we should just watch from the park."

I have never been more grateful to someone in my life.

"Have you seen the Samantha statue?" I ask, immediately regretting it—the Samantha statue is a source of some controversy among the local witch communities. Another diminishment of their culture and traditions, co-opted by watered-down mass pop culture.

"Yes!" Ofira says. "I love her!"

I am once again amazed by how little I can predict about Ofira.

I lead them to the spot in the park where a bronze figure in the likeness of Elizabeth Montgomery as the witch Samantha from the TV show *Bewitched* sits on a flying broom, framed by a bronze sliver of a moon. The statue looks very little like the actress Elizabeth Montgomery, but that doesn't stop every tourist who visits Salem from coming here for an obligatory picture right after they get their Insta pic of the three-gabled Witch House.

"Our girl does not look like herself," Tatiana says. Tonight Tatiana has outdone herself with her Renaissance witch meets Wild West garb. It is only now that I notice she has a coiled black whip snapped into the belt of her corset. It is a bold sartorial move, but one that easily fits in with the rest of the outfits on this evening.

"Why don't they have an Endora statue?" Ofira asks.

"Oh my god, you *are* Endora!" Tatiana says.

We all look at Ofira's vintage black velvet robes. Anita is standing next to her and she takes this moment to adjust Ofira's lapel. Anita is wearing a simple black A-line dress tonight that is once again perfectly tailored to her curves and lets her fiery red mane of hair stand out.

"It's the eye makeup, isn't it?" Ofira says. She turns to Anita. "Too much Endora? Or not enough?"

Ofira has a bright swipe of blue on each eyelid, reminiscent of the outrageous makeup of the character that Agnes Moorehead played on the show.

Anita shakes her head.

"Endora was a fashion icon," she says simply.

"I used to watch the show with my mom and try to see if I could wiggle my nose like Samantha," I say.

"I knew you were a secret witch," Pix says.

*Am I blushing? I am definitely blushing.*

"Well, I couldn't do it," I say, and add, "I guess I needed someone to teach me." This is the closest I come to flirting, but Pix either doesn't hear me or doesn't want to, because she's sitting down now with Ofira and Tatiana in the grass near the statue. I sit down with them.

Anita and Ivy are examining the statue, holding hands as they make their way around it, talking softly to each other. Ivy's dress is the mini version of Anita's black A-line, although she has accessorized with long strings of silver beads and a matching head wrap. I am trying to watch them without seeming like I am watching them, but I must not be succeeding because Pix says quietly to me, "Those two are cute, aren't they?"

"Oh," I say, completely failing to act like I wasn't staring at them. "Yeah."

"Kitchen witch and fashion witch. They've basically been together since junior high. They're totally inseparable. I would be insanely jealous if I didn't love them so much."

"Oh, yeah," I say, my brain moving quickly to spot an opening here. "So you don't have a . . . uh?"

She shakes her head slowly, as if considering it. "No 'uh.' Do you?"

I suddenly feel like we are five-year-olds standing in a playground asking each other if we want to play a game.

"No. But I don't really have friends either, so . . ." I laugh to try to make this sound like a joke.

Pix turns back to the parade. I feel like an idiot. Anita and Ivy sit down in the grass with us, still holding hands. Jealous doesn't even begin to describe the way I feel.

And then the exact thing I was afraid might happen happens.

We hear someone yelling behind us and turn to see what's going on. A boy wearing a *Scream* mask has climbed up onto the Samantha statue and is pretending to hump it. Six guys in various half-assed costumes are cheering him on.

"What the fuck?" Ofira says.

She gets up and starts to head over to them before I can stop her.

"You really want to mess with a witch like that?" Ofira yells at the boy straddling the moon.

"Aw, hey, it's the new girl!" one of the guys on the ground says.

"Witch Bitch!" another one chimes in. "What are you going to do about it, Witch Bitch?"

The boys let out evil witch cackles and another one of them attempts to climb the statue.

Ofira stands her ground. "This witch bitch is going to tell you that your dime-store horror masks are just perpetuating the glorification of violence that is a complete bastardization of Samhain culture."

"What the fuck is this bitch talking about?" A werewolf that sounds unmistakably like Tyler is hanging off someone taller than him who is wearing a Jason-style hockey mask. One of the boys on the statue pushes the other boy off, and he yells in protest and tries to grab the first one. The others laugh hysterically.

"Do you actually find this funny?" Ofira says. She seems to be in disbelief.

The boys simply howl louder with laughter in response. I go to Ofira, trying to keep my head down.

"Just walk away," I say. "It won't do any good."

"I'm not afraid of these assholes," she says, standing her ground.

"Oh, no fucking way." The Jason mask has spoken. Harrison takes the mask off, as if he needs to get a better look at me.

My pulse is racing now.

"We gotta go," I whisper to Ofira.

Tyler catches on a moment later, like always.

"Oh wow, Eleanor Anderson finally found a lezzie cult to join," Tyler says.

Next to Tyler, Harrison's eyes seem to be burning with actual fire. He believes his own bullshit so much, even now, that he is able to conjure up this deep rage at me. He has to, because without his performative anger, his whole stupid story falls apart.

I look behind me, trying to see if there is an easy path of escape out of here. Anita, Ivy, and Tatiana are standing behind me, Pix, and Ofira, like a phalanx of witches ready to do battle.

The air catches in my lungs, and I realize that I am about to have a panic attack. This is a mistake. This whole thing is a mistake.

"Lesbian witch bitches!" Tyler yells, nearly spitting the words.

"Accurate description of a group of people, asshole," Ofira says. "Anything else?"

"Anything else?" Tyler laughs. "Yeah, anything else you want to say, Harrison?'

"Watch how close you get, Anderson," Harrison says. "I'm still working on getting that restraining order." His face is a mask of righteous, stony anger. It's a better costume than the actual mask he was wearing.

I manage to remember to take some oxygen into my lungs, enough to get some words out at least.

"Okay, Harrison," I say. "I'm going. Okay? Have fun humping Samantha."

I turn around and walk quickly through the park, dodging though oblivious families who think this night of horrors is actually entertaining.

"Fucking psycho," comes Tyler's voice trailing after me.

I walk quickly down Washington Street to get away from the crowds and turn left onto a smaller side street. It'll take extra long to get home from here if I'm going to avoid this parade, but I need to keep moving.

"Eleanor! Slow down!"

I stop and turn around to see the whole coven turning the corner behind me.

"I'm sorry," I say when they reach me.

"Why are *you* sorry?" Ivy says.

"Those are some Grade A assholes, my dear," Tatiana says.

"Rule of threes will get them," Ofira offers.

"What's rule of threes?" I ask.

"Whatever you do will come back to you three times over," Ofira says.

"Good or bad," Pix says.

I try to imagine Harrison going through three times the nightmare that he has put me through. It doesn't seem possible.

"I'm just gonna go home," I say. "You should go back to the parade."

"No way!" Tatiana says. "The night is young!"

Pix takes my hand.

"Come with us," she says.

*Of course. Anywhere.*

We walk for about twenty minutes to the nice part of town. Here the Victorian houses have been tastefully restored, with curated lawns and careful paint jobs. Not like our well-worn share with Enid. The Halloween decorations here are less "giant plastic skeleton" and more "tastefully designed pumpkin display."

We stop at one house with no decorations. It needs none, since it already looks like a textbook haunted house—it's painted a dark purplish gray, with bay windows, stained glass, and a pointy gabled roof to top it all off. Ofira's house. It suits her perfectly.

"We're all staying over," Pix says. "You should too."

Her hand is still in mine. Which means that this night can't be a complete disaster, because it is now the night that Pix has held my hand for twenty full minutes.

"Okay," I say. "I'll text my mom and make sure it's okay."

I know that Mom and Susan are planning a Nora Ephron movie marathon after Susan closes the store. I will not be missed.

I don't know exactly what I expect when I walk into Ofira's house, but it is not what I get. I am used to gathering with groups in parent-less houses, holding a blowout party and inevitably trashing the place. "Fun" to the people around me always meant no supervision. Fun meant chaos.

But at Ofira's house we are immediately met at the door by both of her parents.

"How was it?" her mother asks before we even get inside.

"Too crowded," Ofira says. "We did our cleansing and got out of there."

The girls all sit on a bench by the door and start taking off their shoes. I do the same. From out of nowhere we are suddenly swarmed by cats. Four of them. All black. They wind themselves around our legs and examine our shoes.

Pix points at each of them.

"Nyx, Ursula, Maleficent, and Barbara," she says, introducing them.

"Barbara?" I say.

"Ofira's little brother named that one," she says.

"How can you tell them apart?" I ask.

"Different ears," Pix says, as if that explains it.

*Of course Ofira has a herd of black cats.*

"Please tell your sister that you didn't have fun," Ofira's dad says to her. "She's still angry we didn't let her go."

"I can hear you!" comes a shout from the other room.

"It was boring, Lydia, calm down!" Ofira calls.

"I never get to do anything!" Lydia shrieks back.

Ofira stands up.

"This is Eleanor," Ofira says to her parents, motioning toward me. "She's in the coven now."

"Wonderful," her mom says. "Welcome, Eleanor. I'm Sandy, and this is Vincent."

I once again have the sensation that I am being welcomed into a cult. These people are way too comfortable with their daughter talking about her coven.

"You girls have fun," her dad says. "There's pizza in the kitchen."

The other girls make their way to the kitchen with the cat herd trailing behind them, and I follow, trying to take in this house. The entrance to each room is marked with carved wooden latticework. Large paintings fill almost every wall. They seem to be organized by theme to fit the rooms. The dining room contains giant paintings of utensils. The living room has paintings of the actual chairs in the room. I stop to examine them. A boy is sitting in the middle of the living room floor; the contents of a couple of dissected toasters are on the floor around him. He looks up at me.

"Hello," he says. "I'm the brother."

"Hi," I say, taken aback. "I'm Eleanor."

He goes back to what he was doing, and I leave him alone with his toasters.

The girls grab the pizzas and plates and napkins, and I follow them down into the finished basement. The low-ceilinged room includes the traditional elements of a rec room—large TV, Ping-Pong table—but the walls are hung in colorful draperies that make it feel like the inside of a billowing tent. The girls sit on the floor, leaning on large scattered pillows.

"Your house is really cool, Ofira," I say.

"Thanks," she says. "Mom's been messing with everything basically since we moved in."

"I liked the way it was the last time we stayed over," Ivy says.

"I can't even remember, what was it then?" Ofira says.

"The living room was pink," Ivy says. "Remember? Anita's hair was the same color?"

Anita nods in affirmation.

"And there were big bows over every window," Pix says.

"Oh, god, right." Ofira rolls her eyes. "Her bow phase."

"When is she going to do a Renaissance theme?" Tatiana asks, obviously hoping for her particular witch aesthetic to find its ideal environment. "Can I request a room?"

"Please, do not encourage her," Ofira says. She opens the pizza box and passes around plates. "She will settle on something eventually, and I need for that to be sooner rather than later. Moving was hard enough without having to feel like I'm in a totally different house every week."

I wonder if we are in for any more witchiness tonight, but we turn now to more traditional sleepover activities—watching movies and periodically raiding the fridge for more snacks. The only difference being that the coven is determined to watch every depiction of witches in a movie ever. They're on *The Witches of Eastwick* tonight.

It's been a long time since I did something like this. Back in middle school in Mystic I would get invited to parties by the girls who were too nice to not invite everyone in our small class. I knew even then that they were partially pity invites. People didn't actually want me around until Salem. Until Chloe.

*Do not think about Chloe right now.*

The big hair on Cher, Michelle Pfeiffer, and Susan Sarandon in the movie is enough to send everyone into periodic fits of laughter. Everyone except Anita, who has a sketchbook out and seems to be taking notes.

"It's a no on the hair," Ofira says to Anita, "but a yes to Cher in blue velvet."

Anita nods and writes something down.

Pix is sitting next to me on a pillow, and I am finding it very difficult to concentrate on anything that is going on in this movie when her leg keeps brushing up against mine. One of the cats has settled in her lap, and she is absent-mindedly rubbing its ears. Whenever she stops, it nudges her hand to start again. I think this one might be Barbara.

"The devil would have to be significantly cuter than this for me to fall in love," Ofira says, watching the movie.

"Yes she would!" Tatiana says, and they all laugh.

"Hey," I whisper to Pix. "Where's the bathroom?"

"Upstairs," she says. "It's the door on the right in the kitchen."

"Thanks," I say.

I go upstairs, use the bathroom, and check my phone to make sure my mom texted back. She did.

**Sure! Have fun, honey!**

The first floor of the house is empty now. It's only nine, but it seems like the whole family has gone to bed, including the rest of the cats. I am tempted to see if the disemboweled toasters are still spread out on the living room floor, but instead I spot the door to the backyard on the other side of the kitchen and head outside. I could use a minute.

The backyard is an expanse of wild grass with a shed in the back. The door of the shed is open, and it's overflowing with boxes and tools. I sit down on the back porch steps. I can see over the fence into the yard next door. A weeping willow covers most of it, and I realize now where I am. That is Adam Walker's house. Chloe had sex with Harrison for the first time in that house.

*Great.*

There is a joint in my pocket. A lighter in the other one. I don't know what the rules of this seemingly very accepting household might be, but I feel like I might start screaming if I don't smoke this thing.

Or I could just leave. Before this feeling becomes something else. Anger, maybe. Utter despair, perhaps.

"Hey."

I turn around to see Pix sticking her head out the back door.

"I was worried you got lost," she says.

My panic subsides just a little when I see her. It doesn't go away completely, but just that small relief is enough to convince me not to bolt.

"I got a little lost," I say.

She comes out and sits down next to me on the step. We look out at the backyard together.

"Ofira's house is pretty wild, huh?"

"It's really cool," I say.

"My aunt's an artist. When she gets blocked making her work that she actually sells, she just starts redoing every room of their house. And she gets blocked a lot."

"She's your mom's sister?" I ask.

"Yeah."

"Is your house like this?"

"No."

"What is your house like?"

"It's very, very normal. A place for very normal people who do very normal things."

"So how do you fit in there?" I ask.

"Not well," she says, shrugging. "But my mom is kind of in denial about that. I think she gets upset that I spend so much time over here. Like her sister is more fun than her. Which is true. But I think it hurts her feelings."

"Moms are complicated," I say.

"Yeah," she says. "Families are very complicated."

We sit in silence for a moment. I am about to ask her if she wants to share this joint with me when she says, "I'm sorry about what happened earlier at the statue. Ofira doesn't really know when to quit sometimes."

"It wasn't her fault," I say, shaking my head. "I'm a walking target wherever I go in this town."

"I don't like hearing that," she says.

*Do not read my energy, Pix. I do not want my energy read right now.*

"You're not asking me why they hate me," I say. I mean for this to sound like the statement of fact that it is, but I worry that it sounds self-pitying.

"I can't imagine that it takes much more than not being male for those guys to target someone," Pix says.

I take a deep breath.

"Harrison kind of runs Salem High," I say. "Especially now that he's a senior. And if Harrison hates you, it means that everyone hates you. And Harrison has spent the past year and a half hating me."

"Well, he seems like a great judge of character," Pix says sarcastically.

"Oh yeah," I say. "Really astute."

"Uh-huh." Pix nods.

"We dated the same person," I say. "And she chose him. Over me. So."

Have I ever said out loud that Chloe and I "dated"? It seems like such an inadequate word, but I can't think of another one. We were "together"? We were "inseparable"?

We were in love.

"Chloe and I stayed friends for a while after we broke up, and Harrison thought that I was trying to steal her back from him. So he told everyone that I was a jealous psycho lesbian stalker."

"That sounds awful."

"Yup. Pretty much."

I will stop talking now. Now is the moment to end this story. When it still sort of makes sense.

*Don't ask me any more questions, Pix.*

She doesn't. We sit in silence for another minute. I am weighing whether or not to take the joint out from my pocket.

"I like hanging out in Salem," Pix says finally. "But I don't think I would want to live here."

"Why not?"

"It feels like a dumping ground for a lot of feelings. Everyone feels a certain way about it. And they think that's the only way to feel. It's very loud. Energetically."

I am getting more used to this kind of talk. It doesn't sound as silly to me as it used to.

"Did you always read energy?" I ask.

"I think that I always did without knowing it," she says. "When I was younger, I would get really upset for no reason, or really angry or overwhelmed. My parents didn't know what to do with me. I think they thought there was something wrong with me. I mean, I thought there was something wrong with me too."

"You seem like the most well-adjusted person I've ever met," I say.

She smiles at me.

"I was lucky that when Ofira was getting into all the witchy stuff, we started reading about empaths and energy exchange. All of a sudden a lot made sense. And I realized that I could learn how to manage it. And how to protect myself from letting it get to be too much."

I look over at the weeping willow.

"That must be a nice thing to know how to do," I say.

A breeze rustles the leaves of the tree and they sway in our direction.

"Did you love her?" Pix asks. "The girl that you and Harrison both dated?"

I look back at Pix. "Yeah."

She nods. Her long skirt is gathered up in her lap and now she spreads it out on the steps, feeling the fabric.

"How was that?" she asks, not looking at me.

I consider for a moment. "Mostly it really sucked," I say.

Pix looks at me and laughs.

"Have you ever been in love?" I ask, praying for some more information, some details that I don't have to beg for in order to figure out what is going on between the two of us.

She thinks about it for a moment. "I thought I was for a while," she says. "But lately I've been thinking that I wasn't. Not really."

She looks away from me when she says this, and I desperately want to read everything and nothing into what she is telling me.

"It wasn't until I started paying attention to the way that I actually felt," she says, "instead of the way that I wanted to be feeling, that I realized how shitty it was."

"I get that," I say.

"And once I stopped being scared of the way that I was feeling and started just letting myself feel, it was impossible to go back."

"I think that's really brave," I say.

She looks at me.

"I think you're brave," she says.

I nearly laugh at this.

"Are you kidding? I basically ran away from Harrison tonight."

She shakes her head. "That's not what running away looks like. You stayed with Ofira, you got her out of the situation. You stood up to them."

I want to tell her that her version of the incident has nothing to do with what was going on inside my mind in that moment. There was no honor to it, just blind rage and fear.

"I am afraid pretty much all of the time," I say. Saying this out loud suddenly makes me realize how true it is. I feel tears building up behind my eyes.

Pix moves closer to me. She takes my hand.

"I know," she says. Of course she knows.

*What am I thinking now, Pix? Tell me that.*

"Can I kiss you?" she asks. She says it likes she's intentionally changing the subject to something more pleasant.

I look at her, thinking for a second that she must be joking, but her face is serious.

*Don't run away, Eleanor.*

"Yes," I say, my voice steady, still waiting for the punch line.

Pix leans in to me; her lips meet mine.

She is a low hum of electricity. Not the erratic dips and peaks of Chloe's desire but a buzzing, constant vibration.

*Do not think about Chloe right now.*

She puts her hand on my cheek, and I swear the wind picks up. The newly dead leaves on the ground around us start to fly in a small tornado.

This is what it feels like to kiss a witch.

Like she is controlling the weather around us through magic.

Like nature itself is at her disposal.

The kiss ends, and Pix leans back and looks at me.

"Thank you," she says, as if I have done her a favor.

"Yeah," I say, not quite believing that this has actually happened. "No problem."

And then she laughs and I laugh and she takes my hand.

"Come on," she says. "We don't want to give the girls too much to gossip about."

She gets up, and I follow her back into the house, where I will sleep next to her in a sleeping bag on the floor. Or really, I will not sleep at all but instead steal looks at her for most of the night and wonder just how bad an idea this is going to turn out to be.

# STRENGTH

Oh, Strength, we need you now more than ever! That Chariot blazing ahead into the future was exciting, as change can be, but we will burn out without you at our side! You're not about brute strength, although your sweet lion pet could certainly do some damage if you sicced him on someone. But you treat him gently, trust him as your ally in this walk toward the future. You are strength as a pillar, as something to rely on and something we can share with others. Confidence, but also security.

If we believed that we too had a lion walking by our side, what would we feel brave enough to take on? How far could our strength take us?

# 8

If you're going to give someone an ultimatum, it should be carefully planned. You should consider timing, setting, word choice. You must try to imagine the perfect circumstances in order to optimize the chances that things will go your way. Because if you lose, you will lose everything.

Prom was at the beginning of June. Chloe was leaving for her one-month program at FIT in New York at the beginning of July. I had three weeks to figure out how to tell her that she needed to choose. Me or Harrison.

Those weeks would have felt like a strange gray area even if I wasn't in the middle of carefully formulating the perfect ultimatum. I was back at the store full-time after school ended, but the summer tourists were more interested in beaches and boats than witches, and the store was usually empty. Sometimes I would see Chloe walking around town with Harrison or people from his crowd. They never came into the store. At night I would still go over to Chloe's. Often she would text me around ten or eleven to come over, and I let myself in the unlocked sliding door in the backyard.

She never lied to me. She just did not offer up information that I didn't specifically ask for.

I had it all planned for the night before she was leaving for New York. I would go over and help her finish packing, give her a going-away card with a cute picture of us in it from last Halloween when we dressed up as the twins from *The Shining* (even then, her mirror image), and say the following:

*Chloe, I love you and I know that you love me. If you love Harrison and you want to be with him, then you should do that, but I need you to choose. It's me or him. Please take this month away to consider your options and get back to me. Also he will never be able to care about you the way that I do, and what we have is real.*

So reasonable! So calm and collected! So mature!

That's how it was supposed to go.

Instead, four days before Chloe left, I was summoned to her house at midnight. I was already home in bed, and I considered ignoring her text, but then I thought about how few days we had before she left. My ego was simple enough to want to tally up the hours I spent with her before then, make sure that they were more than she spent with Harrison. I wanted hard data to fall back on.

So I got out of bed and threw on a T-shirt and shorts, slipped into the low-top Converse that she had picked out for me, and tiptoed down the hall past my mom's room. The ancient stairs creaked unforgivingly as I made my way down. Enid would be sure to betray me to Mom. But there was no going back now.

Outside, it was a perfect early-summer night, quiet and

cooling off from the hot and humid day. I took a joint out of my pocket and lit it. Since Tyler's party I had been buying from Simon regularly. The stoner kids had become a haven for me that spring whenever I found myself needing a break from the spaces that Harrison ruled over. The stoners were not impressed with Harrison. They were not impressed with much. Plus Simon and his friends had to be nice to me because I was giving them money. It seemed like a fair transaction.

The walk to Chloe's house was exactly a joint's worth of minutes. I arrived high and excited to see her in spite of myself. My stupid body didn't know that I was playing second fiddle to an asshole. It just wanted her.

I let myself into the backyard through a small gate, buried the butt of the joint in a fresh dirt pile in Chloe's mom's flower garden, and went in through the sliding door.

Chloe's room was on the first floor, so it was easy to get to without waking her parents or her sister upstairs. I made my way down the dark hallway and slowly opened her bedroom door, feeling like a burglar. Like someone who didn't belong there.

"Hey," I said to Chloe, closing the door behind me.

She was sitting on her bed looking at her phone. She smiled when she saw me.

"Hey," she said.

I sat down on the bed next to her, and she was immediately on me with sloppy drunken kisses and a hand on my thigh. I smelled beer and something else. Was it just summer sweat? A new perfume?

*Oh.*

I pulled away from her.

"What?" she said.

"I can smell him," I said. "I can smell him on you."

She sat back.

"Were you just with him?"

"Harrison? Yeah. We were hanging out."

"Did you just have sex with him?"

She was watching me like I was an unpredictable animal. I felt a wave of nausea. Her pause meant that I already knew the answer.

"What the fuck, Chloe?"

"What?"

"So why am I here? What is this?"

"I wanted to see you."

"*After* him?"

"You were working before! You couldn't hang out!"

I put my head in my hands. I was reaching back in my stoned brain to try to remember how I was going to fix this terrible situation. If I could just say the right thing, I could fix this.

She touched my arm. "Can't it be, like, kind of hot?"

"What?"

She moved closer to me. Tried to envelop me in her arms. I was stuck, my hands half up to my face.

"Like, I was with him and now I'm with you," she says. "Like, you need to claim me now."

She got on top of me and started kissing my neck, running her hands along my back under my shirt.

That fucking smell.

Something in my brain suddenly zapped into action.

"No," I said. "It's actually not hot at all."

She stopped and looked at me. She didn't move, though. Her weight on me felt crushing, like I couldn't breathe. I wriggled my way out from under her.

"I never agreed to any of this," I said.

"What does that mean?"

"I'm not okay with you being with Harrison."

She sat back and crossed her arms, closing herself off from me.

"I made sure you were okay with me going to prom with him," she said.

"You didn't ask me if you could have sex with him," I said, my voice rising.

Chloe looked at her door, as if a parent might appear at it any minute.

"I think maybe we didn't really understand each other, Eleanor." Her voice calm, as if I was the child and she was the teacher. "I don't want to just be in one relationship. I'm seventeen. I want to date people."

"Yeah, but you love me," I said. "And I love you. We love each other, Chloe."

How many ways could I say the same thing?

"I know."

"Do you love him?"

"It's not like that," she said.

"What is it like?"

She pulled her legs up to her chest.

"It's just interesting, all right? I'm interested in him. I love you because you're my best friend. And then this other thing with you and me is really nice, you know? I'm not trying to say it isn't"—I could feel her search for the right word, one that wouldn't give away or commit too much—"meaningful."

"Uh-huh," I said. I would now hate the word *meaningful* for the rest of my life.

"I really like this," she said. "I wouldn't do it if I didn't. But we're not married or anything, Eleanor."

It was all such a reasonable picture that she was painting. She was the reasonable one. I was the foolish one who expected some kind of young-love cliché, high school sweethearts together forever. It was true that we had never discussed monogamy. She had every right to date whoever she wanted. Except for one thing.

"Everybody knows about you and him, and no one knows about you and me." The words were pouring out of me now. "And I want to be understanding, like maybe you think your parents would freak out if they knew you were with a girl. I get that."

She raised an eyebrow. "My parents don't care about that."

"They don't?"

"No. I had a girlfriend at summer camp two years ago. It's fine with them."

"You didn't tell me that."

"Yes, I did."

She had not told me that.

"You said you had never kissed a girl before," I said.

"No, I didn't."

"Yes, the first time that we kissed. You said it."

"No, I said you had never kissed a girl before," she said.

The math involved in understanding the situation was becoming too complicated for me.

"So, then, what is the problem?" I asked. "If it's not about being with a girl?"

She was annoyed with me now. I could feel her pulling further into herself.

"You tell me," she said. There was a bite to her words.

"Is it that your dad wants you to be with Harrison? Because he works for his dad?"

"What do you think this is? Some kind of arranged marriage? My parents don't control who I date."

"So, then . . ." The math problem was solving itself now. X minus Y equaled Chloe just didn't care. "You don't want people to know you're with me," I said, "because Harrison has status, and I have nothing. So you go to prom with him. You take a picture with him. You post it for everyone to see. You have sex with him at a party so everyone knows about it."

I could feel the tears coming and I wished I could stop them. I was at so much of a disadvantage already.

"And I'm the idiot who comes over here when he's done with you."

She wasn't saying anything. What could she possibly say? I stood up.

"I wanted to tell everyone the first day you kissed me," I

said. "I wanted it published in the newspaper. I wanted to post it online. I wanted to write it in skywriting for everyone to see. And you only want people to see you with him."

"That's really unfair," Chloe said, her face stone now. She had completely retreated from me. There was no getting her back now.

"Yeah, it is." I was crying now. Blubbering. I was a mess. "It's really, really unfair."

She wouldn't look at me.

"You should go," she said.

"Yeah," I said, wiping my eyes with my hand. "Don't worry. I'm going."

I left her house that night feeling like my heart had been ripped into tiny pieces and left in a sad, bloody pile for someone else to clean up. My brain was ringing with all the things that she could have said. How she could have told me that I was wrong, that she didn't realize what she was doing, how she would immediately post a picture of the two of us and write, "Isn't my girlfriend cute?" or some stupid shit like that. Other people got that. Why couldn't I have that?

But she didn't say any of those things. Not that night, and not for the whole next month when she was in New York. I didn't hear from her once. No text. No email.

It was over. And I was completely alone.

The coven is just waking up when I leave Ofira's house the morning after the sleepover. I need to get home and take a shower before I open the store. I say thank you to Ofira's parents on the way out, pet the cats that escort me to the door, and send a quick sorry for leaving abruptly to the group email chain. Ofira's dad is making something in the kitchen that smells amazing, and my stomach grumbles knowing that I will not have time for more than a protein bar.

My walk home mostly consists of me trying to convince myself that last night was real. Pix kissed me. Not in a casual way. Not in a "we're drunk and this is fun" way. In a sober, serious way. And for a very long time.

I want to remember every detail about that moment so I can call it up whenever I need to. Her gentleness. Her hand on my cheek. My body is demanding to know how soon we can make this happen again and when and how, because it is going to be very difficult to think about anything else.

And my brain is saying, *Slow down, cowboy. You still don't know what this means.*

Since last night there has been one thought tugging at the back of my brain—I didn't tell Pix the end of the story of Chloe. Which means that she doesn't actually know me. And she won't know me until she knows everything. And I can never, ever tell her everything.

So that's that.

A few hours later I'm in the store ringing up a woman's well-curated purchases: a small plaque that says, *It takes a coven*, a goblet-sized wineglass with *Magic Potion* on it, and a Salem baseball cap.

"That's for my boyfriend," the woman is telling me.

"That's nice," I say.

"I got him a hat last time I came here, and he really liked

it, so I got him another hat this time."

My phone lights up on the counter next to me. I make very little effort to pretend I'm not looking at it. Susan's no-phone rules be damned.

"That's so, so great," I say to the woman.

It's a text from Pix.

**That was fun last night.**

"People just love it when you bring them something back from a trip." It seems this woman is still talking. Meanwhile my pulse has just doubled itself as I stare at the screen of my phone. "Like, it lets them know you're really thinking of them."

"That'll be sixty-three eighty-five."

The woman hands over her credit card. It never ceases to amaze me what people will pay for this crap.

*That. Was. Fun. Last. Night.*

"Are you okay?" the woman asks me.

I look at her, then down at my hand. I have been holding her receipt and a pen as if I am going to sign it myself.

"Oh, sorry. Here you go."

I shove her purchases into a Salem Gift Emporium bag and try to muster up a smile as I hand it to her.

"Happy Haunted Happenings!" I say.

This must sound as deranged as it feels, because the woman takes her credit card and shopping bag and leaves without saying a word.

I grab my phone.

**Yeah, it was super fun, I type. Thank you for inviting me.**

Send.

*Wait. Wait. Wait.*

Want to talk on the phone later? she writes back.

*What does this mean? Why talk? What is there to talk about? About how great kissing was and that we need to figure out how to do it again as soon as possible? Because that is what I would like to talk about, Pix.*

Sure, I write. I'm done at the store at six.

Cool. Call you then.

I look up from my phone. There are a couple of people browsing in the store, but nothing needs my attention. And I need something to distract me from completely spiraling here, trying to anticipate what Pix wants to say to me.

I pull the tarot book out of my bag. I have turned down the corner on my place, and I open it now.

*Strength.*

Yeah, I could use some of that.

I am walking home from work when Pix calls. When was the last time someone actually called me on my phone? It was probably Chloe. Which means it was more than a year ago.

*Do not think about Chloe.*

"Hey!" I answer, trying to sound cheerful but not overly cheerful and instead sounding like no human who has ever lived. Possibly like a sort of angry, surprised elf.

"Hi," Pix says. "How's your day been?'

"Since I left you guys at eight a.m.?"

"Yeah," she says.

"You know, really, really thrilling," I say sarcastically.

"Oh yeah?" I can hear her smile.

"Basically a nonstop adventure."

"Wow."

"I know."

*Is this charming? Am I being charming?*

"How was breakfast?" I ask.

"Really good. Of course. Banana nut pancakes. Ofira's dad is a chef, so pretty much every meal is an event over there."

"That's so cool."

"Yeah, he used to have a restaurant in Boston that was this Italian/Mexican fusion thing."

"Sounds amazing."

"There was *a lot* of cheese involved."

I laugh. "Do you think her family would adopt me?" I ask, only half joking.

"They've basically adopted me," Pix says. "So probably."

"Sign me up," I say.

"What I wanted to say," she starts. She sounds tentative. "You know how we kissed last night?"

*Here we go.*

"I mean, yes. I was there," I say.

Pix laughs. "Right."

"Look," I say, unable to handle hearing her uncertainty. I will help her let me down easy. "It's okay if it was just a fun one-time thing. You don't have to feel weird about it."

Pix is silent for a moment. I check to make sure my phone didn't drop the call.

"I don't feel weird about it," she says finally. "Do you?"

"No," I say. "I really liked it."

"So did I," she says.

And there goes my ripped-apart heart, barely taped back together after this past year of my life, melting into a useless puddle.

We talk for three hours. Until Mom makes me come eat some dinner long after it has gone cold. Until I forget to smoke the joint that I had saved for tonight. Until my face hurts from smiling.

# THE HERMIT

I knew we were going to need our friend Strength for something. It's you, Hermit, ready to walk us into the darkness of solitude. What does it mean to be alone? To be cooped up in a tower of your own making? No distractions from your thoughts, no respite from your own mind. You'll have to make friends with it, then. Can you make friends with your own mind?

But maybe it's not so dire as all that, Hermit. Sometimes solitude is nice. Recharge your batteries. Get ready for the next thing that life will ask of you. Maybe new information becomes clear, new neural pathways are formed. When you emerge, you can light them up like your own lantern, helping guide others through the dark night of the soul.

There are gifts to be found when you're all alone. Trust that you will know how to recognize them when they come. Trust that isolation is temporary. The world is still out there, turning and churning. And it will be there for you when you emerge from your cave, that much wiser.

# 9

Here is what I learn about Pix over the next four days:

1. She has two much older brothers, one who goes to Harvard Law and is her parents' favorite child; the other is an accountant and is her parents' second-favorite child.
2. Her father is a lawyer, and her mother is a doctor.
3. Her parents have no idea how she ended up in this family, and neither does she.
4. She goes to a fancy private girls' school that her mom picked out, but there are some cool people there. That's how she met Ivy and Anita.
5. Her favorite color is turquoise.
6. Her favorite food is Ofira's dad's baked clams that he only makes on Christmas.
7. She just got her license but refuses to drive on highways, and if she has to drive somewhere she will only take back roads where she doesn't have to go more than twenty-five miles an hour.
8. There's nothing that she doesn't believe in.

This last piece of information comes on day four of talking nonstop on the phone whenever we can. I am washing the dishes after dinner and I have her on speakerphone so that I can hear her over the water running.

"What do you mean you believe in *everything*?"

"I just mean I'm not ruling anything out," she says. "Aliens. Bigfoot. Vampires."

"Wait, vampires?"

"Yeah, I mean, there's such a thing as an energy vampire, someone who lives off the energy of other people. Haven't you ever known someone like that? Where they take and don't give and just sort of exhaust people?"

"Yes, I have known someone like that."

"So. That's a vampire."

I finish the dishes, wipe my hands, and take her off speaker.

"You can't be serious," I say.

"About which part?"

"The whole thing! Aliens?"

"Sure."

"Like, little green men in flying saucers?"

"Not necessarily. It's pure human arrogance to think that we would know what they look like, or even that we would be able to see and hear them."

"So you are proposing that aliens that we can't see or hear have visited Earth?"

"Maybe. Why not?"

I start laughing, and luckily she is laughing too.

"So I guess witchcraft wasn't a big leap for you, huh?" I say.

"Nope," she says, "makes total sense to me."

Pix has to go do homework, so we hang up with the promise to talk again tomorrow. I put my phone down on the kitchen table and try to have a little conversation with myself about what is going on here.

*Is it okay to get used to this?*

*Yeah, why not? Do you have something better to do right now?*

*I feel like I'm lying to her.*

*You're not lying. You're leaving out information.*

*I would rather not get by on semantics here.*

*If she likes you then let her like you. This is the nicest four days you've had in over a year.*

*Yeah, but how long can this go on?*

No answer to this. Such are the limits to talking to myself.

Mom comes into the kitchen to put the kettle on the stove.

"Thanks for doing the dishes, honey."

"No prob."

"Was that Pix again?" she asks. I can tell she's teasing me a little. Anytime she has seen me in the past four days I have been talking to Pix.

"Yeah," I say.

"Susan says she's really nice."

*God, Susan.*

"Yeah, she is."

Mom sits down at the table.

"So is Pix more than a friend?"

My eye roll must be epic because she says, "I know, moms are not allowed to ask about these things! So uncool, Mom! Whatever! LOL!"

Mom's ridiculous impersonation of a teenager overpowers

my being annoyed at her asking about Pix. I can't help laughing at her.

"I don't know," I say. "Maybe."

Mom raises an eyebrow.

"Okay," she says.

She is smiling, but part of me wonders if this whole situation worries her.

"Why don't you invite her over?" she says. "I could make dinner."

Now it's my turn to raise an eyebrow.

"Or order takeout," Mom says.

"I don't know," I say.

She gets up from the table and touches my hair on the way to getting herself a mug from the cupboard. She hasn't done this in a long time, and my first instinct is to squirm away, but something stops me. I feel suddenly like the happiness I have been feeling for the past few days has filled me up in such a way that I have extra to spare. Like I can afford to be generous.

"You sure you want someone coming over?" I ask.

Mom scoffs and pours herself some tea. "I've lived in Salem for long enough that I should know how to entertain a witch," she says.

I mention Mom's invite to Pix on the phone the next day while I'm walking home from the store.

It's only once the words have come out of my mouth that I realize that this might seem like a big step to make so soon. A "meet the mom" step. And we've only hung out twice, in a group. And only kissed once.

"So my mom wants to know if you want to come over for dinner one night," I say, failing at sounding casual.

"Sure, that would be fun," Pix says, succeeding at sounding casual. "I could do Friday. If that's good for you guys."

"Yeah, okay. I'll ask her." As if we have anything else to do on Friday. I text Mom and the answer comes back immediately: Friday's great!

"I'll just need you to give me directions on how to get to your house through only side streets," Pix says. "And it might take me a couple hours to get there."

"That's fine," I say, laughing.


Although my mom manages to downplay the significance of this Friday dinner, Susan has no such ability. The questioning starts as soon as I get into the store that morning.

"So what time is she coming?"

"Like around seven," I say, still taking off my jacket.

"And your mom's cooking?"

"I said we should just order. Probably Thai."

"From Thai Kitchen or Rice World?"

"Thai Kitchen, of course," I say.

Susan nods in approval. "Okay, but you should have something homemade. I'll bring over a cake."

"A cake? When will you have time to make a cake before tonight?"

"Okay, some cookies."

I toss my bag next to Susan's desk and head back out of her office.

"Please don't make a big deal out of this," I say.

"I'm not!" Susan calls after me. "I mean, it is a big deal, but I'm not *making it* a big deal."

I pull back the curtain to her office and look at her. "You can bring cookies. At eight. Okay?"

Susan claps her hands together, delighted that she has been given permission to meddle.

"Peanut butter?"

"Chocolate chip," I say. Then I think for a moment. "Peanut butter chocolate chip."

Susan smiles. "Done!"

It turns out that having Susan come by is actually a great idea, because Mom is so excited to talk to Pix that it seems unlikely that she will ever stop. There are about a thousand questions launched at Pix over dinner, and at some point I realize that Mom is just excited to have a new person to talk to. I almost tell her to stop a couple of times, but Pix launches into answers before I can, so I let the two of them talk while I push my pad thai around on my plate.

Susan's arrival is a party of its own. She tends to blow into places like a hurricane, dropping articles of clothing and various shopping bags in her wake before she presents the inevitable baked goods. Of course the cookies are delicious.

I realize I will owe Susan for the rest of my life when she grabs the bottle of wine that she brought and demands that she and Mom drink it in their usual spot on the front porch. I offer to help Mom down the stairs, but Susan figures out a way to carry two wineglasses, the bottle, and help Mom.

"We're good," she says, winking at me.

The wink feels like overkill, but I am grateful to her anyway, because Pix has let herself into the open door of my bedroom and is now looking at my bookshelves.

I feel suddenly self-conscious looking at my room through Pix's eyes. It looks like the room of someone who never quite moved in, which is sort of true. When I packed up my bedroom in Mystic for the move to Salem two years ago, I remember thinking that I was packing up the stuff of a kid, and that this was the chance to figure out what the space of New Me might look like. I even gave away a lot of my things to Mom's students. All I knew was that my new room needed to be completely different from what it had been before. I figured the rest would become clear as I went. It hasn't yet.

I met Chloe only a month after we moved here and proceeded to spend pretty much the next nine months at her house. And after that I didn't care much about what the space around me looked like.

"I don't have a lot of stuff," I say to Pix.

She shrugs. "Stuff is overrated."

She sits down on the floor. "Your mom is so great," she says.

I sit down next to her.

"Yeah," I say. "She has Lyme disease." I suddenly feel weird saying this, as if it was not my information to tell. "Sorry. That didn't come out right. I mean, yes, she's great. She just doesn't feel well most of the time."

Pix does that thing where she doesn't ask any questions,

she just looks at me with a kind of listening face, which then of course makes me want to tell her everything.

"She got it when we lived in Mystic," I say. "There are a bunch of different strains of it, and some people just get one and they have pretty mild symptoms. But she got a bunch of them. It makes her really tired all day, and she has really bad joint pain. She saw one doctor who said she should just get used to having the body of a ninety-year-old woman even though she's in her forties."

"That must be really hard for her," Pix says.

"We left Mystic so she could be near Susan, who basically keeps us alive. Mom's family didn't really know what to do with us."

"That must be hard on you too," Pix says.

"Oh. I mean, I just go to work." This is not a response, really.

"What did your mom used to do? Back in Mystic?"

"She worked at the aquarium. I spent pretty much my whole childhood there. The handlers used to let me feed some of the fish. I thought it was normal to help feed entire tanks of eels."

"You fed eels?" Pix sticks her tongue out. "Were they disgustingly creepy?"

I laugh. "They were," I say.

"Do you miss it?" Pix asks.

"Mystic?"

"And the aquarium? Your family?"

I try to think back to what our life was like there. It feels like we were two different people than we are now. It's a world that belongs to BL—Before Lyme.

"It seems like a long time ago," I say. "We see my grandparents at Christmas. I think that's enough for my mom. They aren't very sympathetic about the Lyme thing."

"Why not?"

"My grandpa was a doctor. I mean, he was a podiatrist. But he tends to have a lot of opinions about medical stuff."

"Ah," Pix says. "They think she's faking it."

I nod. "Yup, they think that a forty-seven-year-old woman who had a job she loved and who was financially and physically independent is faking a disease that pretty much ruined her life."

"Does she say it ruined her life?" Pix asks.

I think about this. Mom would never talk that way.

"No," I say. "But it obviously did."

Pix looks at me. That look that is waiting for something.

"What?" I say.

"Well, she still has you," Pix says. "She has Susan. You guys have this cute apartment. Maybe her life is difficult in new ways, but you can't say it's ruined."

I want to say that I was probably talking about my life. Which wasn't ruined by my mom's limitations at all. I managed that one completely on my own.

"And if it hadn't happened, you probably wouldn't have moved here," Pix says. "So I never would have met you. And that would have been really sad."

My heart grows about three sizes in this moment and I

want so badly to kiss her, but I suddenly feel shy, as if we are not the two people who have talked for hours every day for the past week. As if she is not the person who kissed me a week ago. As if I am not the person who hasn't gotten high for days because I was so excited to talk to her and wanted to be sharp and seem smart on the phone.

Pix spots the tarot guide on my dresser.

"I brought something," she says. She reaches into her bag and pulls out a deck. "I thought we could do a spread. If you want."

For all of my reading this guide and playing with Susan's display deck, I have never used these cards for their actual purpose—a reading.

"I don't know," I say. "What if something scary comes up?" I know there are ominous cards lurking at the back of the guide that I have yet to read about. Death and dark moons and towers falling.

Pix shakes her head. "There are no scary cards," she says. "Just cards that reflect an intensity back to us. They're reading the energy that already exists in this moment."

"Okay," I say, "why not."

Pix shuffles the deck. Then she hands it to me.

"Think about your question," she says.

"What if I don't have a question?"

"Then think about something in your life that you would like more information about. The cards respond best to specificity. And remember that it has to be a two-way conversation."

"What does that mean?"

"People expect a concrete message about the future to be handed to them when they use tools for divination, but the cards are just presenting you with a different perspective to consider. What you do with the information is up to you."

I close my eyes and hold the deck and try to think about something.

*Not love, not love, not love.*

But then I wonder if by doing this I am simply encouraging the cards to talk about love.

*Okay, how about hanging out with the coven?*

This seems safe enough, and it is Pix adjacent, so if any of this really does work, maybe I can find out something about what's going on with us.

I open my eyes.

"Now put the deck down and cut it," Pix says. "Cutting it into three piles is traditional, but you should do whatever feels good."

I cut the deck into three piles.

"Now put them back together however you like."

I do. Pix picks up the deck. She holds it to her heart and closes her eyes for a minute. I watch her. I think about kissing her. I think that this is probably not an appropriate moment to kiss her. She opens her eyes.

"We'll do a really simple spread," she says, laying out the top three cards. "Past, present, future."

I see some familiar faces. The Hermit. The Hierophant. And in the middle, a figure mostly covered in a shroud-like cape looking at some cups that have spilled out on the ground.

Pix looks at the cards and nods.

"Bad?" I say.

"Interesting," she says.

"I just read about that guy," I say, pointing to the hermit. "He sounds like tons of fun."

"Interior work," Pix says. "Period of contemplation. Solitude. Sometimes solitude that we didn't choose for ourselves, but it turns out that it was important for our journey toward becoming ourselves."

I don't say that I think my solitude has completely formed who I am now, and that I don't think that's such a good thing.

"That's in the past, though," Pix says. "You're done with that. And in the present you have the Five of Cups."

"That doesn't look great. All those cups have spilled."

"But look." She points at the right side of the illustration. "There are still two cups upright behind him. He's just choosing to only see the spilled cups. He's not seeing what's still there after he lost the thing he thought he needed. All he has to do is turn around and see that he still has so much."

I don't have a lot to say about that.

I point to the Hierophant. "So in the future I'm going to be a wise teacher?"

"In the future you are going to have a strong connection to your intuition that is going to bring you important wisdom that, yes, you'll share with others."

"And how is that going to happen?"

"Well, let's ask for some advice." Pix pulls another card

off the top of the deck. It's a hand holding a big stick that is growing leaves. The hand is emerging out of a curly cloud and seems to be glowing.

"Ace of Wands," Pix says.

"What does that mean?"

"It means that if you want to get here"—she points to the Hierophant in the future—"you need to believe in the possibility of new beginnings. Inspiration. New energy."

"And what if I have a hard time believing in those things?"

Pix pulls one more card. The image is a person sitting up in bed. They are covering their face with their hands. Above them, the wall is filled with hanging swords.

"Okay, that definitely doesn't look good," I say.

"Nine of Swords. Worry, anxiety, depression."

"Oh, sounds fun," I say.

"But remember what question you just asked. What will happen if you don't believe in the idea of new beginnings? Here's your answer."

"So what do I do?"

Pix smiles. "You choose to believe."

This from the girl who admittedly believes in everything. Can someone who believes in everything believe in me too? Even if I can't believe in myself?

"It looks like good news to me," she says.

"I mean, it looks like complicated news," I say.

She picks up the cards and puts them back in the deck. "No one said it wasn't going to be complicated." She shuffles the deck a couple of times and then puts it back in the box.

"You don't have a deck, do you?" she says.

"No. I just play with the one in the store until Susan starts yelling at me that I'm messing it up."

"You're not going to learn how to read if you don't have a deck."

"Am I learning how to read?"

She hands me the box. "This one's yours now."

"What? No. Why?"

"I have about fifteen different decks. This one's supposed to be yours. I can just tell."

"Is this because of that rule where someone else has to give you your first deck?"

I had read that somewhere, that the only authentic way to procure a tarot deck is to receive it as a gift, ideally from another reader.

Pix shakes her head. "I don't like that rule. Are we just supposed to sit around and wait for someone else's permission to read? What if you don't know any other readers? Plus there are so many cute decks to buy."

The box is a little worn around the edges. It has been well loved. Maybe I'm being influenced by all of Pix's talk, but I can feel the energy of it in my hand.

"I don't think I can accept this," I say.

"Well, I'm not taking it back. And you just had me over for dinner, so it would be rude for me to not give you a thank-you gift."

"It's too much," I say.

"I'll make a deal with you," she says. "If you don't want it in a month, you can give it back to me."

"Okay," I say. "Thank you."

She smiles, and because I don't know what to say beyond this, I stop talking and I lean over and kiss her. Finally. She runs her hand through my hair and pulls me closer to her. I realize, as I am overcome with the intensity of this gesture, that Pix kisses the way she does everything: deliberately, thoughtfully, and fully. She kisses with her whole self. And it makes me feel like I'm standing at the center of the universe.

We only stop when we hear Mom and Susan coming up the stairs laughing. I can feel that my face is flushed. But I don't feel embarrassed. I feel too alive to be embarrassed.

Susan and Mom come down the hallway, and Susan stops in the doorway of my room.

"You girls conjuring spirits?" she asks.

"Just reading a little tarot," Pix says, holding up the deck as evidence.

"I've been thinking about getting someone to read in the store," Susan says.

"You have?" I say.

"Sure, why not?"

"Because in October every store in Salem has a tarot reader."

"So, maybe I'll get one in November," Susan says, half making fun of me.

Mom calls Susan into the kitchen, and we are left alone again.

"You should learn to read," Pix says to me. "Then you could read in the store."

I laugh. "Okay, that is not happening."

"Why not?"

I can't quite explain to her the complexities of why not. Maybe because no one in this town would want to have their fortune told by me of all people? Because I am the self-professed least witchy person in Salem? Because the only reason I started paying attention to tarot at all was that this weird book arrived at the store and I was bored and then I met Pix and somehow the book and Pix have become wrapped up together in my mind, but that doesn't mean I actually believe in any of this?

"I think you would be a really good reader," Pix says.

"Yeah, but you believe in aliens and vampires," I say.

"So?"

"So, you have a lot of faith in some pretty improbable things."

Pix smiles.

"Yes," she says, "I do."

# WHEEL OF FORTUNE

Wheel of Fortune! Do you know that game show named after you? The one with the big wheel and the hopeful contestants mustering up all their strength to spin that wheel as hard as they can so it goes tick tick tick tick tick, tick, tick, tick . . . TICK.

So we each take our spin and see what we get. And sometimes we end up with a place on the wheel where we have been before. Maybe we have landed there many times and are starting to get a little sick of this particular spot. *Again?* we think. *Really? Shouldn't I be past this by now?*

But here's the thing—we know more this time around. We are wiser, more patient, more mature than we were before, when we spun the wheel back then with such blind optimism and found ourselves so disappointed. When that wheel comes back around to the same place again, we will know what to do. And if we can get it right, maybe this is the last time we will see this part of the wheel. Something can get cleared, forgiven, released. It can be different this time, if we want it to be.

# 10

The next time the coven gets together, it's not for a circle but for "an organizational meeting for Samhain."

Samhain is the pagan name for Halloween. Pagans have eight holidays spread throughout the year. A lot of them have provided fodder for the more traditional holidays: Bring a tree into your house! Light candles! Celebrate eggs and bunnies! Those were all originally pagan traditions. Pagan spirituality honors nature above all else. Not all pagans are witches, but a lot of witches are pagans.

These are the kinds of things you learn when you are dating a witch.

Although Pix and I haven't used the D-word yet. Or the G-word, the one that ends with *friend* and somehow means way more than friends. Even though we talk almost every day, I can count the number of times we have hung out on two hands. It's only been a month since she and Ofira first walked into the store, and somehow it feels both like it's only been two days and that I've known her forever.

But for the first time in a long time it feels like something in my life is working. And maybe it can continue to work if I manage to not completely screw it up. I keep thinking of that Five of Cups guy. Have I finally turned around to see the full cups behind me that I never noticed before? Is it possible that I can keep them from getting knocked over?

The miracle of October having arrived and me actually being okay is pretty remarkable. I have spent the past year dreading this month and how I was going to feel when it arrived. And now it's here and I'm even looking forward to being around people who enjoy Halloween and find meaning in it beyond binge drinking and scaring people.

Pix explains to me that Samhain is the witches' New Year. It's also when the veil between the living and the dead is supposedly the thinnest, so it's easiest for us to communicate with the other side. It's related to the Mexican Day of the Dead, when people build altars of photographs and food for their deceased loved ones and families get together and eat and play music and basically have a party for ghosts. Even if that sounds pretty implausible, it's a much nicer idea than a night that glorifies horror and fear.

So, like most things with the coven, even if I don't quite get it, I can get into the spirit of the thing. No pun intended. Especially if it means more time with Pix.

The coven's Samhain meeting is being held in a place that has played a significant role in my life, even though I've never actually been inside—the Vagina Vase store. The Vagina Vase Store is not actually called the Vagina Vase Store. It's called

Collective Witch, and turns out they do in fact have vagina vases. They also have handmade salt and pepper shakers shaped like boobs in different skin tones, and posters that say things like *The Moon Is Your Mother.*

This place is so much cooler than anything else in town, it makes me even more embarrassed about working at Susan's store. Even the more traditional witch store items are better here—mini cauldrons and crystal palm stones and hand-carved incense holders have been tastefully arranged to create a vision of aspirational witch life. If being a witch looks like this place, maybe it's kind of cool after all.

The girls are gathered at the back of the store when I arrive. Tatiana is wearing yet another Ren faire tunic dress. Anita and Ivy are huddled together, both in meticulously tailored silver dresses that I'm sure Anita designed. Pix is in a long prairie dress. One of my favorites. I love that I am starting to know her well enough to have favorites.

Pix sees me when I walk in and comes over.

"Hey," she says. She takes my hand and kisses me on the cheek. I try not to look and see if the other girls have seen this. I try not to care if she has told them about us yet. I try as hard as I can.

"This place is so much cooler than Susan's store," I say.

"Aw, I like Susan's store," Pix says.

"Susan's head would explode if she actually came in here."

I spot Ofira at the back. Tonight she's in all blue, with streaks of blue woven into her hair.

"Okay, lovebirds," Ofira calls out to us. "Let's get started, please."

*Lovebirds. Pix told her.*

Pix leads me to the back of the store, where the girls are sitting down on the floor in a circle. I am trying not to grin like a complete idiot, and I am failing.

And then I see that someone new has joined the circle. Someone joining us now on the floor. She's done up in full goth glam—oversized black clothes with a chain around her neck, dark kohl applied perfectly around her eyes. It takes me a minute to register that I know this person. It's Gillian, Simon's girlfriend. Crossover between the goths and the stoners. Ofira's classmate at Salem High. My former classmate at Salem High.

*Shit shit shit.*

I have to remind myself to keep my cool. I try to take deep breaths while I sit down next to Pix in the circle. Maybe this is fine.

*This is definitely not fine.*

"Welcome, everyone," Ofira says. "Before we begin this planning meeting, I want to thank Liz and Taryn for letting us meet in their store tonight."

The couple who own the store are sitting behind the counter, and they smile and give a little wave. They are as impeccably dressed as the store is well curated. I suddenly feel like I need an entirely new wardrobe.

"And I have invited someone new to join us tonight, with the hope that she will be interested in joining the coven. This is Gillian."

Gillian offers up a half smile. She was never one for cheerfulness. I hope my face looks normal as I'm looking at her, but then I see her eyes register my presence, and I know that I have failed at hiding the dread I am feeling. She looks away.

Ofira leads us through the agenda for the meeting. We do a lot of voting—on where to hold the Samhain circle, what to wear, what supplies we will need. Anita will organize costumes. Ivy will bake the cakes that are required to eat after a circle for grounding (and also for deliciousness). Tatiana is in charge of logistics.

"It has to be at the memorial," Tatiana says. "If we're in Salem, we need to *do* Salem."

"It's right in the middle of town, though," Ivy says. "My parents brought me to Salem once on Halloween when I was little and it was like the Haunted Happenings Parade times ten."

Ofira turns to Gillian.

"What do you think?" she asks her. "Too crazy to try to get to the memorial that night?"

"It won't be easy," Gillian says.

"What about the cemetery?" Tatiana asks. "That's right next to it."

"The Burying Point," Gillian says, the disturbingly literal name of the historical cemetery in downtown Salem. "They close it at sunset on Halloween." She is not looking at me. I want her to look at me when she says this. When the next thing out of her mouth is going to be the explanation for why they close the cemetery early on Halloween now.

"Maybe it's worth trying to get to the memorial," Ofira says, "and if it's too crowded we'll move to plan B."

The details of plan B are now hashed out. Pix absent-mindedly touches my hand. It is clammy. I am sweating. She looks at me.

"Okay?" She mouths the word.

I give a little nod.

"For our last order of business"—Ofira looks to Gillian—"we wouldn't normally do this with you present, but since I've already discussed it with most of the girls, let's take a vote on confirming Gillian as part of the coven. Tatiana? Yea or nay?"

"Yea times one hundred," Tatiana says.

Ofira makes her way around the circle.

"Ivy?"

"Yea."

"Anita?"

Anita gives a nod.

*Oh goddess help me, it's my turn.*

"Eleanor?"

*Please sound normal. Please sound normal.*

Except that I do not manage to sound normal. Instead I say, "Yea!" like I am excited about something and pump my fist.

Gillian looks at me and quickly looks away.

Yeas from Pix and Ofira, and that is the end of my little safe circle away from all the old madness of Salem.

After the meeting is over, Ofira and Ivy and the women who run the store put out some snacks on one of the display tables. Ofira is pretty obviously smitten with both of these women. They must be in their early thirties and maybe Ofira sees her future in this fashionable witch life. At least they seem to be amused by her and our ragtag group.

"Will you be able to come out on Samhain?" Pix asks me. "Will Susan need you at the store?"

"It should be okay as long as I'm there all day beforehand."

"It's a pretty wild night, huh?" Pix says.

"Yeah."

"Gillian was saying there's a back way we can take to the memorial that would help us avoid the crowds."

I pick up a boob-shaped saltshaker and pretend to be deeply fascinated by it.

"Hey," I say, "did you guys vote on me? Like, when I first started coming?"

Pix nods.

"Yes. It was unanimous."

"To keep me out, right?"

Pix smiles. "Oh yeah, but I fought for you."

She takes my hand and gives me a quick kiss. On the lips this time. She is kissing me on the lips in front of other people. It's a tiny gesture, but my heart surges with happiness. No one has ever kissed me in public before. And she did it so casually. Like it was nothing.

While a person who could literally ruin all of this is standing less than ten feet away from me, watching.

"Hey, Pix," Ofira calls from the back of the store. "Stop sucking Eleanor's face and come help me with the drinks."

I think I see Pix blush a little. She squeezes my hand and

goes to Ofira. I think about following her, but by the time I decide to do it, it's too late. I'm stuck lingering at the snacks. Gillian is the only person close to me. I try to focus on spooning out a very particular amount of hummus onto a small paper plate.

Gillian comes over to me. "So are we going to pretend we don't know each other?" she asks. She twists the chain on her neck back and forth with her fingers, a seemingly nervous gesture. It occurs to me that Gillian is probably not high right now, and that it's possible that I have never actually spoken to Gillian when she wasn't high before, since 100 percent of our interactions have been at parties.

"Hey," I say. "No, I mean, I was waiting to say hi. I didn't know you were coming. To this."

"Ofira just asked me, and I thought it would be cool," she says. "I didn't know you were in the group."

"I met them about a month ago," I say. "In the store."

Gillian and I stare at the tiny plate of hummus that I am holding for a moment.

I start to say, "How's Simon?" even though I see him once a week and he's the only person in Salem I actually talk to, but she starts to say something at the exact same time. "Sorry," I say, "you go ahead."

"I was just asking if, um, you guys are dating?"

"Oh. Yeah. Me and Pix," I say. "It's new."

Gillian nods. "That's cool."

I look at the rest of the girls; they are all in the back of the store helping Ofira get cups and bottles of soda. If I am going to say something to Gillian, this is the moment to do it.

"They don't know about everything," I say quietly. "And I would just . . . could you not tell them?"

Gillian looks at me, and for a moment I think she might pretend that she doesn't know what I'm talking about. But then her face softens. "Yeah," she says. "No problem."

"It's just nice to be around people who don't automatically hate me."

"People don't hate you, Eleanor."

I raise an eyebrow.

"I'm serious," she says.

I shake my head. I do not want to discuss this.

"It doesn't matter," I say. "It's just nice to not have to think about it sometimes."

"Yeah, okay," she says. "I get it."

I breathe a sigh of relief. Although Gillian's aesthetic has always seemed kind of intentionally intimidating, she never made me feel unwelcome in her and Simon's stoner corner of the world. Maybe it was because she felt she didn't quite fit in there either. She was the goth to Simon's hacky sack goofball, a girl and one of the few people of color in Simon's predominantly white group of stoner boys.

"Thank you," I say.

She nods, and the girls come over with the sodas.

The truth is that even if the others don't find out about last Halloween, someone in this room does know about it. Which means that I am no longer a blank slate, starting over. I am pulled back into an old idea about myself.

*Yeah, but what if you don't let that happen, Eleanor? What if this time you make a different choice?*

I look over at Pix, who is laughing with the women who run the store.

Things are different now. I know they are. Because these girls all voted to have me here. And Pix sees something in me that is worth spending time with, and worth talking to on the phone for hours, and worth kissing in front of her friends.

This is not Chloe. This is Pix. This is new.

*So give it a chance.*

# JUSTICE

Justice! We've taken a turn on the old Wheel of Fortune, and, silly us, we expected it all to come out right in the end. Surely the pros and cons of a situation will be weighed and we will all come to the same fair and practical conclusion, won't we? Surely the universe wants to reward the good and punish the bad?

We can ask for Justice, but we might not always get her. And we might not always understand her ways. If we disagree with the outcome she has determined, we can either fight against it, or learn to live in the new world that is formed by her decision.

But remember, Justice, we're not at the end. Not yet. And injustices sometimes have a way of correcting themselves even when we've given up on them.

# 11

Without any communication from Chloe for the entire month that she was away at FIT, I spent my time at the store imagining all the amazing new friends she must be making. Sometimes I would check her social media accounts on my phone when Susan wasn't looking to actually see pictures of these new friends, follow their tags to their pages, find out everything I could about them. All really super healthy behavior.

I had about two hundred drafts of potential text messages, emails, and DMs to Chloe in my notes app. Some that directly addressed the problem. Some trying to pretend there was no problem. Some asking for forgiveness. Some accusing her of being unfair. Some accusing Harrison. Some finding a brand-new scapegoat. In the end all I really wanted to say to her was:

"It's okay if we're not together, but I feel so alone without you I can barely stand it."

She had told me the dates of the program when she first got in, and now I found myself counting down the days to her return. As if it mattered. If she wasn't talking to me, her return home wasn't going to help the situation. And once she got back, I would have to see her around town with Harrison again, which would make me feel even more pathetic than I already did.

But if she was here, at least there might be some chance that I could fix things. Maybe some genius idea would suddenly occur to me out of nowhere. Or maybe Harrison would do what Harrison does, find someone else, and I would be there to catch Chloe when she fell.

And then she texted me the day that she was coming home.

Hey, can we meet up tomorrow?

No part of me had the ability to wait to respond.

Sure, I wrote. I'm at the store 10-5.

Meet me @ 5:30. At the bandstand.

The bandstand on Salem Common somehow manages to feel like both the most private and most public place in Salem. The common is a large expanse of grass that is either dead in the winter or trampled in the summer. Trees line the perimeter, framing the gray concrete domed structure, set in the middle in a position indicating that it is something much grander than it is. No one actually hangs out in the bandstand. It is the fishbowl of Salem Common.

So it was impossible to tell what kind of gesture asking to meet at the bandstand was. If she really wanted privacy, wouldn't she just invite me over? Unless she really did not want to invite me over.

Yeah, I wrote back. See you then.

*

I got to the bandstand at five twenty and Chloe was already there, as if she needed to prepare for this meeting. The bandstand was just its usual environment of discarded cigarette butts and a couple of stray beer cans. On the metal railing that runs between the concrete columns, someone had locked a bike lock that had yet to be removed. It made me think of that bridge in Paris that I've seen in pictures—the one where people in love attach locks with their initials on them to become permanent fixtures of the bridge.

Chloe was wearing an FIT tank top, jean shorts, and flip-flops. Somehow she looked tan, as if she had been to Florida instead of New York. She didn't see me approach the bandstand, or maybe she was intentionally looking at her phone. I stood on the steps for a moment, waiting for her to notice me. When she didn't, I finally gave in to saying, "Hey."

She looked up.

"Oh, hey."

I stepped into the strange coolness of the stone structure. Something about it always reminded me of a crypt.

I wanted to be the kind of person who just waited for her to start. She was the one who had asked me here, after all. But I felt like I had waited a lifetime to talk to her again, and I couldn't help myself.

"How was New York?" I asked.

"It was really great. The program was super fun."

"Oh, cool."

"Yeah, they pretty much let us do whatever we want. Like go out at night and everything. I've got this killer fake ID now.

It works, like, ninety percent of the time."

"Nice."

*Okay, that's all I've got, Chloe. Your turn.*

A long pause. Then, finally: "I'm sorry I didn't text or anything," she said. "It was kind of full-on, like, nonstop."

"Yeah. No, that's okay. I'm sorry I didn't either. I didn't want to bother you."

"I missed you, though," she said.

*Oh, what words. What magical words.*

"You did?"

She nodded.

"I figured you were mad at me," I said.

She looked down. "I just needed some time to think."

"I really didn't mean to say all those things the way I did," I said. "Everything came out really wrong."

"No, it's okay," she said. "I could tell that you had been upset since prom, and I was just kind of hoping it would go away and you would be okay with everything."

"Yeah," I say.

"But you weren't," she says.

I wondered if she meant this as a question. I shook my head.

"I guess I'm just a monogamy person," I said.

*Right. Make it your fault.*

"And that's okay," Chloe said. "Like, that's cool. I guess I'm just not."

We were both conveniently leaving out what I had said the night that we fought, which was that it wasn't just Harrison that was the problem, it was the fact that she had placed him higher than me. Our relationship had been written out of the narrative of her life. But by this point I had been put so firmly in my place I started to believe that I belonged there.

All I knew in that moment was that the month I spent without her was torture, and I would do anything to have her back in some way, even if we weren't together.

"I missed you too," I said. "A lot."

"Yeah?" Chloe smiled.

"Yeah."

Her phone chimed, and she checked it to see who had texted.

"Got places to be?" I said.

"No," she said. She put her phone in her pocket. "It was my mom."

*What are the chances that that's true, Chloe?*

She looked at me.

"Maybe we could be friends again," she said. "Like, if you still want to hang out."

My ridiculous heart jumped for joy at this. "Yeah?" I said.

"I mean, maybe that's weird."

"No," I said, too quickly. "I think it would be good."

She smiled.

"Okay, then," she said. "Friends again."

She hugged me. And I tried to take her in, let this feeling of holding her refill the empty place inside me that had been aching so badly. This would have to be enough. At least it was something.

Maybe it was simpler this way. Maybe we were always supposed to just be best friends forever, share an intimacy even beyond the physical. Didn't this prove that we had an unshakable bond? Didn't this put me back on top, in a position of status even above Harrison?

The sad thing is that I really believed this was a good idea. Because it meant that Chloe was back in my life. And that was all that mattered.

# THE HANGED MAN

You are a bit different from how you sound, Hanged Man. When we hear the word *hanged*, we tend to think the worst. We assume that this is the end for you. But you're hanging upside down, holding on to that branch by only your foot. It seems like you could get down if you really wanted to.

But for some reason it isn't time yet. You are literally in a holding pattern, waiting for something to change, some shift to happen that will signal the right moment to be released from this. You look pretty comfortable there actually, arms behind your back, angelic halo around your head.

The question is, Hanged Man, are you waiting for someone else to come along and cut you down? Do you expect to be saved? Or are you willing to get down off this branch yourself? Dust yourself off and realize that you spent far too long with the blood rushing to your head, clouding your judgment and telling you that you should tolerate this discomfort for far longer than you need to. Soon it will be time to move forward again on your own two feet. Will you be ready?

# 12

Two days after my reunion with Chloe, she texted me that Harrison was going to take his family's boat out for an afternoon sail that day and would I like to join? It would just be us and some of Harrison's friends.

*Would I like to join??? OF COURSE I would like to join! We are going to be friends after all, Chloe! Therefore there is no reason at all why I wouldn't want to spend an afternoon stuck on a boat with the person who you chose to be with instead of me with no possible escape except potential drowning!*

My actual response?

Sounds fun!

The thing about Harrison is that he likes people to feel indebted to him. There is no generosity without the expectation that you will now owe him something, even if it's just loyalty. So that day, the *Well Appointed* was stocked with supplies that were meant to impress. The best bottles from his father's belowdecks liquor cabinet. The best caviar that he and his friends had no idea how to eat (it would eventually get thrown overboard, at eighty dollars an ounce). It seemed that Harrison had even conjured up the best possible weather to show that perfection could be purchased, willed, and manifested for his own enjoyment.

Harrison and his friends were already aboard the *Well Appointed* when Chloe and I got there. He reached out a hand to help her step onto the boat and at the last minute grabbed her and pulled her into a kiss. His friends hooted behind him in appreciation.

I stood there, still on the dock. Still time to save myself, to make a different decision. Instead I stepped onto the boat.

"Elea-NOR!" Harrison said my name like it was a football fight call, raising a hand for a high five on the last syllable. I obliged.

"You ever been on a party boat, Elea-NOR?" Evidently this was a new way of saying my name that was going to stick.

"No," I said.

"Well, get ready to get wild."

For half a second I felt a small pang of sympathy for Harrison. He was involved in such an elaborate performance. His whole life consisted of a mix of things he was supposed to be based on stuff he must have seen on TV. There had to be a part of him that was separate from this performance. But that part was not planning on coming out anytime soon.

A round of shots was poured before we set off into the late-afternoon sunshine. Chloe had two. I abstained but pulled out a joint and lit it, not offering it around.

*See how independent I am? How I don't need this? How I am above all of this?*

Harrison started up the boat's engine, and it occurred to me to wonder about the potential legal consequences of all of us being underage on a boat carrying an entire liquor store's worth of alcohol.

*Too late! We're off!*

We had only been out on the water for a few minutes when Tyler sat down next to me and Chloe. He handed Chloe an imported beer with a fancy label. She took it.

"Thanks," she said.

"How was New York?" Tyler said.

Ah, Tyler—the younger, poorer, chattier version of Harrison. Tyler, who, by aspiring to be the kind of asshole that Harrison was, somehow became even more of an asshole.

"It was so fun," Chloe said.

"Art school, huh?"

"Yeah, it was a foundational class, so I got to do everything. Drawing, painting, sculpting."

I wanted to grab Chloe's hand, whisper in her ear that being genuine with this person was not going to go well. Tyler was the kind of person who set traps and grinned as he watched you fall into them.

"Sounds pretty faggy," Tyler said.

Chloe laughed.

*Chloe laughed.*

"What did you just say?" I said.

Tyler took a swig of beer and grinned at me.

"Fag—gy." He broke up the syllables, delighted to have a word powerful enough to get a reaction from me.

"It was a lot of cool people, yeah," Chloe said, taking a sip of her beer.

I looked at her. What was she imagining that he had just said? What imaginary dialogue was going on in her head to drown out Tyler's very real voice?

A couple of the other guys had caught the scent of Tyler's troublemaking and were now eyeing our area, ready to join in if needed. I felt like fresh meat, and Chloe was throwing me to the sharks.

"That's not a great word, Tyler," I said, feeling my half-stoned brain attempt to snap into action.

"What? Faggy? Sorry, should I say 'that's gay'? How about dykey? Is that even a word?" He laughed and looked at his audience. "Super dykey!" The others gave a supportive chuckle in response, still waiting to see if one of us was going to take the bait.

Chloe, unable to continue to pretend that she had suddenly lost her hearing, looked down at her beer.

My heart was pounding.

What kind of joy must it bring him to say a terrible word to someone's face? What kind of power?

"Do you have a problem, Tyler?" I asked. This seemed like the right kind of thing to say now, to try to convince the person hurling such a word that they hadn't succeeded in making you feel smaller than you have ever felt before.

"Oh, I love lesbians. That shit is hot. But, like, the pretty ones. Not the fucking ugly ones who go to Home Depot."

Suddenly Harrison kicked the engine into a higher gear,

and now we were moving swiftly out onto the open water of the sound.

*Please say something, Chloe. Please don't leave me alone in this.*

"Oh my god, Harrison! You're going so fast!" Chloe yelled over the noise of the engine.

"You ain't seen nothing yet, baby!" Harrison yelled back at her.

I silently watched the dock retreating with deep longing. This was my fault for thinking that I could do this. It was my stupid pride that was flattered that Chloe invited me and wanted to prove to her that I could be "cool" enough to join this part of her life. If I couldn't figure out how to navigate this, I was going to miss out on my summer with Chloe. Harrison would win, and I would lose what little I had left of her.

We were half an hour out when Harrison turned off the engine and declared that we were in the perfect sunset-watching spot. To me it looked like we were in a perfect "get eaten by sharks" spot, but at least the relentless bouncing of the boat through the water was over for now.

About half the alcohol had been consumed, and now it was evidently time to consume the other half as quickly as possible. At Harrison's request, Chloe joined an assembly line of shot drinking. Harrison lined up the glasses and poured, splashing indiscriminately onto the deck. As soon as the assembled drank one, slamming their shot glasses back down, he poured another.

I counted five refills before I decided I had to do something.

"Hey, Clo." I grabbed her arm. "Maybe you've had enough?"

"We're just having fun."

"Okay, but maybe, just, like, take a little break from fun?"

Chloe slumped her head on my shoulder, which seemed to be half drunken affection and half involuntary loss of control over her own body.

"Yeah, let's go sit down," I said.

I led Chloe over to where we had been sitting before, and she immediately slumped down in the seat. When I sat down next to her, she put her head in my lap and grabbed my legs as if they were a pillow.

"This is comfy," she said. "Wake me up for the sunset."

I put my hand on her head, touched her hair. She drooled a little on my bare leg, and I felt the purest pang of desire I had ever experienced. How was it possible for me to know someone's body so well and never get to be with it again?

*This will be enough. This has to be enough.*

The sun, as anticipated, did set. It was a perfect sunset for Harrison's perfect fucking day. And as dusk settled on the water around us, it occurred to me that we still had a thirty-minute ride back ahead of us. Now in the dark. And my high was starting to wear off. Why hadn't I brought more with me?

I gently moved Chloe, who had been in and out of dozing for the past forty minutes, and got up to get myself something to help me calm down.

Most of the guys had gone in the water, continually acting out a seemingly endless cycle of pushing each other off the side of the boat, getting back on the boat, pushing each other off again. But Harrison had remained on board, keeping watch over his domain.

I managed to find a clean plastic cup and tried to find a bottle that hadn't been emptied yet.

"Can I get you something, Eleanor?" Harrison asked.

My name, said normally, suddenly sounded very dangerous.

"Sure, I'll just have whatever."

He took the cup from me and started searching among the bottles.

"So it's cool that Chloe invited you today," he said.

"Yeah, it's been . . . fun." I could barely get the word out.

"I would just appreciate if you would keep your fucking hands to yourself."

I froze.

"What?"

"I know the two of you used to scissor or whatever, but I don't really need to be reminded of it, okay?"

I didn't even have words available to me to respond.

Suddenly Harrison was in my face, his breath hot and reeking of alcohol.

"And may I suggest that you keep your fucking mouth shut about whatever you think you and Chloe were? She may think it's cute to call herself 'bi' or whatever, but that's not how we do things in my family. Got it? Mouth shut, hands off. Simple."

He picked up a bottle with a black-and-gold label and a liter of Coke. He poured the two together until they slopped over the side of the cup.

"Here," he said. He handed me the cup. "You'll love this."

I wish that I had said something, anything, to Harrison in response. Even something idiotic, something embarrassing, even just a nice simple "Fuck you" would have done the trick. But instead I said nothing, went back over to Chloe, careful now to sit a few inches away from her, and quickly drank down the entire contents of the cup he had handed me.

Chloe started throwing up first. The swimmers were climbing back onto the boat and drying off for the trip home. Chloe leaned over the side of the boat, and I held her hair back, unable to continue to follow Harrison's instructions to not touch her.

Harrison was watching us.

"What's wrong with her?" he said, as if Chloe had suddenly contracted some sort of mysterious disease.

"What's wrong with her is you gave her fucking alcohol poisoning," I said. I tried to spit out the words, but they felt weak and harmless coming out of my intoxicated mouth.

Harrison didn't respond. He turned on the engine, and the boat growled back to life.

"Everybody hold on," he said.

And then we were flying through the water, faster than before. The light at the prow of the boat barely made an impression on the rapidly deepening darkness in front of us. Chloe tried to sit back down normally, but another wave of nausea hit her and she had to lean over the side again. I held on to her waist as the boat bounced violently through the waves and Harrison's friends whooped into the noise of the motor.

"Harrison, slow down!" I screamed. But the sound of my voice was lost in the wind.

I looked at him, and his eyes met mine suddenly. For the first time I saw the rage behind his competitiveness, his complete inability to deal with the idea that someone was interfering with him having something that he felt that he deserved.

He smiled as his eyes blazed. His hand moved on the gear, and he tugged it hard. At this new speed even his friends protested. But he was on a mission now.

*He wants to throw me off this boat. And he will send Chloe off with me if that's what it takes.*

As soon as Chloe let up, I started throwing up, the two of us now holding each other through this nightmare roller coaster ride.

"Elea-NOR, don't fucking barf in my dad's boat," Harrison managed to yell above the noise of the engine.

Twenty minutes later we arrived back at the dock, Harrison seemingly invigorated by the ride back. Chloe and I were draped over each other. She grabbed my hand.

"We made it," she whispered to me.

Suddenly Harrison was in my face.

"You better head home if you're so sick," he said.

"I'm just gonna help Chloe get home," I said.

"She's fine."

Chloe let go of my hand.

"Yeah, I'm okay," she said to me. "I'll call you later."

All eyes were on me, Harrison's friends watching behind him. It was time to go. It was time to go three hours ago.

"Are you sure?" I asked Chloe.

She nodded. Tried to smile. "I guess I just got super seasick."

I stood up, unsteady on my feet. It felt like the boat was still moving. Someone had put the gangplank out, and I made my way over to it, put my hand on the railing. I felt a shove on my left shoulder and tried to catch myself but fell to my knees on the ramp.

"Oh, you okay?" Tyler said. He was behind me. "Tried to grab you there so you wouldn't fall."

I looked at the black water that I had just nearly tumbled into lapping up against the dock, and looked back at Tyler. Chloe was leaning on Harrison with her eyes closed.

"Okay," I said. "I'm okay." As if anyone actually cared. I got up and made my way slowly onto the dock and away from the *Well Appointed*. I did not look back.

The walk home that night was woozy and unpleasant. But even within the cloud of my poisoned brain I was holding on tightly to three thoughts:

1.  Chloe told Harrison about us.
2.  Harrison was jealous.
3.  Somehow it was all Harrison's fault that no one could know about my relationship with Chloe.

And of the many mistakes that I made in those months, one of the biggest ones was thinking that any of these things made any kind of difference.

# DEATH

Oh dear. Our first "scary" card.

But of course there are no scary cards, really, are there? Dear Death, we've been taught to fear endings, to believe that holding on to what we have is more important than anything, even if it's really time to let something, or someone, go. But you exist as a natural part of this cycle, another manifestation of existence. It is perhaps time to transmute into something else, to release what is not working, no matter how much it hurts.

If we are honest with ourselves, we know when it is time to leave the party.

# 13

I spend the first two weeks of October getting a crash course in witchiness from Pix in preparation for Samhain. Nights when she doesn't have too much homework and I'm not at the store, she comes over and brings me witchcraft books and I pretend to read tarot for her, making up ridiculous meanings for the cards.

"I see you coming into a large inheritance, but beware of men in red hats!" I say. And then she throws the cards at me and I laugh and we kiss and everything is perfect.

Meanwhile the list of "improbable things that Pix believes in" continues to get longer.

"You really think that dead people talk to you?"

"Of course," Pix says. "Our ancestors for sure. And then we each have guides, who may or may not have been human at some point. They communicate with us in lots of different ways."

"Our what now?"

Pix picks up one of the books she has loaned me and flips until she finds the page she's looking for.

"You have not been doing your homework," she says. She points to the chapter heading—"Spirit Guides."

"Are you going to stop dating me if I say that I find all of this pretty implausible?" I ask.

I say it without even thinking. The D-word.

"Isn't it a nice idea, though?" Pix says. "That energy can communicate even beyond our understanding of tangible existence?"

*Did she hear me say the D-word?*

"Yes," I say. "It's a nice idea."

Pix seems to be reading the book for a moment. Then she says, "And no, I won't stop dating you if you don't believe in this stuff. You're my girlfriend."

She looks up at me.

"Right?" she says.

*Nothing has ever been more right in the whole world.*

"Yes," I say. "Yeah." I know that I am not succeeding in holding back a very goofy grin.

She smiles and looks back at the book.

"As long as you don't make fun of me for believing in this stuff," she says.

"Why would I do that?"

"Some people just aren't very open-minded."

"Like who?" I ask.

She shakes her head. "It doesn't matter," she says. "There are just some people who refuse to accept things that they don't understand."

I want to ask her more about this, but I think about how

she never pushes me for more information than I am ready to give. If she wants to tell me something, I'm here to listen.

My tarot deck is spread out on the floor in front of us. I am definitely failing in the "always respect and take good care of your deck" department. The death card is turned faceup, and Pix picks it up.

"On Samhain the concept of death is really more about transmutation," she says. "Honoring what has been, but releasing what needs to go."

She hands me the card. A skeleton in knight's armor riding a horse. Are those people being trampled at the horse's feet, or just humans bowing down in awe at Death's power?

"Sounds good to me," I say.

I waited a day after Harrison's boat ride from hell to recover from the haze of my hangover before I texted Chloe. I assumed that she was in worse shape than I was, and probably embarrassed about the whole thing. I doubted that even her desire to be with the most popular boy in school could survive the experience of him basically trying to kill us.

You feeling okay? I texted.

No response. For hours. And then she showed up at the store. She was wearing a baseball cap low over her eyes. I had never seen her wear a baseball cap before.

"Hey," I said.

"Can you go on a break?" she asked.

"Uh, yeah, probably."

We left the store together and walked down Essex without

saying anything. We seemed to be heading back to the common, but then Chloe stopped abruptly in front of Hawthorne Hotel, the location of Bridget Bishop's infamous hauntings of her old orchard.

I stopped and looked at her.

"Are you okay?" I asked.

She took the baseball cap off nervously and smoothed back her hair, then put it back on. I caught a glimpse of her eyes, red and tired.

"I wanted to believe that we could do this, but we can't," she said.

"Do what?"

"Like, be friends. Include you in my life."

My heart started racing. This was not the conversation that I was expecting to have in this moment. "What are you talking about?"

"I invited you on Harrison's boat, and you were totally rude to him."

I felt like I had been kicked in the stomach.

"He said that *I* was rude to *him*?"

She nodded.

"Chloe, he basically threatened me. He told me that I shouldn't ever touch you."

"Well. Maybe you shouldn't."

"What?"

She started to walk away from me now, quickly, toward the common. I followed her, running to try to keep up.

"I'm not supposed to touch you?"

"If this is going to be too confusing for you, and you can't just be my friend because you're obviously still attracted to me, then we can't do this."

She was a little ahead of me, and the words were floating back to me like exhaust, like a black cloud. I grabbed her arm. She stopped.

"Is that what he said?"

"Let go of me," she said, her voice firm. I did.

"You're telling me that Harrison said I'm too attracted to you to be friends with you?"

"Yes. And I think he's right."

I looked around us. People were catching Frisbees on the common. Several picnics were in progress. It was a perfect summer day in Salem.

"Tyler pushed me," I said.

"What are you talking about?"

"When I was getting off the boat. He pushed me and I fell. You were too drunk. You didn't see it."

"I'm not talking about Tyler," she said. "Tyler's an idiot."

"Oh, what makes you say that?" I asked sarcastically. "Maybe because he likes to throw around words like *dyke* and *faggy* just for fun?"

She crossed her arms in front of her chest.

"People just talk that way," she said. "It doesn't mean anything."

I put my hands up to my face. I could feel myself turning red from anger.

"Do you even hear yourself?" I was trying not to yell. I wanted to scream.

"Even if Tyler pushed you," she said, "I'm not dating Tyler."

"Harrison threatened me, and then Tyler pushed me. He's like his little henchman or something."

Chloe rolled her eyes. "Henchman? Harrison's not a villain in a comic book, Eleanor. He's a person. And he's my boyfriend. And he's trying to protect me."

"From what?"

She just glared at me from under that stupid hat. A hat that must have belonged to Harrison. Just another way he was slowly taking over her life. She used to dress me in her clothes, now she was wearing his.

"What do you need protection from, Chloe?" I asked. I wanted to hear it from her, whatever hateful words Harrison had poured into her brain. "From me? Or from yourself? From you not being some kind of virginal, straight, perfect little princess for him to stand next to in the family Christmas card?"

I was yelling now. The words coming out of me were on fire.

She stared at me for a minute, as if she couldn't believe that I had spontaneously grown enough of a spine to say these things to her.

"Fuck you, Eleanor," she said finally. Then she turned and walked quickly down the common. I watched her go, unable to believe what had just happened. Then I turned and started walking in the other direction.

I walked for hours, reliving the entire conversation over and over in my mind. I didn't stop until I reached the water at the eastern edge of Salem, the beach at Winter Island. I sat on a low stone wall and looked out over the sand. The beach was filled with sunbathers and swimmers. Families and people playing volleyball and building sandcastles and all the things you are supposed to do in a summer. All the things I would not do. Because I had to work and I did not have a family and I did not even have friends.

It was over.

Harrison had won.

And the worst part was that he was right. About all of it. I did love Chloe too much to just be her friend. And every time I touched her it brought all of it back, all my desire. All of what I thought had been our desire. I would always want her back.

Why was she allowed to do this? To decide what both of our lives would be like now? And what power could he possibly have over her to blind her to the fact that he was nothing more than an insecure rich bully spending every minute of his life overcompensating? That he was trying to control everything about her, including who she was?

Why wasn't she willing to fight for me?

After holding them back for hours, the tears came in full force now, and I pulled up my legs so I could cry into my knees, a pathetic ball of despair surrounded by nothing but the pure joy of a beautiful summer day.

All the promises that I'd made to her in my head had been taken away from me one by one. And the last one left was the hardest to let go of—"I will be there for you. I will protect you."

I couldn't protect her from Harrison. She wouldn't let me.

I reached in my pocket reflexively for my phone. Was there any chance there was a text from her? Some expression of regret, now that she had said the words to my face?

Nothing.

Just a text from Susan asking where I was. I managed a halfhearted response about feeling sick and going home, not even bothering to cover my tracks by texting Mom.

Then I opened my text chain with Chloe and stared at it.

My text from the day before—You feeling okay?—stared back at me. My finger hovered over the screen. What could I say to her now if she had nothing left to say to me?

*You're making a huge mistake*

or

*He will never love you like I do*

or

*You don't know what you're missing.*

Some kind of cocky line that Harrison would send?

*But Chloe knows exactly what she's missing.*

I went to messages and swiped left on my thread with Chloe.

*Would you like to delete this conversation?* my phone asked me.

Eleven months of texts. Thousands of them. Sometimes fifty in a day. Pictures and GIFs and bad memes. An entire relationship from beginning to end.

"Yes," I said. I said it out loud and hit the delete button again. Then I got up, put my phone in my pocket, and started the long walk back home.

# TEMPERANCE

So, Death was a little intense. Even when we accept inevitable endings, even when we let go, there will always some mourning that follows. Here you are to help us with this, oh angel of Temperance!

Can you show us how to maintain balance in this moment? Bring us calm? Ease? Not too much of one thing or the other? Pouring the water back and forth between your two cups, you allow for flow. We want to live in balance with you!

In the wake of tragedy, can we employ healthy coping mechanisms? There's a gift of patience here, of learning how to be self-sufficient. What if you could survive without the excuses that you thought you needed? What if you were enough all on your own?

# 14

I don't know if I intentionally have not been smoking pot around Pix, but I have not been smoking pot around Pix. It's not that I think that she would disapprove; it's just not a conversation that I want to have in case she does. I don't want to have to explain what it means to me, and what I'm worried I would be like without it. Times when I've really tried to cut back, I stop sleeping, stop eating. I jump at my own shadow.

Simon and I have been meeting up on Thursdays for almost a year and a half now. It's the most consistent force in my life. But October in Salem tends to disrupt all regularly scheduled programming.

I'm in the store behind the counter, trying to keep up with ringing up such important items as a T-shirt with a cartoon ghost on it that says *My Boyfriend Ghosted Me!* when I get a text from Simon.

Can you meet me at work tonight? Thought I had the night off but the Frankenstein called in sick.

Most people who need work in Salem take on a second job in October.

**Where's work?** I text back.

**I'm part time at Professor Scary's.**

Professor Scary's Haunted Extravaganza is one of the many seasonal haunted houses that pop up in empty storefronts in town in October. They are usually cheaply made, with second-rate animatronics rescued from shuttered theme parks, and staffed by teenagers who are instructed to bring their own costumes and to jump out from behind the displays and scare people.

**What time?**

**I've got a break at seven,** he texts back.

I am supposed to be at Ofira's house at seven to start work on the headdresses Anita is going to help us make to wear on Samhain. But missing Simon is not an option.

**Ok. See you then. And I think you mean Frankenstein's monster.**

He texts back a ?

**Frankenstein was the doctor. Not the monster.**

**We don't really have time for semantics at Professor Scary's,** he texts back.

Pix was supposed to meet me at the corner after Simon stopped by the store at six thirty and we were going to walk over to Ofira's together. I call her, and she puts me on video chat.

"Hey," I say. I prop the phone up next to the cash register so I can see her and ring up a woman buying some fairy wings at the same time.

"Hi," she says. "Ready for craft night?"

"Yeah, I just need to do something right at seven. Can I meet you at Ofira's?"

"Excuse me, you just rang those up twice," the woman buying the wings says. She is staring daggers at my phone as if it were personally responsible for trying to scam her out of money.

"Nope," I say. "These wings just cost thirty-seven dollars."

"That is very overpriced!" she says.

"That's Salem in October," I tell her.

She hands me her credit card, and I go back to my conversation with Pix.

"You still there?" I ask.

"Yeah, where do you need to go at seven?"

"I just need to pick something up from a friend."

A long pause. Pix knows that I have no friends. If I had friends, she would have heard about them in our three-week-long nonstop conversation.

"Uh, you know Simon?" I say. "Gillian's boyfriend?"

"I don't think so."

"I just need to get something from him, and then I can head over to Ofira's."

"Okay. I'll just go with you," Pix says.

*Ah. Okay.*

"Sure," I say.

"See you in a bit."

She hangs up.

Since it's only a Thursday, the crowds on the pedestrian mall aren't as overwhelming as they already are on the weekends. These are the more experienced October tourists. Only an amateur heads to Salem on a weekend in October. So my anxiety moving through the crowd tonight is manageable. And it helps that I know an even bigger antidote to my anxiety is promised at the end.

This task is also made much easier by the fact that I am holding Pix's hand. I have used the fact that I know where we are going as a very thin excuse to grab her hand, and now I am leading her down the mall to Professor Scary's thinking that I don't know exactly how I am going to handle this interaction in front of her but that I'll somehow figure it out when we get there.

There's a line to get in outside Professor Scary's. It's got the novelty factor of being a new attraction this year, so Salem haunted house completists need to get there so they can post video reviews online or whatever they do.

I take Pix to the front of the line. A guy who I thankfully do not recognize is sitting on a stool at the door like he's a bouncer at some kind of exclusive club.

"I'm looking for Simon," I say.

He doesn't even bother to look at me. Just points inside.

"Door on the left," he says.

I wonder how much business Simon has been doing out of Professor Scary's.

Inside the entrance there is a door half-hidden behind a curtain that says *Staff Only*. I push through it, and Pix and I find ourselves in a makeshift locker room that has been fashioned out of hanging black curtains. A single ghost light illuminates the space.

"Simon is here?" Pix says.

"He's playing Frankenstein's monster," I say. "Or he's filling in for Frankenstein's monster? I wasn't really paying attention."

"Thank you," Pix says.

"For what?"

"For knowing that Frankenstein was the doctor," she says.

On cue, Frankenstein's monster and a particularly shabby-looking vampire pull back a curtain and come into the make-shift space.

"Did you see that kid kick me?" the vampire says. "He was only like six years old! Fully kicks me in the shin."

"You gotta move quicker, man," Simon says. "The little ones are the worst."

"I want that kid banned," the vampire says. He takes off his cape and throws it on a chair, then pushes open another curtain and goes through it, calling out, "Pee break!"

Simon turns to us. He has patchy green makeup on and plastic bolts hanging crookedly off his neck.

"Do not laugh, Sanderson," he says. He goes to a locker.

I was trying not to, and this puts me over the edge.

"Did you stick your face in a can of green paint?" I say, laughing.

"I'm not even supposed to be on the floor. I got hired for electronics. This Frankenstein thing"—he turns around to face us and gestures at his ill-fitting costume—"is bullshit."

"Frankenstein's monster," I correct him again.

"Sanderson, gimme a break."

210

"Simon, this is Pix," I say. "She knows Gillian."

"Hey." Simon nods at her. "You part of the cult?"

"It's a coven," Pix says, one eyebrow raised. "Not a cult."

"Well, please tell my girlfriend not to hex me or whatever."

"If you get hexed, it'll be because you deserve it," I say.

He hands me the bag.

"We don't hex," Pix says, watching.

"Just make sure she knows that, okay?" he says.

I shove the bag in my pocket.

The vampire comes back in the room, grabs his cape, mutters something to himself, and heads back into the haunted house. He holds the curtain back for a moment, and we can see the eerie blue lighting and the jerky movements of some ancient witch animatronics. A soundtrack of recorded screams floats back to us.

"So we'll tell Gillian to hex the crap out of you, got it," I say. I grab Pix's hand, and we make our way to the exit.

"You're funny, Sanderson. You should be in comedy."

"Good luck in there, Monster!" I call back. "Careful of the little ones. I hear they kick!"

Pix and I move past the bouncer at the entrance and back onto the pedestrian mall. We're still holding hands as we walk back toward Essex, but neither of us is saying anything. Am I imagining that she's mad at me or is she actually mad at me?

"I just needed to restock," I say. "Supply tends to run a little low in October."

Pix starts to say something but then stops. She stops walking too.

I turn around, about to say, "Are you okay?" but I see that she's stopped in front of a small crowd that is waiting to get into the Salem Wax Museum.

"Evan?" she says, a look of disbelief on her face.

One of the boys in the line turns around.

"Oh, hey, Penny," the boy says. He is a tall, thin white boy with curly brown hair, wearing a long army jacket. "How's it going?"

"Fine," she says. Her hands are on her hips. She does not look fine.

I walk over to them. The group around this guy is eyeing Pix but keeping to their own conversations.

"I'm Eleanor," I say to the boy, because no one is saying anything.

"Hey," he says.

"This is Evan," Pix says. "What are you doing here?" she asks him. She is annoyed. I have never seen her annoyed before.

"We just thought it would be hilarious to go to the wax museum. It's supposed to be really dumb."

"You came to Salem to make fun of a wax museum?" Pix says.

"Yeah. This whole scene is hilarious," Evan says. "Salem in October is, like, full-on kitsch central."

Something seems to be being communicated between these two people that I do not understand, because Evan starts defending himself as if Pix has accused him of something.

"This has nothing to do with your witch stuff, Pen. How

are you going to manage to take it personally that I'm in Salem?"

"I'm not taking anything personally."

"That would be a first," he says.

I don't want to overstep, but I also suspect that Pix would be happy for this conversation to be over.

"We've got someplace to be," I say.

Pix nods.

"See you around," he says, as if he is not looking forward to this possibility.

Pix starts walking away and I walk quickly to catch up with her.

"Hey," I say as we turn onto Essex Street. "Who was that?"

Pix keeps looking straight ahead, frowning.

"That was my ex," she says.

We make our way quickly over to Ofira's house, and it is clear to me that Pix does not want to talk, even though I've got about a billion questions.

*Pix dates boys?*

*Or Pix has dated at least one boy?*

*And Pix has an ex she hasn't told me about?*

*And she didn't introduce me to him?*

*And she doesn't want to talk about it?*

As I struggle to keep up with her, I go over these questions one by one.

*Pix can date boys, that's fine. Who cares? She's dating me now. Not that jerk.*

But there's one question I can't talk myself out of.

*Why didn't she introduce me to him?*

All my old fears come rushing back. Suddenly nothing from before this night matters anymore—not Pix kissing me in front of the coven, not us walking around town holding hands, not her calling me her girlfriend. Because the real truth, the only truth that matters in this moment, is that Pix did not introduce me to Evan as her girlfriend. Even if this guy is a jerk, couldn't she have taken my hand, declared loud and proud, "This is my girlfriend, Eleanor, who makes me much happier than you ever did," and then kissed me passionately in the middle of the pedestrian mall? Would that have been so difficult?

We arrive at Ofira's house, and I try to calm myself down.

*Pix is not Chloe, Eleanor. It doesn't have to be the same.*

But this is not enough to get my heart to stop racing. I pause at the gate.

"Hey," I say. "You go ahead. I'll be in in a minute."

Pix looks at me. I can't quite read her expression. She feels far away and preoccupied.

"Okay," she says, and goes in the house.

I pull a joint out of my pocket and walk around the corner to smoke it. If the energy feels all wrong now, I've got to do something to change it, and this is the only thing I can think of.

*Everything's okay, Eleanor.*

I keep telling myself that until the smoke makes my body almost believe it.

Inside the house, Anita has commandeered the large dining room with piles of headdress-making accessories. Twigs, feathers, yarn, construction paper, beads, paint, and glitter cover the dining room table.

"How are you making your sticks stand up straight?" Tatiana is asking Ofira.

"Hot glue," Ofira says, handing her a glue gun. "Lots of it."

Jazzy music drifts in from the kitchen, and I can see Ofira's dad bustling around in there. Whatever he's making smells incredible.

Pix is sitting at the table with her back to me. She doesn't turn around when I come in. I get a "Hey, Eleanor" from Ivy and Tatiana. The rest of the girls are too absorbed in their work. And Pix is maybe ignoring me, although my altered state of mind allows me to not completely panic over this information.

*Is this a fight? Is this our first fight? And if it is, then what does she have to be mad at me about?*

Ofira's eleven-year-old sister, Lydia, is sitting next to Pix, and the only open seat is next to her, so I sit there.

"Headband base or crown base?" Lydia asks me immediately.

"What?"

She picks up a headband and a crown. "You have to pick a base, depending on the look you want. I would go with crown if I were you. It's more stable. You can get a lot of stuff on there."

"Okay," I say.

She hands me the crown, and I look at it, completely lost as to what I am supposed to do next. I look at Tatiana across from me.

"What is it supposed to be?" I ask.

"Just something fabulous," she declares.

"Anita recommends that we start with the natural materials and then add from there," Ivy offers as her girlfriend's spokesperson. She holds up her creation. It has a circle of upright twigs with black ribbons wound around them. "But you can make whatever you want."

Gillian is sitting next to Ivy, and she nods a hello.

"Just saw your bf," I say.

"Oh yeah?" she says.

"He asks that you not hex him."

Gillian rolls her eyes. "Idiot," she says, but the affection those two have always had for each other is obvious. Imagine a relationship that could actually weather years of high school drama.

Anita is going around the circle, checking on everyone. She stops for a moment longer behind Ivy, rubs her girlfriend's shoulders with a show of affection that suddenly makes me ache. I look over at Pix. She has her eyes on a pile of black feathers that she is sorting into different sizes.

I look down at the crown in front of me. Am I too stoned for this activity, or exactly stoned enough?

"Do you want help?" Ofira's sister says a little too enthusiastically. She grabs my crown before I can answer. "I'll just start for you."

I spend the next hour watching Lydia make an elaborate headdress that no one would ever be able to actually balance on their head. For something to do, I eat the fancy popcorn that Ofira's dad has made—it's covered in herbs and the perfect amount of butter. Pix doesn't even look in my direction until Lydia turns to me with her finished product.

"Ta-da!" she sings out.

I nearly spit out my popcorn. The crown is about three feet tall and covered in black glitter.

"Oh wow," I say, attempting to sound enthusiastic. "Thank you."

She nods, satisfied with herself, and hands it to me.

"Put it on," she instructs.

"Now?"

"Yes!"

I do as I am told, holding very still so I don't topple this intricate creation. That's when Pix finally looks over. She can't help but laugh.

"What?" I say. "Too much?"

But she turns back to her own work and the interaction is over.

Now left without an activity, I head into the kitchen to refill the popcorn bowl.

"Hi there!" Ofira's dad says when he sees me. He's enthusiastically stirring something in a pot on the stove.

"Hi. Uh, is there more popcorn?" I ask.

"In the pantry, second shelf on the left."

I open the pantry door and nearly scream when I see that Ofira's brother is in there, sitting in the dark.

"What?" he says, annoyed.

"I'm looking for the popcorn," I say.

He hands me a large Tupperware container and shuts the

door. I am pouring popcorn into the bowl when Ivy comes into the kitchen.

"You want something to drink, Eleanor?" she asks me.

"I'm okay," I say.

She gets herself a soda from the fridge. Ofira's dad is now loudly singing along to Nina Simone.

"What's on the menu tonight, Vincent?" Ivy asks him.

"Enchiladas," he says. "We just unearthed my grand-mother's recipe for the sauce. I never felt like I got it right at the restaurant. Here."

He holds out a spoonful of sauce for Ivy to try. She tastes it.

"Is it habanero or ancho chili powder?" she asks.

"Habanero," he says. "Too much?"

"I think you could do more," Ivy says. She turns to me. "Eleanor? You want to taste?"

"Oh, no, thanks," I say.

She comes over to me.

"You doing okay?" she asks.

I am not sure what this means. Does it mean, "Why are you so stoned right now?"

*Do not drift into paranoia, Eleanor. That defeats the whole purpose.*

"Yeah," I say. "Why?"

Ivy shrugs. "Energy seems off," she says.

This is definitely the downside to hanging out with a bunch of witches. You can't get away with anything.

"I guess something kind of weird happened before we got here," I say.

Ivy pops her soda tab and takes a sip. She is wearing dangling silver earrings that look like fish scales and I am attempting not to become mesmerized by them as they sparkle.

"We ran into this guy Evan on the way over," I say.

Ivy's eyes get wide. "Pix's ex," she says.

"Yeah," I say. "She's never mentioned him before."

"Evan was not into all of this." Ivy gestures toward the dining room in a way that seems to encompass the activity, the people, the house, and the entire town.

"Yeah, I got that."

"Pix is a real empath, you know?" Ivy says. "Not like the way people use that word casually. Or to mean that they are really sympathetic. She absorbs the energy around her. So especially for her to have someone toxic in her life. . . ." Ivy raises an eyebrow. "It was not good."

"So Evan was a jerk about the witchy stuff?" I guess.

"He basically told her he couldn't date someone who actually believed in all of this. So she made a choice."

"Sounds like she made the right choice."

"It's fine if someone doesn't believe in it, you know? But most people can manage to live and let live, or at least have a sense of humor about it. Like, it's all in good fun. But I think Evan found it threatening for some reason. Have you ever heard of the broom closet?" she asks me.

"I mean . . . I have heard of broom closets," I say.

"That's what we call it when someone can't be out as a witch. I'm in the broom closet with my family."

"You are?"

"They're pretty religious," Ivy says. "It was hard enough telling them I was dating a girl. I don't need to add witchcraft onto it. Never mind that I am one hundred percent certain that our ancestors practiced what my mom would call witchcraft way before Christianity showed up."

"Have you tried to talk to her about it?" I ask.

Ivy shakes her head. "Not all of us live in a house like this," she says, looking at Ofira's dad, now belting out "My Baby Just Cares for Me."

I almost say, "I don't either," but then I think about my mom and Susan. For all the things that might be wrong with my home life, not being accepted isn't a problem.

Instead I say, "I'm sorry you have to be in the broom closet."

"It's okay. It's how I became a kitchen witch. Now most of my witchcraft just looks like cooking, which my mom loves. As long as I call them recipes instead of spells, it's fine."

"So Pix seemed really shook up by seeing Evan," I say, hoping to get more information out of Ivy.

"I don't know him that well," she says. "They met a long time ago at summer camp. So I don't know if he used to be less of an asshole, but we all agreed that it was time for him to go."

"Not everyone can have what you and Anita have, I guess," I say.

"I mean, it's not always easy," Ivy says. "I end up doing about ninety percent of the talking with her. But we love each other, so we figure it out."

I suddenly feel like crying. Could Pix and I say that about each other?

"I know what you mean about Pix being a real empath," I say. "I've never met anyone like her before."

Ivy smiles. "Yeah, she's a special one. Ofira might be leader of this coven, but Pix has always been the heart of it. I'm glad you two are together," she says.

"You are?"

She nods. "She deserves to be with a good person."

A chill runs through me when she says this. I am not sure that I meet that requirement. And something else occurs to me.

"When did she and Evan break up?" I ask.

"Uh, I guess it was August."

August. Right before Pix met me. Which makes me her rebound.

*Don't do that, Eleanor. Don't assume the worst.*

But if I was more than a rebound, wouldn't she have proudly introduced me? Shown me off as proof of how well she was doing? Or is that what she would do if I *was* a rebound?

Ofira's dad turns toward us and gestures at the pot that is bubbling on the stove. "Ivy, I think I may have overdone it now on the chili powder."

Ivy goes over to the stove, and I leave them to their kitchen witchery and head back into the dining room.

At some point during the evening, Pix starts acting like her normal self again, and I allow myself to relax into the idea that the earlier weirdness might have simply passed us by, and we will now be able to continue on as if nothing happened.

But I still have questions. Not that I'm planning on asking them.

Once the headdresses are all completed and the food is all eaten, Pix and I leave Ofira's house together after saying goodbye to everyone. I follow her lead, heading down Chestnut Street back toward the center of town, where she parked by the store.

I don't realize that I am counting the seconds of silence until Pix says something. I get to thirty-two.

"How often do you buy pot from Simon?" she asks me suddenly.

"Oh. Uh, I don't know," I say, wondering if there is a good answer to this question.

I receive silence in response to my lie.

"I guess like once a week," I amend.

Pix stops and looks at me.

"But you're not always stoned when we're together, are you?" she asks.

The way that she says this makes me want to cry. There is genuine fear in her eyes, as if I have changed from something stable and stationary into a messy blob of uncertainty. And I so want to be that stable, stationary person.

"No!" I say. *Does this sound defensive?* "I started smoking a lot last year when things were really stressful in my life. And honestly, since I met you, I've been smoking way less."

"But you're high right now," she says.

*Deep breath.*

"I'm . . . yes, I am a little high right now."

"You stayed outside to smoke before you came into the house."

"Yes."

"Why?"

We are standing in front of a house that has covered its large front yard with fake tombstones with ridiculous sayings on them. *Here Lies My Ex-Wife: DO NOT DISTURB* and *I TOLD You I Was Sick!* I assume that these people are vying to win the Salem house-decorating contest, because they have also set up timed lights to go off to periodically illuminate strategically placed skeletons around the yard.

"I was just feeling kind of stressed tonight," I say.

"Why?"

I don't want to have to say why. I want her to already know why.

"I don't understand why you didn't introduce me to that guy," I say. I feel like the most pathetic whiner in the world saying it. Like someone desperate. Like someone who I used to be, and secretly suspect that I still am.

"Evan?"

"Yeah."

She crosses her arms in front of her chest. Even the mention of this guy's name causes her to close herself off.

"I didn't introduce you because he's a jerk, and I didn't want to be seeing him in the first place," she says.

"Yeah, but . . ." I don't know how to say it. How to say it and not be that girl.

"What, Eleanor?"

"Wouldn't it have been nice to be like, 'This is my new girlfriend, so, like, fuck you'?"

Pix looks around as if the solution to this problem might be hiding behind one of these fake tombstones. She lets out a sigh and takes my hand. "Come here," she says. I follow her up onto the lawn, and we sit down behind a skeleton that seems to be crawling up from out of one of the graves.

"I don't want Evan to know anything about my life," she says. "He was basically my best friend, and then he was my boyfriend, and it took me a really long time to realize that the passive-aggressive judgmental things that he constantly said to me really hurt my feelings. And yes, he does it because he's insecure and he can't learn how to accept himself, but I felt responsible for that for a long time and I don't anymore. So, no, I didn't want to introduce you to Evan, and I don't ever want to introduce you to Evan. He's the reason why I barely post anything online. I don't even want him to see me."

I can't imagine anyone making Pix feel small and insecure. How would it be possible to make someone so glorious and self-assured doubt themselves?

"I'm sorry he did that," I say quietly.

"It's okay," she says, softening. "It just took a really long time to realize what I actually needed from another person. And it's not that."

I look around at the tombstone next to us. *RIP My DIET!*, it says. The lights around us flash off and on.

"Ivy told me that you guys just broke up in August," I say.

"I mean, officially, I guess. It was off and on for a while there."

"So does that make me your rebound?"

If she is able to read into my energy right now, then she can tell that this is not a joke. When I so desperately want it to sound like a joke.

"Eleanor." She says my name like I should know better. Like she is disappointed in me. "Do you really think that?"

I shake my head. "I don't want to."

She leans back. "You don't trust me," she says.

"It's just . . ." I can't believe I am about to pour out my heart here, next to *RIP My DIET!* "My ex-girlfriend, the one who dated Harrison . . ."

"Chloe," Pix says.

It feels so weird to hear Pix say her name.

"Yes. Chloe," I say. "She didn't want anyone to know that we were together. And Harrison went on this whole campaign to make sure everyone thought that I had this obsessive unrequited love for her. But it wasn't true. And no one knew the truth. Because Chloe was, I don't know, ashamed of me or something."

It's the first time that this word had occurred to me to describe the situation. *Ashamed.* What a horrible word.

"That was about her, then," Pix says. "Not you."

"Yeah, but it kind of was about me," I say. "If I had been someone she thought was worth showing off, she would have shown me off. I wanted to tell everyone in the world that we were together."

I hate that these words feel so hard to say, that thinking

about Chloe can still make my stomach tighten and stupid tears build up behind my eyes.

Pix takes my hand.

*Come back to the present, Eleanor.*

"I want the whole world to know that we're together," she says.

"You do?"

She nods. "And it's not that I don't want Evan to know about you. It's that don't want him to know about anything in my life. I don't want him to have energetic access to me. It was too hard cutting that cord once; I don't want to have to do it again."

I smile.

"What?" she says.

"I just like the way you talk. 'Energetic access.'"

Pix smiles. "That's why I like being with you," she says. "That is not the reaction Evan would have had to those words."

"Well, I hate him," I say. "Because everything about you is the best."

The light next to Pix flashes on, and I think I can see her blushing.

"I guess things turned out okay, then," she says.

I take her other hand.

"And I really am smoking a lot less," I say. "I think I just panicked tonight."

Pix nods. "We all have our coping mechanisms," she says.

"Yeah, I think I forgot to get some more of those," I say.

She moves closer to me.

"Maybe I can help you find some," she says. She leans toward me and begins to kiss my neck. She travels up to my ear, my cheek, now my lips. I wrap my arms around her and I let myself trust this feeling. This is a person I can talk to, who listens to me, and I listen to her. And if I can fully accept the pleasure of what it feels like to hold her, to feel her lips on my skin, then there is no more Evan, and no more Chloe, and no more Harrison. This feeling is so wonderful that it takes over the entire world and makes everything so beautiful that anything and anyone not in the service of this feeling is banished. Nothing but this feeling is allowed from now on.

Here, in a fake suburban graveyard, among the plastic skeletons and commodified witchery of Salem, finally, is some real magic.

# THE DEVIL

Well, look who just showed up. The iconic fallen angel himself, chaining all of humanity to its darkest inclinations. If the Hierophant, the Magician, and the High Priestess operate up in the high-vibe realms, showing us big and beautiful truths about the universe, existence, and how we are all connected, then you, Devil, are interested in the low vibe. You want to tie us back down to earth, to forget all those big beautiful lessons and believe that each of us is alone and must fend for ourselves. That humanity is inherently evil and self-serving. That we must not trust each other, rely on each other, believe that we can take care of each other.

What will we do when we meet the Devil? And what if he is not a horned demon dressed in red at all but a way of thinking, a way of being, a place, a situation, a feeling? How will we hold on to the things that we have come to know as true in the face of the Devil's tricks? How can we protect ourselves from him?

# 15

If I were to cast Harrison as the Devil in my life, it would only mean that he created the circumstances for me to realize the worst parts of myself. I was the one who took the bait, who carried through on instincts that I knew were wrong. Even if what he did was worse than what I did, he wasn't wrong about the fact that I couldn't let Chloe go.

That's how the Devil gets you. By knowing you better than you know yourself.

When I deleted Chloe from my phone, I basically deleted my entire existence since coming to Salem. There was no backup plan, no other friends ready to take my side. I spent the rest of that summer working in the store, getting high, and dreading school starting in September, when I would not be able to avoid seeing Chloe and Harrison together.

As it was, I was already torturing myself by checking both of their social media accounts incessantly. I told myself it was because I wanted to make sure I knew where they were so that I wouldn't run into them, but there was an undeniable pang of horrible pleasure I would feel whenever I opened up a social media app on my phone and saw the two of them at the beach, her hanging off him.

It was the day before school started again when Chloe first wrote the words "I love you" publicly to him. Harrison had posted a picture of her playfully sticking her tongue out for her birthday with the caption "good thing she's got a good personality" underneath. Chloe's response in the comments? "LOL I love you baby."

That day I got more stoned than I had ever been before.

Mom was also struggling a lot that summer; the heat and humidity made her joint pain worse, and we couldn't afford air conditioning. I would get high and watch movies with her while she rested. Some days she just stayed in bed with the fan that Susan had brought over making a halfhearted attempt at circulating the air in her room. She asked me a few times where Chloe was, but I lied and said she was still away for the summer.

Since I had never even told my mom that Chloe and I were together, how could I tell her that we broke up? There didn't seem to be any point. And Chloe was the last thing I wanted to talk to anyone about.

Once school started, I managed to put on a pretty good performance of normalcy. My grades even improved because I had nothing better to do than spend hours on my homework. Even though I didn't have any actual friends, people were still talking to me at this point. I picked a lunch table far away from Harrison's regular spot and ingratiated myself with the math nerds who sat there enough for them to tolerate me. If anyone noticed that the formerly inseparable team of Chloe and Eleanor was no longer in business, they didn't say anything to me about it. Maybe they chalked it up to the typical "best friend gets a boyfriend and doesn't have time for anyone else anymore" phenomenon. But in the end, the royal couple of Harrison and Chloe eclipsed all other topics. They were Salem High's greatest celebrities. And I was no one.

Something in me knew that the only way that I could keep up this performance of calm in the face of my worst nightmare would be to feed something horrible inside me—a need for some kind of power. It would be one thing if Chloe had just broken up with me, but the fact of us not even being able to be friends anymore was Harrison's fault, and a result of the fact that he outranked me now. He had taken everything from me and then a little extra, just because he could. And all I could think to do was to try to take something back.

The problem started when I took myself out for a walk late one night when Mom and Susan were watching TV. September was a good time to walk the streets of Salem while listening to my best moody playlists and feeling appropriately sorry for myself. There was a new autumn chill in the air. The relentless pumpkin and wheat bale and scarecrow decorations had just started to go up downtown. And only a few houses had begun the preparations for the one-upmanship of front yard Halloween decorations. There was a quiet anticipation in the air, as if we were all saving our energy for the coming onslaught.

I could say that I didn't know that I was walking to Chloe's house that night, but it wouldn't be true. I knew the way so well. Even if it wasn't my brain's idea, my body was taking me there.

Chloe's house was west of downtown, on the way to the country club, where Salem started to look just like any other American suburb. Here the streets had wide sidewalks, the houses had bigger lawns. There had always been something calming to me about how generic Chloe's neighborhood was. The houses felt private and contained. It felt like you could hide there.

When I got to Chloe's house that night, I stopped on the other side of the street and looked at it. Her room was in the front on the first floor. Her light was on, the window curtain half-open. I could see her inside sitting on her bed. I sat down on the curb and just watched. And watched. And watched.

Completely stoned, I sat there that night for at least an hour, watching Chloe go back and forth between homework and her phone. At one point someone video chatted her and she held the screen up to her face to see them, laughing.

I sat there long enough that I believed that I was in her room with her, like I had been so many times. The two of us doing homework, then stopping to make out, then doing more homework. I was back there, and Harrison didn't exist, and nothing had changed, and she still loved me, even if she didn't know how to tell other people about it. I sat there and forgave her for that, forgave her for not standing up to Harrison when he told her the two of us couldn't be friends anymore. I forgave her for not being able to see how he was manipulating her. She hadn't heard what he said to me on the boat, hadn't seen Tyler push me. So she didn't know. And so I forgave her for all of it.

Chloe wanted us to at least be friends. Hadn't she told me that? It was Harrison who screwed that all up. I was just correcting things.

After that I came back almost every night. It was easy enough to just tell Mom that I was going to Chloe's house after work, technically the truth. After blaming my summer without Chloe on her absence, it only made sense that she and I had become inseparable again now that school had started. Plus Mom's summer symptom flare was getting better with the cooler weather, and I could tell that she felt guilty about the summer, thinking that she had been the reason I stayed inside every day.

I became so focused on the details of my plan to get Chloe back, I didn't realize that the weeks were stretching on with me still stuck in the first part of my plan. Number one: wait. And hope that maybe Chloe would come out of her house and see me casually walking down the street.

"Oh, hey," I would say. "I've just been out for a little evening run."

A run? Would she believe that?

Backup plan: work up the nerve to walk up to her door, ring the doorbell, tell her I just needed to talk to her for a minute.

"I know things have been weird," I would say. "I'm sorry if I did something that upset you, but I think we can fix this."

So reasonable! Any day now I would enact one of these very reasonable plans!

And then I saw Harrison there.

He was in Chloe's bedroom with her when I got there, telling some animated story, and Chloe was laughing. A fake laugh. It had to be fake.

When his story was finally over, Chloe went to him and kissed him. And then he kind of picked her up and threw her on the bed and I couldn't see them anymore. They kissed all the time in public, but it made my stomach turn to actually see the two of them in this intimate moment. Was that what he did? Picked her up and threw her down? As if he had complete control over her body? Was that what she wanted?

I walked home that night telling myself that I would not go there again. My plan only made sense if there was a clear path between me and Chloe. Seeing Harrison there was all wrong. I would need to find another way to get through to her. Maybe a letter. Or a gift. Or skywriting. Or maybe she would just show up in the store one day and say "I miss you," and everything would be okay again.

Or maybe I would ignore every smart instinct I had and go back to Chloe's house the next night.

It was a little earlier when I headed out on my walk that night. Mom had ordered us pizza, and it was waiting for me when I got home from the store, and we were done with dinner early. So it was still dusk when I turned onto Chloe's street.

I hadn't given much thought to Chloe's neighbors on the

nights that I had spent on her street. Cars would pass by and pull into and out of driveways, but a teenager smoking on a curb wasn't much of a sight in a town used to much more unusual happenings. So it didn't occur to me that my watching was being watched.

The curtain in Chloe's window was closed, and I sat down on the curb, wondering if she was home or out with Harrison. Maybe this would be the night when I would catch her arriving home at the perfect moment. Could I even make it seem romantic?

*I can't stay away from you.*

I could pull that off, right?

A sharp tap on my right shoulder nearly caused me to jump out of my skin. I looked up. A woman in matching pink sweatpants and sweatshirt was staring at me with her hands on her hips.

"Hel-lo!" she said, drawing out the word, as if she had been trying to get my attention for hours.

"Hi," I said.

"What do you think you're doing?" she said.

"I was just taking a walk and I got, uh, tired."

"Um-hm," the woman said. She crossed her arms. "And is that your explanation for sitting here every night for the past two weeks?"

There was no time to come up with an answer to this because across the street Chloe's mom and her sister were coming out of the house, followed by Chloe.

The woman in pink looked at me.

"I called them," she said. "You're lucky I didn't call the police."

I saw Chloe's mom recognize me and turn to say something to Chloe. Then a look of recognition registered on Chloe's face.

"Eleanor?" Chloe called out.

I considered running. But then I thought that maybe this was my moment. Sure, there were more people around than I had envisioned, but maybe I could make that work to my benefit. A declaration of devotion in front of others!

I got up and walked over to Chloe. She met me halfway in the driveway. Her mother gave the neighbor a little wave and took Chloe's sister back to the front door, where the two of them watched. The neighbor remained standing in her yard with hands on hips.

"What are you doing?" Chloe asked me.

"I was just walking by," I said. "I was hoping I could talk to you."

"Mrs. Albertson says you've been sitting out here every night for weeks. Is this true?"

*Admit it, Eleanor. She'll understand.*

"I just miss you," I said, hoping that these words could sound sweet and not desperate, in a moment when I was feeling more desperate than I ever had in my life.

"You can't just sit and stare at someone's bedroom window," Chloe said. Her voice was cold and on the verge of anger. I had to turn this around.

"Can we just talk?" I asked. "That's all I want."

"You wanted to talk to me so you started stalking me at my own house?"

My heart sank.

*Is that what this is?*

"That's not what this is," I insisted.

"It actually is, Eleanor," she said.

And just so that this terrible moment could turn into one of the most terrible moments ever, a car pulled up and Harrison got out.

"Hello," he said, slamming the car door behind him.

*Why do everyone's hellos sound like weapons today?*

"Eleanor was just leaving," Chloe said, already walking away from me.

Harrison spotted Chloe's mom and sister in the doorway and the neighbor watching from across the street.

"What's going on?" he asked, ready to step into action.

"We're just talking," I said, realizing too late that I was the only one talking. There was no "we" here. I was standing alone on one side of this battle, somehow surprised to be abandoned there.

"I need to know that you know this isn't okay, Eleanor," Chloe said to me.

"Can somebody explain to me what is happening?" Harrison said, his voice a warning.

Chloe took his hand.

"I'll tell you inside," she said.

"I wasn't stalking anybody!" I yelled. I saw Chloe's mom pull Chloe's little sister closer to her, as if I was about to attack.

This woman who used to make me snacks after school and bring me fresh lemonade in the backyard on warm days. Sometimes I would help Chloe's sister with her homework. My first indication that I had turned into a monster was the look in their eyes when they stared at me from the doorway that night.

I took a deep breath and lowered my voice, tried to lower my blood pressure with it.

"I just needed to talk to you, and you're always with him."

"I'm always with him because he's my boyfriend," Chloe said. "You seem to be having a lot of trouble understanding that."

Harrison stepped between me and Chloe in a ridiculous show of protective strength.

"You need to go now," he said.

My pulse was racing. I couldn't let this happen like this. It wasn't supposed to happen like this.

He moved closer to me, towering over me.

"Now," he said.

"Are you going to hit me, Harrison?" I said, but quietly, so only he could hear. I was furious. Daring him. "Go ahead and do it." Let Chloe see who he really was.

He glared at me.

"You're pathetic," he said, the words spitting out at me.

He turned away from me and went to Chloe, put a hand on the small of her back.

"Inside," he muttered. A command.

Chloe's mom and sister ducked in the front door, Chloe

following them, obedient. Harrison slammed the door behind them. I heard a loud click as the dead bolt on the door engaged.

And because I am a complete idiot, even in that moment I believed that she might come back out. That she might realize how wrong this all was.

"Okay, now I am calling the police." The woman in pink was still standing on her lawn, phone in hand, watching me.

I glared at her and pulled up the hood on my jacket, walked away from her as quickly as I could.

I felt like the smallest piece of dirt that had ever existed. I felt like a creature sent back to live in its home in a cave. I was destined to sit in the dark alone for the rest of my life. Unlovable and unloved.

It's amazing how quickly five hundred people can be turned against you. It can happen in a matter of hours. A few texts, a couple of DMs, and it's all over. By the next morning I was branded a stalker who was dangerously obsessed with Harrison's girlfriend.

Becoming Salem High's pariah seemed like a logical next step after officially losing Chloe. It was just externalizing how I felt on the inside. I had already lost everything; now everyone knew it.

I deleted my social media accounts, kept my head down in school, ate lunch by myself. I was completely and utterly alone.

And this time it was my fault.

What I had done wasn't romantic. It wasn't a way to get Chloe back. It was wrong. And it did make me an unhinged lesbian stalker who wanted to steal Harrison's girlfriend away from him. It was all true.

I spent the month of October working late at the store after school. It was only my second October in Salem, and the year before I had been distracted by my new friendship with Chloe. Now I had nothing to do other than assist Susan through Haunted Happenings hell. I have never hated monsters, zombies, devils, and witches more than I did that month.

I smoked before school, at lunch down the street, after school, after work, and before bed. My entire salary that month went into Simon's pocket. I didn't care. I responded to direct questions from Susan and my mom with one-word answers at that point. I locked myself in my room at night to keep my mom away from me. I was impossible.

But some tiny, wildly stupid part of me had not given up hope completely on fixing some part of this situation. At least I could apologize to Chloe. Explain to her that I meant well. That I was just trying to figure out how to approach her. A text wasn't an option. What if Harrison saw it and sent it to people? Same with a letter. If I called, I could easily imagine a screenshot of Chloe's call history being circulated in the ongoing case against me.

And that's when I heard about Harrison's Halloween party.

Having a party on Halloween in Salem was a completely redundant activity. The entire town was a nonstop party for twenty-four hours, with a costume parade, carnival rides, food stands, and fireworks. Downtown, the bars and restaurants overflowed with costumed drinkers overindulging. There was no reason to differentiate between one set of festivities and another. Unless you had something that you were trying to prove. Harrison always had something that he was trying to prove. And it usually involved flexing his privilege in a way that no one else would even dare to attempt.

The Burying Point looks like a movie set for a cemetery, like it must be the original creepy cemetery that all subsequent creepy cemeteries were based on, with crooked headstones etched with winged skulls, buckling ground, and gnarled old trees. No one buried there has been alive for the past two hundred years. And this was where Harrison would be throwing his party. It seemed like a test to see how far Harrison's privilege could carry him. My guess was pretty far.

Word of the party spread quickly around school in the week before Halloween. The talk of it was so blatant that even I, who no one was speaking to directly at this point, was hearing about it nonstop.

I didn't know for sure that I was going to sneak into this party until the afternoon of Halloween. I had been mulling it over in my head since I'd first heard about it. Chloe would be there, of course, and if Harrison was hosting, he might be occupied enough that I could get a few minutes with Chloe alone. And although trying to talk to Chloe around a bunch of people was risky, if I timed it right, they would all be so drunk that no one would even notice I was there. It's not hard to slip through the cracks on Halloween in Salem. Everyone on the streets is so desperate for attention that a person not on intentional display is basically invisible.

So.

I would go to the party.

And I would apologize to Chloe.

And she would accept my apology.

And understand why I did what I did.

And tell Harrison that she and I would always be friends and he couldn't get in the way of that.

And everything would be okay again.

I really believed that.

# THE TOWER

Finally, inevitably, here we are at the Tower. Death was difficult—accepting an end to something. But often we can see it coming. It is part of a natural process, one that must be integrated into life if we are to understand the complexity and beauty of existence.

And then there's you, Tower.

There's no way to put this nicely. You are unexpected, often devastating, complete destruction. A deeply flawed situation has gone on for far too long, and we have done nothing to fix it, so now fate must intervene, and the entire structure comes tumbling down. All that we thought we had reveals itself to be an illusion. There is no foundation to withstand this sudden flash of lightning.

But if this is a forest fire, that means the trees must burn to make way for new growth. Beauty will return. From the ashes, new life will emerge, carrying the knowledge of this history. But first, the Tower must fall.

# 16

The coven preparations during the final week before Samhain take on a new level of intensity. Anita is working on everyone's costumes, Ivy has reconfigured the menu about twenty times, and Tatiana and Gillian continue to brainstorm alternate possibilities for our route through town to the memorial. The group text chain is epic.

I'm worried that I'm not contributing enough, until Pix informs me that she and I are organizing the offerings for the witch trial victims at the memorial.

"We'll do all the traditional stuff," she tells me over the phone while I attempt to hear her over seven children fighting over the last talking magic wand in the store. "Pomegranates and sweets. Ofira will get some marigolds to honor Day of the Dead traditions."

"Okay," I say as I watch Susan try to convince the kids that the non-talking magic wand is just as good as the talking one. "You need me to go buy that other stuff?" I ask.

"No, you're busy at the store. I can get it all. If you could just help me come up with one more idea. We need something that feels personal."

"Personal?"

One of the kids has now thrown themselves on the floor. A full-on tantrum seems imminent.

"Like something that feels personal to the people we're honoring. Something that we make that we can leave there for them."

"Okay," I say.

Susan is breaking out the big guns. Halloween candy. She shoves a Kit Kat under the nose of the tantrum child. It seems to be working.

"Whatever you come up with will be great," Pix says.

I spend any free moments that I have the rest of that day trying to think of what I could make. Then something occurs to me during a late-afternoon lull. I go back into Susan's office.

"Do we still have those mini ships in bottles?" I ask her.

"The ones from last summer that barely sold? Probably. They would be on the shelf in the back with the beach towels if we do."

"Can I use some of them?" I ask.

"What for?"

"It's just a thing," I say. "Something I'm making."

Susan swivels around in her chair. "A *coven* thing?"

Although I can tell that Susan is excited that I actually have friends to hang out with again, she also cannot stop herself from teasing me about the coven.

"Yes, it's a coven thing, okay?"

I go to the shelf in the storage room where we stashed last summer's unsold stock. The bottles are in a box with the painted conch shells. I grab a handful of them and go back into the store behind the counter. Susan follows me.

"What if I say you can only have them if you tell me about your coven thing?" she says.

I roll my eyes.

"It's nothing," I say.

She looks at the bottles now on the counter in front of me and jokingly picks one up and hides it behind her back.

"No info, no bottles."

"Come on, Susan," I beg. "I need them!"

She puts the bottle back on the counter, one eyebrow raised. I pick it up and take out the tiny cork.

"It's for this Samhain thing," I say. "Witch's Halloween."

I look inside the bottle at the little ship. How am I going to get it out of there? I stick a pen in and try to fish it out.

"I think the whole point of those things is that you can't get the boat out," Susan says.

I jam the pen in more.

"The coven wants to do this thing where we honor the victims of the witch trials by leaving offerings for them. I thought I could make little copies of cards from the major arcana and put them in the bottles."

"You're really getting into this tarot stuff, huh?"

"I guess," I say, not wanting to give Susan anything else to tease me about.

246

"Very well," she says. "You may have the bottles." But she isn't quite done getting information out of me. "And you and Pix are officially an item?"

"An 'item'?" I say. I would roll my eyes again, but Susan will inevitably tell me that they will get stuck that way.

"I just mean, are things good with Pix?" Susan asks.

"Yeah," I say, unable to keep from smiling. "Really good, actually."

Susan pretends to clutch her heart.

"I'm sorry, did Eleanor Anderson just say that things are 'really good'? Did I hear that correctly?"

I am blushing and fighting the urge to throw something at her.

"Yes, okay?" I say. "For once, things are going really well."

"Are you . . . in loooooove?" Susan says, poking me playfully.

"Stop!" I squeal. I hold the pen up threateningly. "I have to get this done for Halloween."

Susan stops poking me.

"What's happening on Halloween?" she asks, her voice suddenly serious.

"That's what this is for. We're doing this whole ceremony thing at the memorial that night," I say. I do not look at Susan. I am very deeply absorbed in what I am doing.

"Is it a good idea to do that on Halloween?" she asks gently.

Is it a good idea to go to the witch trials memorial, which is right next to the Burying Point, which is where Harrison had his party last Halloween? No, it's not a good idea.

"I told them it'll be really crowded in town," I say. "They want to do it anyway."

"You know that's not what I mean."

I throw the pen down on the counter in frustration.

"I want to do this," I say. "And even if I didn't want to do it, I don't want to explain to them why I don't."

Susan nods.

"Okay," she says.

"Do you have tweezers or something?" I ask, exasperated.

She goes into the back room and comes back a minute later with tweezers. She hands them to me without saying anything, and I get back to work on removing the tiny ships from their tiny bottles.

The fact that Pix and I survived our first sort-of fight makes me feel very proud and adult. We are obviously both incredibly mature people who are very good about talking about our feelings, and this means that we can survive anything and we will be together forever.

I think back to times when I was so afraid to tell Chloe how I really felt. It seemed like I should measure every word, consider the issue from all angles, before I even tried to talk to her. Any conversation about anything real had to be initiated by me, run by me, and resolved by me. So now when Pix and I talk to each other, I feel almost giddy with victory.

We have not used the L-word yet. One thing at a time. The G-word is in effect. The L-word has to come soon after, right? And even though I know for sure, in my bones, that I am in love with this person, I also think that I should not be the first one to use this word.

*I might be the first one to use this word.*

A few days before Samhain, we are all summoned to Ofira's house for a final planning meeting to review everyone's contributions. I wrap the twenty little bottles in tissue paper and put them in my bag, hoping that they will be approved. I'm worried that they might be too cheesy. Although one thing I have noticed about witches is that they seem to have a pretty high tolerance for cheesy things.

The girls are all in the living room when I arrive at Ofira's house, the members of Ofira's overly involved human and animal family circulating around them. Anita is fitting a black corset on Tatiana, who keeps yelling, "Tighter!" which makes Ofira's little sister break out into giggles.

Pix comes over to me as soon as she sees me and gives me a kiss on the cheek.

"Thank goddess you're here," she says. "Ofira is freaking out that we don't have enough offerings. I told her the flowers are going to take up a lot of space, and we're not getting those until the day before."

Behind her I see Ofira consulting with Ivy and Gillian over a stack of plates and picnic blankets.

"Will it be safe to light the candles?" she asks Gillian, who has been made into our local Salem Halloween expert. I am happy for her to have been designated this position.

"Depends who's around," Gillian says. "The cops are so busy that night, it should take them a little while to catch on."

Ofira's mom comes into the room and stands next to Ofira. She puts her hands on her hips, and the two of them are instant twins, surveying the supplies.

"I would put the candles in jars," her mom says. "It could be windy."

I open my bag and take out one of the tiny bottles.

"I brought my offerings," I say to Pix.

I unwrap the bottle and hand it to Pix. She holds it up and examines the tiny copy of the hermit that I drew and stuck inside.

"Eleanor," she says, amazed, "this is beautiful."

"I have twenty of them. One for each."

"I can't believe you had the time to do this!"

She hugs me.

*I would do literally anything that you asked me to do under any circumstances.*

I unwrap each of the bottles and add them to the pile of things being inspected by Ofira.

"Look how great these are," Pix says, showing one to Tatiana, who oohs and aahs in appreciation.

I do not attempt to hide the fact that I am blushing.

Ofira's dad comes in the room with hot apple cider, and I sit on the floor to drink mine out of the way of the bustle of preparations. One of the cats comes over, lies down next to me, and demands a belly rub. I think it's Barbara. I remember too late that she's a biter.

Gillian sits down next to me and holds up her mug for a cheers. We clink.

"You good?" she asks.

I nod. "I didn't know this was going to be quite so elaborate," I say.

"You haven't even gotten your fitting yet," Gillian says. We look over at Pix, who is being pinned into a long Victorian mourning dress by Anita.

"I am not wearing that," I say.

Gillian smiles. "I think she's got something different for the two of us," she says, indicating our black jeans and ratty T-shirts.

Across the room, Ofira picks up one of my little bottles.

"These are good, Eleanor," she calls over to me matter-of-factly.

"Was that a compliment?" I say out of the corner of my mouth to Gillian.

"As close as you're going to get to one," she says.

"Gillian, can you check the grimoire for the order of the benches at the memorial?" Ofira asks. "I wrote it down in there with the other notes for Samhain."

"Sure." Gillian grabs a large leather-bound book from the scattered pile of supplies. She sits back, opens the big leather cover, and starts flipping through the pages.

"What's a grimoire?" I ask, watching her. I manage to feel only slightly jealous that Gillian has more familiarity with something about the coven than I do.

"A grimoire?" Gillian repeats. "It's like a coven's diary slash recipe book slash scrapbook. Ofira puts all her notes for everything in here."

The pages have dried flowers and herbs glued on them. Some have clippings from recipe books or Anita's drawings for one of Ofira's outfits.

"This all seems pretty familiar to you," I say to Gillian. "You've been doing this kind of thing for a while?"

She nods. "I was what's called a 'solitary practitioner,'" she says. "You have no idea how ironic it is to live in this town and not be friends with any other witches."

"There was no one at Salem High before Ofira?" I try to think back to the different cliques at SH.

"No one who was fine with everyone knowing that they actually believe in all this stuff," Gillian says. "It's a pretty judgmental place."

"Yeah," I say. "I know."

She looks at me. "Right."

She turns more pages in the book. We see instructions for spells to do during the waxing and waning moon, pasted-in pictures of different tourist attractions in Salem where Ofira hopes to do energy work on behalf of the victims.

"But what if there were always actually a bunch of solitary practitioners," I say, "and it was just that none of you ever knew it because you were too worried about letting other people see you?" The words leave my mouth, and I wonder who this wise person talking is. I realize that I sound like Pix.

"I guess that's possible," Gillian says. "We aren't all as fearless as Ofira, though."

Gillian turns another page of the grimoire and suddenly I see a cut-out image of a familiar figure. A jaunty man with a small dog at his side. A stick resting on his shoulder holds a tied-up bag of his possessions. The sun shines brightly behind him.

In big letters on the top of the page it reads, *The Fool.*

"Hold on a second," I say. "Can I see that?"

"Sure."

She hands it to me. I examine the text under the print-out of the Fool. Underneath the image, in very familiar neat handwriting, is written out the entire first page of "The Major Arcana, A Magical Guide to the Story Cards of the Smith Rider Waite Tarot Deck."

I feel myself start to sweat.

"This is weird," I say.

"You okay?" Gillian asks.

"I don't know." I flip to further along in the book. They're all there. The High Priestess, the Emperor, the Wheel of Fortune.

The Tower.

"I know this," I say. "This is from a book that we got at the store."

Gillian shrugs. "Maybe Ofira got the same book."

But that doesn't make any sense. There are notes in the margins here, words crossed out and replaced in the handwritten text. This is a draft.

"Pix?" I call to her.

She is standing with her arms up while Anita makes the final adjustments on her dress.

"One sec," she says. "I'm currently being stuck with pins."

I get up off the floor and go to her, holding the book open for her to see.

"What is this?" I ask.

She looks at the page.

"Those are Ofira's notes for her tarot book," she says.

"'The Major Arcana, A Magical Guide to the Story Cards of the Smith Rider Waite Tarot Deck,'" I say.

"Yes," she says, a funny look suddenly crossing her face.

"Why do I have this book?" I ask her. Anita has stood back now. Most of the girls have stopped when they are doing and are listening. "Someone sent it to the store at the beginning of September. We got it in the mail the day that I met you. Ofira wrote it?"

"Yes," Pix says carefully.

"You didn't say anything when you saw I had it." My brain is attempting to put a puzzle together with about a million pieces missing.

Pix doesn't say anything. She looks over at Ofira. Their look seems to have some secret meaning in it, and I am starting to panic.

"What is going on?" I ask.

Pix takes my hand.

"Let's go outside," she says, urging me.

I suddenly feel very strongly about not going outside.

"I want to talk here," I say, looking around. Even Ofira's mom is listening.

Pix releases my hand.

I look at Ofira.

"Did you send me the book?"

She doesn't say anything. I have never seen Ofira look unsure of herself before. I don't like it.

"I sent it to you," Pix says quietly. "I felt it was important that you have it."

"Why? You didn't know me."

She doesn't say anything.

"Okay, I don't like this," I say. "You need to explain this to me right now."

Pix takes the grimoire from me. She turns to the back, where some pages have been stapled in. She flips through them. They're all printed-out articles about terrible things that have happened around Salem. Car accidents. A shark attack from last summer. A family that lost their home in a fire. A robbery at the gas station.

I know what is coming. My heart sinks.

Pix stops flipping.

*Tragic Accident*, the headline reads. *Teens' Halloween Out of Control.*

Gillian is close enough to see what I am seeing, and I look at her.

She shakes her head. "I didn't tell them," she says.

There in the corner of the article—Chloe and Harrison's prom picture.

I consciously take a deep breath, because if I don't, I think I might stop breathing altogether.

"Ofira was working on the tarot book all last year," Pix says, "and when she was done I had this idea that we should send it to people in Salem who had experienced something difficult, as part of her healing Salem thing. She heals places. I wanted to do something for people."

"You wanted to *heal* me?" I say in disbelief. I look around at the faces of the others. Have they all known about this? Am I some kind of coven charity case?

"Just because we read about what happened and I felt I had to send it to you," Pix says.

Pix and her intuition. Everything can be explained by "*I felt.*" How am I supposed to argue with that?

"And then we came into the store because I wanted to make sure that you got it."

I am trying to run the memory of those first two times meeting Pix through my mind. She and Ofira came into the store looking for a map. Pretending to look? Pix commented on the Fool. . . .

"I didn't expect you to join the coven, Eleanor," Pix says. Her voice is gentle now. I can tell she is trying to keep me calm. But there's a small glint of panic in her eyes.

"Why didn't you tell me that you knew about last Halloween? And that the book was from you? Why not just give it to me in person?" I still don't understand what is going on, but I feel like I might start screaming if someone doesn't make this all make sense.

Pix gives me a look.

"If I had walked into the store and said, 'Eleanor Anderson, we're witches and we read about what happened to you and we want to help heal you energetically, so here's a tarot book that you should read and please come join our coven,' you would have taken us seriously?"

"But why didn't you tell me later?"

Pix doesn't say anything.

"Eleanor," Ofira tries to start, but I stop her.

"I want to hear it from Pix," I say.

Pix takes a deep breath.

"I didn't expect to like you," she says. "And then when we were at the Witch House I realized that I really liked you, and I could tell that you would freak if you knew that I knew. Especially after you bolted from the boat. I was so excited to like someone again, I didn't want to mess it up. I didn't want to scare you off."

"I can't believe this," I say. "Were you ever going to tell me any of this?"

Pix nods but doesn't say anything.

"You weren't," I say. "You were going to let me believe that I was starting over. That I was with someone who would always be honest with me." I go to the corner of the room where my jacket and bag are and grab them.

"I was trying to make it okay for you . . . ," she starts to say.

"Yeah, but you don't get it!" I'm yelling now. I can't stop. "Nothing is ever okay for me. And I had actually gotten really used to that, and then you came along and sucked me into this fantasy world that I started to think was real, and of course it's not. None of this is real." I gesture at the entire room and everyone in it, preparing for a made-up magical holiday that is just as fake and stupid as Halloween ever was.

Pix steps back from me, as if ducking the blow of my words.

"I happen to live on planet Earth," I say, "where we have certain rules, and one of them is that we don't lie to people we care about, even if the 'vibe' is off or whatever. It's great that all that matters to you is how everything *feels*. But some of us have to deal with reality. Unlike you, who does whatever you want and justifies it by saying some fake, invisible alien told you to or something."

I pull on my coat.

"Grow up," I say, a command to the room, to myself, to Pix. Two words that explode like a bomb.

"Eleanor," Ofira says, coming toward me, "we should talk about this."

But I am out of there before she can draw me back in with her very reasonable Ofira-speak, in which she can justify energy clearing and talking to dead people and "healing" the town. I can't believe I was stupid enough to think that it was all harmless and well-intentioned.

Out the front door, down the steps of Ofira's house and out into the October night, I walk as fast as I can in the direction of home, as if I can outrun my own stupidity.

*Nothing good gets to stay.*

*Nothing that seems good was real in the first place.*

I almost make it home before the tears come, but I turn onto our street and here they are, hot and relentless, like a dam has opened, and won't be shut for a very long time.

*

Halloween, almost exactly one year ago.

I was going to Harrison's party at the Burying Point.

I was going to fix things with Chloe.

It was all going to work out.

It was nearly one a.m. when I was finally able to head to the cemetery. Susan had decided to keep the store open late, and we were nearly sold out of every witch hat, plastic broom, and black cape that we had.

"You okay to get yourself home?" Susan asked me. "Or you want me to walk with you?"

Susan looked beyond exhausted. And I had no intention of heading home.

"I'm good," I said. "I'll go the back way to avoid the crowds."

The official festivities of the night were over by this point, but that was when the real madness started. The cops basically gave up, just trying to keep a lid on any drunken fights that might break out and any reports of open flames. Besides that, Salem was left to run wild.

I pulled up the hood on my jacket and headed down Essex into the crowd as if I were trying to push through an arctic squall. Between dodging drunk monsters and weaving around the impromptu photo shoots that seemed to be happening every three feet, I made it to the cemetery in twenty minutes.

I had already calculated that the easiest way in to the officially closed tourist attraction would be through the Witch Trials Memorial. They locked the gate to the cemetery at ten p.m. back then, but a low stone wall separates the memorial from the cemetery, and one of the little benches with one of the victims' names on it supplied a leg up. I hopped over the wall easily, landed between two ancient gravestones, and made my way farther into the cemetery.

I followed the sound of boisterous laughter to the large tree that marked the middle of the cemetery. The partygoers seemed to have chosen a round patch of grass with a few scattered graves surrounding the tree as its headquarters. I wish I could say that as I walked toward a group of people who hated me and definitely did not want me there that I started having doubts. That I asked myself, *Is this really a good idea?*

But I didn't do that. I kept going.

I didn't see Chloe. Tyler, in a half-assed werewolf costume, was manning a keg, and I marched up to him.

"Oh shit!" Tyler said. He was so drunk that his eyes were barely open. "It's a dyke party now! Dyke party!" Then he howled and the idiots around him joined in. I cursed Harrison for the millionth time that he could throw an illegal rager with underage drinking and trespassing with literally zero consequences.

"Where's Chloe, Tyler?" I asked. Not even this idiot was going to stop me.

"Wouldn't *you* like to know?" Tyler said, offering up what barely constituted a comeback.

"Chloe and Harrison and some guys went over by the Tombs," said a girl who was dressed in a cat costume that involved very little actual clothing.

"Thanks," I said.

The Tombs was an area of the cemetery that had large rectangular concrete blocks scattered haphazardly among the regular tombstones. They were raised graves, but they looked like something that you might see at a construction site—massive building blocks ready to be hoisted onto a giant's brick wall.

I made my way down the path, passing various sub-parties that had broken off from the main tree, squinting in the dark to try to make out people's faces. None of these people were Chloe. And all that mattered was that I find Chloe.

I reached the section where the Tombs started, and I paused for the first time. It had rained earlier in the day and the ground was muddy here where there was less grass. My canvas sneakers were no match against this centuries-old grave dirt. I attempted to wipe my shoes on a rock that I hoped was not someone's final resting place.

The scene around me was *not* not creepy. It was way past midnight on Halloween, and people had been known to do some freaky stuff in this graveyard. I was now far away enough from the party that no one would hear me cry for help if something weird happened.

But these were silly fears. The fears of a little kid on Halloween—*What if a real witch comes? A real zombie? A werewolf? What if it's all real?*

I kept moving, calling out, "Chloe?"

All the chaos of the party and the town and the night faded around me as I heard a noise that sounded half like a laugh and half like a cry. It came from behind one of the tombs. I followed it.

"Chloe?"

I heard a muffled noise, definitely not a laugh this time, and then, "I said . . . fucking no!" It was Chloe.

I ran behind the tomb and saw them both on the ground. Harrison was on top of her.

My first instinct was to run. This wasn't for me to see. Once again I was where I wasn't supposed to be. But then Chloe saw me, and I saw the look in her eyes. She was terrified and angry.

"Harrison!" I yelled, running over to them.

"What the fuck?" he yelled.

He sat up enough that Chloe was able to mostly pull herself out from under him. He was so drunk he almost tipped over.

"Are you okay, Chloe?" I asked.

"What the fuck are you doing here?" Harrison yelled. "Fucking stalking my girlfriend some more?"

"Are you okay?" I asked Chloe again. I stepped toward her, hoping I could grab her and get her farther away from him.

She was even drunker than Harrison was. She started crying, lying there in the dirt, still partially pinned under him.

"I said I didn't want to do it out here," she sobbed. "My costume is ruined!"

She was wearing a witch costume, and she tugged at it now, trying to pull the black lace top down over her stomach.

Harrison looked from me to Chloe, panicked.

"What the fuck are you talking about?" he said. "You're drunk."

That was enough. I ran at Harrison and shoved him with everything that I had in me. He didn't move much, but it was enough to get him off Chloe. She pulled herself away from him.

"You're really starting something, Anderson?" Harrison yelled at me. "Is that really what you want to do right now?"

"Just get away from him, Eleanor, he's being fucking stupid," Chloe yelled.

I was standing only about a foot away from Harrison now, my fists clenched. I did not know how to punch someone, but in the next thirty seconds I was going to figure it out.

"Come on, Eleanor!" Chloe yelled. "It's not worth it!"

She got up, stumbled a few steps, then tried to run, tugging her skirt down as she ran.

Running in the dark on the uneven dirt and old gnarled tree roots.

Running between large stone monuments.

Running until she slipped in the mud.

And fell.

And hit her head one of the tombs with a terrible thud that seemed to reverberate through the ground.

"Chloe!"

I pushed Harrison away from me and ran, sliding onto the ground in a patch of mud as I reached her.

She was lying on the ground, not moving. There was a gash of blood and dirt on her forehead.

"Chloe? Can you hear me?"

Nothing.

Behind me I heard Harrison say, "What the fuck?"

"Go get help," I called back to him.

A pause, then he yelled at me, "What the fuck did you do, Anderson?"

"What?" I looked back at him.

"Did you push her?"

"Harrison, she's not responding," I yelled.

I took my phone out of my pocket and dialed 911 with trembling fingers. I vaguely heard Harrison running off behind me.

"I'm at the Burying Point and my friend hit her head really badly," I said. "She's unconscious. We're near the south exit."

The nonchalant voice on the other end of the phone: "All right, we'll send someone when we've got someone."

I hung up.

I put a hand on Chloe's chest. It rose slightly, then went back down, rose again. I felt like I was holding her heart in place.

My tears fell down onto my hand.

"It'll be okay, Chloe," I whispered, not even believing it myself. "You'll be okay."


I sat in the hospital waiting room until past four a.m., when one of the policemen finally told me to go home. They wouldn't tell me anything about how Chloe was doing, especially once her mom arrived. I watched as she came in the entrance of the ER. For a moment I thought I should try to talk to her, but she was rushed in by a nurse, and I missed my chance. What would I say anyway?

I called Susan, waking her up, explained the bare minimum

of what had happened, and asked if she could come get me. By the time we got home, Mom was up waiting for us.

Over the next two hours I told them the whole terrible story from the beginning. My relationship with Chloe, Harrison, prom, the boat, sitting outside Chloe's house for weeks, everyone hating me. Ending with that night, the end of everything. They listened and said very little. I didn't give them much of a chance to anyway. I thought if I stopped talking I wouldn't be able to get it all out.

Around six thirty, Susan went back to her house and Mom went into the kitchen to make some coffee. The sky was lightening outside the windows. The worst night of my life was officially over.

I went into the kitchen, where Mom was watching the coffee drip into the pot. After my talking nonstop for hours, the silence between us was disconcerting. I needed her to say something.

"I'm sorry I didn't tell you about everything with Chloe," I said. "I didn't want to bother you with my problems."

She looked up at me. "You know that you can always tell me what's going on in your life," she said.

"You just haven't been feeling well," I said quietly.

"That doesn't mean I can't listen."

"I feel like I stress you out."

She shook her head. "What makes you think that?"

Now I was crying. "It just feels that way sometimes," I said. "When you're not feeling well, I don't want to make things worse for you."

Mom came over to me and grabbed me in a hug. It was the first time I had let her hug me in a long time.

"You are the most important person in the world to me," she said. "And I will always be here for you. No matter how I'm feeling."

We stood like that for a long time, until the coffee beeped that it was ready. Then Mom poured us two cups and we sat at the kitchen table and watched the sun rise through the window.

"Do you think she's going to be okay?" I asked after a while, as if my mom could know.

"I'm sure they're doing everything they can to make her comfortable," Mom said. Not an answer, but something.

"I don't know what's going to happen," I said.

"Well, first off, I'm going to kill that kid Harrison," Mom said. "And we'll go from there."

*Right. Harrison.*

I couldn't stop seeing the image of him on top of her, her crying out for him to stop. If there was any justice in the world, this night would ruin Harrison's life.

Instead, of course, it ruined mine.

Chloe was in a coma for four days. Which was plenty of time for Harrison to have his story firmly in place by the time she woke up. The idea of me as a crazed stalker had already been well established, so no one had trouble believing that I had followed Chloe to the party and interrupted her and Harrison innocently making out in a fit of my own jealous rage. From there the details of the story became conveniently murky. Some people said I tried to punch Harrison. Some said Chloe fell because I pushed her.

I didn't even care what people were saying anymore. I just needed her to be okay.

Mom and Susan let me stay home from school and the store. It was like I was the sick one now, except my version of Mom's exhaustion was to smoke myself into a catatonic state—sleep and then smoke and then let her try to get me to eat and then sleep again. Every once in a while I would sign into Mom's social media accounts on her computer to see what people were saying about the situation, just to torture myself more.

The only thing that made any sense in my brain was the single thought, repeated over and over: *Chloe has to wake up.*

And then she did.

And she was okay.

And then she went away.

There was a *For Sale* sign on her front lawn by Thanksgiving. Chloe's mom was blaming the incident on Chloe falling in with a "bad crowd" and drinking too much, and had insisted on the move. There was a rumor that Harrison's dad was threatening to fire Chloe's dad over even the possibility of the incident reflecting badly on Harrison, so Chloe's dad quickly accepted a job offer in another state.

But Harrison didn't have to worry about Chloe not corroborating his version of the story. Evidently she had no desire to talk about any of it. No one heard from her at all.

Only three people knew the truth of what happened that night, and only one of us would be listened to.

Someone had to pay for the harm that was caused. Some-one had to be the target of everyone's anger. And in the end, weren't the things that everyone was saying about me mostly true? I followed Chloe to the party that night. I spent weeks sitting outside her house. I violated every boundary she had set between us. I had been blindly determined to get her back, even if it was just as a friend. And if I actually admitted the truth to myself, I knew that being friends with her wasn't enough for me. There was no defending myself, because there was no denying the heart of what was being said about me, even if the details were wrong. Any defense I might have provided would just be used against me.

In a town famous for scapegoats, I was a perfect target. Already alone and weird and sad, I was easily pushed even further to the edge of town.

Here in Witch City, the witch gets determined by who points the finger first.

# THE STAR

Well, look at that! We survived! All that strife and drama. It sure was exhausting. Time now for some hope, some faith, some renewal!

Star, you shine down on us, one foot on land and one in the water, bringing new sweet energy in to irrigate the fields of our existence.

Oh, Star—how can we be a star like you? How can we believe in the sweet hope and promise of the future? We've been knocked down a few times by the major arcana, and now we want to embrace our inner optimist.

Can we take a moment to pause and tell ourselves that, after all that, everything is going to be okay?

# 17

Yeah. No.

# THE MOON

Even though we are embracing optimism now, there's just a little more work to be done in the darkness. You, Moon, teach us to flow with your phases. The ebb and flow of life is a natural phenomenon, and there's no reason to fight it. Sure, you're only a reflection of the sun, but you bring us a taste of that light, illuminating the dark night sky.

With you, Moon, there is no need to fear this strange wilderness that we find ourselves in. You will guide us through the confusion of the dark. If we listen closely to you, Moon, you will light the path back home.

# 18

The thing about having your life turn into a complete disaster multiple times is that you're very familiar with what to do when things inevitably become horrible again. Reverting to not eating, never leaving the house, and refusing to go to work would probably give me unwelcome flashbacks to last year if I wasn't getting so stoned that I can't even muster up the brainpower to care.

All I know is that I need to stay in bed until Halloween is over. And maybe for a few months after that just for good measure. But unfortunately, Susan has other plans, something that becomes undeniably clear when I wake up early on Halloween morning to the sound of a heated conversation going on in the hallway in front of my bedroom door.

"Well, have you tried to talk to her?" I hear Susan ask.

A muffled response from my mom.

"If you won't do it, Hannah, I will."

There is a perfunctory knock on my bedroom door. Perfunctory because Susan opens the door a second later, not waiting for a response.

"Okay, sleepyhead," Susan says to me. "You better have a fever of about a hundred and twenty if you are planning to miss work today."

I pull a pillow over my head. Susan grabs it away from me.

"I don't feel good," I mumble.

"Exactly how bad do you feel?" Susan asks. "As bad as someone who has worked fifteen-hour days with very little help since Friday? Who is about to face her biggest sales day of the year short-staffed?"

I pull the covers up over my head.

"Is that all you care about?" I say. "The stupid store?"

It is the wrong thing to say. I look out from under my cave of covers. Susan is glaring at me.

"I care about being a person who takes my responsibilities seriously. I care about paying my bills. And I care about you and your mother being able to pay your bills."

She walks into the hallway. I pull the covers back over my head, embarrassed that I am being such a brat. But I just want to be left alone. I don't want anyone to try to fix this or to tell me that everything is going to be okay. I know better than that by now.

Mom comes into the room and sits down on the bed.

"We're just worried about you," she says. "You haven't been like this in a while."

I don't say anything.

"Did something happen?"

I don't say anything.

"With Pix?"

I bury my face in the pillow.

"Did you break up?"

"Please, Mom," I say, muffled by the blankets. "I really don't want to talk about it."

I think back to a year ago, staying up all night pouring my heart out to her and Susan. I can't do it again. I don't want them to know that I just repeated the same stupid mistakes, trusted someone who I shouldn't have trusted yet again. There's no fixing this, so what is the point in talking to anyone about it?

It is quiet for a minute, and I wonder if Mom has silently left the room. I look out from under the blankets. She is holding the tarot deck that Pix gave me.

"Can I look at these?" she asks.

"Yeah," I say.

"You're supposed to shuffle them?"

I nod. Mom shuffles the cards. Susan is standing in the doorway now, watching us.

"Now what?" Mom asks me.

I sit up.

"You think of a question," I say. "And cut the deck if you want. Then pick a card."

Mom holds the deck in her hand for a moment, then puts it down on the bed and cuts it, puts the deck back together. She picks the card off the top and looks at it.

"What did you get?" I ask.

She shows me the card.

"The Wheel of Fortune," I say.

"Is that bad?"

"None of the cards are bad or good, really," I say. "They're just reading the current energy."

"And what's Wheel of Fortune energy?"

I think for a moment. I can picture that page in the little book. Ofira's book. I have shoved it deep into the back of my closet, not able to bring myself to just throw it in the garbage. I couldn't let my stupid life ruin that book along with everything else.

"It can mean literally luck, good or bad," I say. "Just, like, is it your time for things to go your way? Or your time to get the crappy spin on the wheel?"

"Okay," Mom says.

"But in a bigger sense it's about the cycles of our lives. How life doesn't always feel neat and linear. Sometimes it seems to go in circles, and you find yourself back in a place you've been before, feeling things you never wanted to feel again. And maybe you're really angry because you thought you were done with this."

Mom is staring at me intently.

"But the thing is," I say, "it's not exactly the same as last time because, if you were paying attention, last time you learned something. So something hard that you went through serves a purpose. You know more now than you did before."

There is silence for a moment, then Susan says, "That's really nice, Eleanor."

I pull the blanket up around me. This is the most I have spoken in days.

"It's just the meaning of the card," I say. "You can read about it in any tarot book."

"Well, I like the way that you said it," Susan says.

I look at Mom. "You can pull a clarifying card if you want," I say.

"What does that mean?"

"A second card that can give you more information about the first one."

Mom takes another card off the top of the deck and looks at it. "The Moon," she says.

She hands the cards to me.

The last page I read in the book before I put it away. Light in the darkness. A way back home.

"I don't know about this one yet," I mumble.

Mom puts the Moon down on the bedspread next to the Wheel of Fortune.

"I'm heading to the store," Susan says. "I expect to see you there in an hour, Eleanor."

She goes down the hallway, and I can hear her clomping down the stairs with her trademark Susan urgency.

Mom gets up from the bed.

"I'm going to make some pancakes," she says. "If you're hungry."

I look at the cards in my hand. It suddenly feels like Pixie herself, the original Pixie, is speaking to me through these images.

*The Moon looking at the Wheel of Fortune asks you to see these cycles as a natural part of life, like the phases of the moon. Where there is darkness, there will always be light again. Nothing is perma-nent. Not even feelings.*

"What was your question for the cards?" I ask Mom.

She looks at me for a moment, then says, "I asked, 'What does Eleanor need to know to help herself right now?'"

# THE SUN

Sun! After trusting the limited light of the stars and moon, we now go to the source of light, life, and happiness! There is no doubting anything when we are basking in your beautiful rays, Sun. You are a gift to all living things, and we are able to see the truth in all that is around us as the dark corners are lit up with your glorious rays. Maybe we thought something scary was hiding there, but no! Corners are just corners. And we can face anything with the generosity of life and light on our side.

This is true abundance. Crops will grow, creatures will thrive, and you will have enough to move forward into a new phase of life, love, and confidence. What you thought was impossible is revealed to be within your reach. Just point the Sun in the right direction and you will find that you are able to light up all the darkness.

# 19

I feel bad enough about abandoning Susan that I manage to get myself out of bed, make a halfhearted attempt to put on clean clothes, inhale some of Mom's pancakes, and get myself over to the store. When she sees me arrive, Susan, to her credit, pretends like nothing is wrong, and we settle into the familiar Halloween crunch of restocking quickly emptying shelves and answering tourists' idiotic questions. At least it provides some kind of distraction from the mess that is my brain right now.

I am attempting to bring some kind of order to the T-shirt shelf when a woman holds a black witch hat up in front of my face and says, "What witch is this for?"

I stare at the hat.

"What do you mean?" I ask.

She looks at the hat again, as if she needs it to back her up on this.

"Like, which witch? From a movie? Or a book?"

Susan is behind the counter and she generously saves me from this interaction.

"Oh, that can be for any witch character," she says. "It's adaptable."

I attempt not to laugh at the seriousness with which Susan says this, and mostly fail.

The regular Halloween madness is going on outside. The big candy crunch comes midafternoon when school lets out and about a million kids descend on downtown to trick-or-treat at the stores. I have convinced Susan to put out a bowl of mini chocolate bars with a sign that says *Take One* and just hope for the best.

It's when the sun sets that this becomes a town for grown-ups who want to act like children. Watching the crowded sidewalks through the window, I have to keep taking deep breaths to not feel claustrophobic, like I am stuck inside a fishbowl.

"Should I put the brooms outside?" Susan asks me.

Susan's Halloween anxiety partially manifests in her thinking that we have to unload every witch-themed item before midnight or the store will go under.

"If you want a bunch of stolen brooms," I say.

"Should I have marked them down more?" she asks. This will continue until closing. I just have to let her go through it.

"I think we're good," I say.

The truth is that I am glad to be back at the store. In the regular timeline of "Eleanor's life is in shambles," spending all my time working at the store is the next natural step. And luckily there is a lot to do and not much time to think about anything. Like Pix. And Halloween. And the coven. And obsessing over that last night at Ofira's and wondering if I overreacted, if there was some way to salvage what had been broken.

*Nope, no time to think about any of that.*

It's just *Life's a Witch and Then You Get Cursed* T-shirts and pewter fairy goblets for the foreseeable future.

Until Gillian and Simon show up at the store.

I don't see them come in. They have to push through the hordes of people messing up my perfect T-shirt piles to get to the counter where I am trying to fix an inventory mistake that one of Susan's part-time workers made on the computer.

"Eleanor," Gillian says.

I look up. My immediate reaction is to be worried that she's here. Did the coven send her to deliver some message about how I will now be cursed for all time? But the presence of Simon complicates things. What does he have to do with any of this?

"We need to talk to you, Sanderson," he says. "ASAP."

"Can you take a break?" Gillian asks.

I look back at the computer.

"Not really," I say. "We're pretty slammed. Halloween, ya know?"

This comes out harsher than I mean for it to.

Susan, who seems to hear everything, has of course overheard this interaction.

"You can take fifteen, Eleanor," she says. "I'll hold down the fort."

Sometimes I wish that Susan would not be so very helpful all the time.

"Okay," I say.

I grab my coat, and Simon and Gillian and I push through the shoppers and make our way out the front door. I slip into the alley next to the store to escape the relentless foot traffic. They follow me.

"What's up?" I say.

"I hear you threw a hissy fit in front of a bunch of witches, Sanderson," Simon says.

I am not in the mood to be teased by him.

"Yeah, that's none of your business," I say. I turn to Gillian. "So?"

"We need to explain a few things to you," she says.

Across the street, a guy dressed as Jesus is holding a two-sided sign that he keeps flipping. On one side it says, in big scrawled letters, *It's Not Too Late*, and on the other, *You Can Still Be Saved*. I wonder if this is an actual protestor, or just someone who has decided to dress as Jesus for Halloween.

"Pix was totally devastated when you left Ofira's the other night," Gillian says.

My heart sinks a little hearing this. But then I remember that Pix is not actually the person that I thought she was, the person I would have done anything for.

"I haven't heard anything from her," I say.

"Yeah, well, you said some pretty shitty things to her," Gillian says.

"You were always a champion in the ring, Sanderson," Simon says.

"I'm sorry," I say, turning to him, "why are you here, exactly?"

"Because you've got everything all wrong," Simon says,

suddenly serious. "I've been trying to tell you for a year, and you won't listen. And I'm sick of it. So now you're going to get yelled at."

Simon actually saying something real that's not couched in a joke is shocking enough to get me to shut up and listen.

"You're wrong about Chloe and Harrison," he says, "you're totally wrong about this town, and it sounds like you've got everything all wrong about your girlfriend and your witch club too."

"Pix lied to me," I say, my face turning red.

"Yeah, but she lied to you because you've got this complete block about what happened last Halloween," Gillian says, "and you think that everyone hates you because of it."

"Everyone does hate me," I say. "Did you see what people said online? It was months of abuse." I feel myself getting hot just thinking about this. They don't know what I went through, and I don't want to have to explain it to them.

"So you were the hot goss for like a minute," Simon says. "It sucks, but it's just people talking shit. You wait it out until they've moved on to the fact that Olivia was hooking up with the drama teacher."

"She was?" I say.

"Evidently like three girls were," Gillian says. "It's a big mess."

"The point is that people can talk shit all day," Simon says. "But everyone knows that Harrison is an asshole sleazebag whose entire life is going to be one long, empty, meaningless cry into the void."

"People know he's a monster, Eleanor," Gillian says. "He's

groped pretty much every girl who has ever walked past him.
And maybe like ten awful people thought it was fun to gossip
about you in a really mean way last year, but at the end of the
day, no one actually thinks that what happened to Chloe was
your fault."

I do not want to cry in this stupid alley on stupid Halloween about stupid Harrison, but I feel the tears coming.

"I just wish people knew the truth about everything," I say.
"But no one would believe me."

"Fuck it," Simon says. "Start telling the truth, Sanderson.
We'll believe you. I bet a lot of other people will too."

The man across the street flips his sign. This time he cries
out along with it, "You can be saved!" He is looking at me.

"There's another thing I need to tell you," Gillian says.
Her hand goes up to the chain around her neck in that anx-
ious way that I noticed before. "I know you really cared about
Chloe, but she wasn't the person that you thought she was."

"What does that mean?" I have never talked to anyone
other than my mom, Susan, and now Pix about Chloe. It feels
weird, like I am betraying her.

"Chloe collected people," she says. "Like little projects.
Pretty much a new one every year. And then she would drop
them when she got bored. You only met her two years ago,
so you hadn't seen it go down before. We've known her since
kindergarten, and it happened like clockwork."

I want to protest, to defend Chloe's good name, to insist
that what we had was real, but something keeps me from
doing it.

"She did it to Gillian in eighth grade," Simon says. "Picked her up in September, dressed her up all year, did the whole best friend routine, then dropped her in June."

Gillian gives a little nod to confirm that this is true.

"Luckily you had a really hunky guy there ready to pick up the pieces," Simon says to Gillian. Gillian rolls her eyes, but she gives him a trademark Gillian half smile.

My stomach sinks. Was I really just Chloe's school year project? Had I been that naïve?

"Why are you telling me all this?" I ask.

"Because you mixed up what was real and what wasn't," Gillian says. "Chloe was not who you thought she was. And Pix is exactly who you thought she was. She made a mistake, but she didn't mean to hurt you."

Across the street, the Jesus man has begun singing "Glory, glory, hallelujah" at the top of his lungs.

I feel like I am standing in the rubble of the Tower card with the broken pieces of my life scattered around my feet, and I have no idea what parts to save or how to put them back together again.

"But what am I supposed to do now?" I ask. "It's not like there's a way to fix this."

"You could come to Samhain tonight," Gillian says. "Give Pix the chance to apologize. Explain everything to her. Tell her how you're feeling."

"What the hell is Sow-when?" Simon asks, dragging out the word.

"Shut up, Simon," Gillian says.

I shake my head. "I can't imagine that anyone wants to see me there," I say. "I completely freaked out in front of everybody."

She shrugs. "You can only fix what you decide is worth fixing," she says. "But I think that when you find someone who is worth fighting for, worth it for real, you should fight for them."

"She knows this from experience," Simon says, jokingly grabbing her hand. "I was very difficult to catch."

She must spend half her day rolling her eyes at him.

"We'll let you get back to work," she says to me.

She pulls Simon out of the alley and back onto the crowded sidewalk.

"Just think about it, Eleanor," she calls back. "Remember that it takes a lot more than some big emotions to scare a bunch of witches."

Back inside the store, I push my way to the counter, where Susan is paying the pizza guy for the pie he has just delivered for us. He is wearing a vampire outfit, looking like the most stressed-out Dracula I have ever seen.

"You doing okay out there, Jeffrey?" Susan asks him, handing him a big tip.

Jeffrey just shakes his head. "Every year," he says, and leaves.

Susan looks at me. "You okay?" she asks.

"Yes?" I must not sound very convincing because she grabs my hand and pulls me behind the counter.

"You're not okay," she says.

"No," I say. "I guess not."

"What's wrong?"

I shake my head.

"Honestly, I don't even know where to begin."

"Try me."

I look around. "It's too complicated to explain in the middle of all this," I say, gesturing at the crowded store.

Susan looks at the browsing customers.

"Hey!" she shouts at them. A few turn around to look at her.

"Everybody out!" she says. "We're closed!"

No one moves until Susan starts literally herding people toward the door.

"Susan, you can't!" I insist. "It's Halloween!"

"Out out out!" She pushes the last werewolf out the door, locks it, and hangs up the *Closed* sign.

"What are you doing?" I ask, horrified.

She comes back to the counter.

"It's fine. I'll open up again in half an hour. This way we can eat our pizza in peace."

I look at Susan as she puts out two paper plates and piles them with enormous gooey pizza slices. An overwhelming urge to hug her comes over me. So I do it.

"Hey," she says, surprised. "What's that for?"

"Everything," I say.

She smiles and hugs me back.

"All right, start talking and/or eating, kid," she says, "before these monsters break down the door."

I spend the next half hour telling Susan about what happened with Pix, and she attempts to give me advice, but ends up mostly making self-deprecating remarks about her own failures in love. At one point she insists that we get Mom on video chat so the two of them can compete in giving me the worst advice they can possibly think of from their own lives.

"Did you try texting her 'where are you?' twenty times a day?" Susan asks. "I've heard people love that."

"Or did you propose on the third date, Eleanor?" Mom says. "That's the key to a healthy romance!"

I don't know what it is about this ridiculous night or my mom and sort-of-second-mom responding to my drama with pure silliness, but I am laughing so hard I almost pee in my pants. I can't remember the last time I laughed like this.

"Okay, in all seriousness," Susan says finally, wiping tears from her eyes from hysterically laughing. "What are you going to do, Romeo?"

"I don't know," I say, completely at a loss. I wish the two of them would really just tell me what to do.

"Listen," Mom says over the video chat, "there's no way to guarantee protection against a broken heart."

Susan raises a can of soda to toast that sentiment.

"But it sounds like Pix cares about you," Mom says. "And if you care about her, then maybe you owe it to yourself to see if you guys can work this out. If she's sorry and you're sorry, then maybe there can be a second chance here."

*Right. Second chance.*

*Pix was my second chance.*

"Here," Susan says. She grabs the display tarot deck from its spot on the counter. "Let the cards pick."

I look at the deck. Am I really ready to let a stack of cards determine the future of my life?

*What do you have to lose?*

I open the box and shuffle the deck. Put it on the counter and cut it into three piles, then put it back together. I take a deep breath and pick up the card on top.

And there he is. In all his stupid glory.

The Fool.

I start laughing.

"What is it?" Mom says.

I show her the card.

"It's the naïve joker who is about to blindly step off a cliff and hope that something catches him."

"Well, that sounds like a pretty good metaphor for love to me," Mom says, smiling.

I know that the coven was planning to start their Samhain procession at Ofira's house at seven. It is now seven twenty. If I go directly to the memorial, I can probably catch them when they arrive. It occurs to me that I might see a lot of other people that I would rather not see on this walk through town, so I grab a plastic kids' witch mask from a pile by the register before putting on my coat and heading out.

Susan unlocks the door for me and flips the closed sign back to open.

"You sure you'll be okay without me?" I ask her.

"Oh yeah. I'll just beat them off with a broom if I have to," she says. "Now go get your witch."

Outside, I pull the mask down over my face and start dodging through the crowd in the pedestrian mall. I realize that if I can get over my anxiety about the crowds and the people who I don't want to see, there actually is something kind of beautiful about how over the top everything is. I pass a family dressed as the Addams Family, complete with a baby wearing a mustache, and some dachshunds dressed like hot dogs. Even a team of giant dinosaurs running down the street doing high kicks is kind of glorious in its silliness.

And then the night becomes truly magical. As I'm moving along the edge of the crowd, I see it part suddenly in the middle to let something come through—a procession of seven figures wearing tall headdresses with long black veils and beautiful Victorian dresses. The two figures at the front hold lanterns to guide their way. A wind picks up the veils and flutters them behind as the group walks down the street.

It's the coven.

One of the figures is smaller than the others, and I realize that Ofira's sister, Lydia, has taken my place. I feel a sudden pang in my heart, as if I am a ghost watching my own funeral.

Even on a night with many surprising sights, the coven makes an impressive picture, moving down the street toward the memorial. I worry for a moment that someone is going to mess with them or make fun of them, but wherever they walk, the crowd moves out of their way, the normal level of noise dimming to a murmur.

Everyone else is just pretending tonight. They are the real thing.

I follow behind the procession, my plastic witch mask feeling too symbolic of the truth of this situation. I am the fake here. I don't fit in this picture.

But I keep walking.

The procession reaches the memorial, and the few people who were interested in looking at a tourist attraction that is basically stone benches on the biggest party night of the year quickly clear out. Tatiana and Ofira start setting some things up in the patch of grass in the middle of the memorial.

I stop across the street, suddenly doubting my decision to come. Even though Gillian thought it was a good idea, that doesn't mean that Pix actually wants to see me. And now here I am, once again going after someone who didn't ask for me to be here.

But then Pix looks over at me.

I take off the mask and wave. She lifts her black veil and waves back.

"Hi," I say.

She looks back at the girls, who are still setting up, then crosses the street to me. I see Gillian watching as she does.

"Hi," Pix says.

"I didn't know if I should come," I said.

"I'm glad you did."

"Really?"

She nods.

She looks amazing in a ruffled black Victorian dress and

long black gloves. Her headdress is made up of tangles of black yarn and flowers that flow down her back.

"I'm really sorry, Pix," I say. "I feel like I messed everything up."

She shakes her head.

"No, I'm sorry. It was my fault. I should have been honest with you," she says. "I was trying to protect you and, I don't know, make things better for you."

"I could have told you that would be impossible," I say, attempting a half smile.

"I'm learning," she says, "that sometimes I just need to let people go through things and understand that I might not be able to make it all better. That's hard for me. To know that I can't fix everything."

She looks down at the ground, and my heart aches thinking that I could ever have thought this person didn't really care about me. She cares too much. I'm not used to that kind of problem.

"Yeah, but you were right," I say. "I wouldn't have been able to be with all of you if I thought that you knew about what happened. I was so convinced that I was unlovable, I thought that I had to hide my entire history from you for you to want to be with me."

Pix shakes her head. "You're not unlovable, Eleanor. I love you."

I can feel the anxiety leaving my body, everything that I have been holding on to this past year. All my fears that no one would ever say those words to me again. That I didn't deserve them. And here is this perfect person saying them to me.

Well, not perfect. But isn't that part of it? Maybe we aren't supposed to be perfect. Even if we are witches, we are still human.

"I love you too," I say.

Pix smiles, a little smile to match my half smile. Maybe it's the other half? She takes my hand, and I feel the smooth silk of her glove.

"You forgive me?" she asks.

I look over at the coven, now congregating in a circle around the temporary altar that Ofira has set up. I feel a sudden surge of pride to be here with them, these girls who part the crowd when they walk down the street. Who don't seem to be afraid of anyone.

I have wasted so much time being afraid.

Less than fifty feet away is the place where the worst moment of my life happened—the thing that I have let define me for the past year. The moment when someone I loved got hurt, and I thought that making myself miserable would somehow make up for my mistakes.

"Of course I forgive you," I say to Pix. "You forgive me?"

She squeezes my hand tighter.

"Of course," she says.

And we both smile.

And I kiss her.

And suddenly Halloween isn't so bad after all.

*

Pix leads me over to where the girls are setting up the circle.

"Nice to see you, Eleanor," Ofira says when she sees me.

"Thank you for having me," I say. She continues to light the candles.

Spotting Gillian, I give her a goofy thumbs-up, and she nods in response. I know she and I will have more to talk about soon. There's so much that I still need to understand about what she has told me.

"Thank you," I say to her, meaning it in about a hundred ways.

"Glad you came," she says.

I join the circle with Pix, and when Lydia sees me she gets up and puts the headpiece on my head. I start to say, "No, really, that's okay," because the thing is so big I can barely balance it, but it is such a sweet gesture that I just spend the next thirty minutes trying to hold it steady on my head with one hand.

After the ceremony, we walk around to the different stone benches and present our offerings to the dead. Pix has brought mine with her, and I place my little bottles carefully down next to the names of the victims.

As we move from stone to stone, I feel a kind of shimmer in the air. Ofira says that tonight the veil between the living and the dead is at its thinnest, and I feel as close to magic as I have ever felt. It's not what everyone else thinks of Halloween—ghosts and hauntings and zombies. It's not something to be afraid of. It's just a part of this night that I think I have always felt, but never understood before. It's the promise of unseen forces. The feeling that anything is possible.

Since no one seems to mind our presence, and the streets around the memorial are now even more packed with people, we decide to stay and sit on the grass for a while after we have presented our offerings. Ivy lays out the food and drinks that she has prepared for us to ground ourselves after the circle, and soon this patch of grass is transformed into a decadent witchy picnic.

Lydia is helping Ivy set up, and I take off the giant headdress and bring it to her.

"I think it looks better on you," I say, handing it to her.

She looks up at me with big eyes.

"Oh, okay," she says. She puts it back on her head and looks like an amazing witchy child of the forest. It's the best costume of the night.

Pix gets some food, and she and I sit next to each other in the grass and eat pomegranate seeds and cheese and chocolate. I feel like I have never actually tasted any of these things before. I feel like some part of me has just woken up, and I had no idea that it had been asleep for so long.

I'm think this might be called feeling happy.

The coven is talking and laughing, and I move in closer to Pix and take her hand.

"Can I ask you something?" I say.

"Sure," Pix says.

"How did you find me? Like, I get that you decided you wanted to send me Ofira's book, but how did you know where to send it?"

"I had your name, and Susan's website lists you as an employee. You're not as hard to find as you think you are."

I laugh.

*Of course. Susan's stupid website.*

"And you just felt that I needed the tarot book?"

She nods.

"I know that I don't always have normal reasons for why I do things. Or reasons that will completely make sense to other people," she says. "I know that."

I shake my head. This part is my fault, making her feel like there is something wrong with her. When her witchy intuition is what I like best about her.

"I probably sounded just like your stupid ex that night," I say. "But I didn't mean those things."

"It's okay," she says. "You were upset. And I was the one who complicated everything by going into the store to make sure that you got the book. And then inviting you to the full moon circle. *And* getting a crush on you at the Witch House."

I know that I am blushing. She says these things so easily. I am still getting used to that.

"But what made you think that I wasn't a horrible person?" I ask her. "Anybody who knew about what happened last year thought I was a crazed stalker."

"Witches don't tend to automatically believe what crowds of people decide about others," she says.

*Ah, right.*

"The thing is," I say.

*The thing is what I don't want to say.*

"The reason why it's been so hard for me to deal with what

happened," I say, forcing the words out of my mouth, "is that a lot of what people were saying about me was kind of true."

She looks at me, that face that I remember from that first night on the boat. I need to say what I'm thinking before she just goes ahead and reads my mind.

"I was in love with Chloe," I say, "and I was jealous, and I was obsessively following her, and I kept making one wrong decision after another until they all just added up into catastrophe and someone got hurt. She was running away from Harrison that night when she fell, not me. But with all the rest of it . . . they weren't wrong about me, Pix."

She raises an eyebrow. "Maybe you made some mistakes," she says. "Maybe they were even really big ones. Maybe you have things to be sorry for. But you didn't hurt Chloe. You tried to help her."

I am overwhelmed with the enormousness of this feeling. As if Gillian and Simon opened the door to the possibility of a different reality, and now Pix is walking me through that door.

A tear falls down my cheek in spite of myself. Pix takes off her glove and wipes it away from my cheek with her thumb.

"You're allowed to be sad that she's not in your life anymore," she says, "and to feel bad that something terrible happened. And you're allowed to be angry at the people who were horrible to you. But that's not the whole story of your life. You don't have to hold on to that anymore."

I remember what Pix told me before about letting things go on this night, and I look over the stone wall to the Burying Point.

*I'm sorry.*

I say it to myself and to Chloe.

*And I forgive you.*

And then I let go. Of her, of that old version of me, of the sad, small life that I confined myself to, that I thought I deserved, all of it.

And something flies away from me, lifts off me.

And I am as close to free as I have ever felt.

As if on cue, the fireworks display starts in the distance, and the girls stand up to get a better view of the sky.

I take Pix's hand.

"So what is the story of my life now?" I ask.

She smiles and leans over and kisses me.

"Whatever you want it to be," she whispers in my ear.

Lydia is shrieking at the explosions, and the other girls are laughing like the cackling witches that we all are.

"It's beautiful!" Lydia declares.

Ofira raises a cup of sparkling cider in a toast.

"So mote it be," she says. "So it is."

# JUDGEMENT

Here, at nearly the end of our journey, we meet you, Judgement, asking us to decide—are we ready to level up? To devote ourselves to a higher purpose? To embrace all that is good in us and allow ourselves to be elevated into some high-vibe living? It is time to bring together our minds and our hearts to see the situation clearly. There is no more room for a false sense of self in this existence!

Judgement, you ask us to take true and honest stock of our lives and our selves, realizing that there may be much more beauty and goodness there than we ever allowed ourselves to see before. Our past wounds have been healed, and we are ready to step forward into the bright future.

# 20

"But why can't you just tell me what college I should go to?"

Simon is sitting across from me at the tiny folding table that Susan has set up by the bookshelf in the back of the store.

"That's not how this works, buddy," I say. "The cards just help you look at things in a new way. You still have to make your own decisions."

"Seems wrong," Simon says, examining the Celtic cross spread on the table between us.

"All right, fine," I say. I pull another card. "You should go to BU."

"Is that really what it says?"

"No, it says you need to focus and not worry about what other people will think about where you go to college." I hand him the card. It's the Five of Wands.

"*That's* what this says?"

"Yup."

Simon shakes his head.

"It seems a little too convenient that the tarot cards are saying the same thing that my witch girlfriend says."

"She probably pulled the same card," I say. "Anyway, I'm applying to BU."

"Aw, Sanderson, you're going to college?"

"If they'll have me."

"We could be roomies!" I am hoping that Simon is kidding when the kitchen timer that I set next to us on the shelf goes off. It's been an hour.

"Therapy's over," I say cheerfully.

"Must mean I'm cured! It's fifty for the reading?" Simon asks, getting out his phone.

I shake my head.

"First one's on the house," I say.

This is the first time I've seen Simon since Halloween. I wonder if he's hurting from the lack of my business. A free tarot reading is the least I can do.

"That's no way to make a profit, Sanderson," he says.

"Sometimes it's more fun to give magic away for free," I say. "Plus I still owe you for your intervention."

He looks at me questioningly.

"Halloween," I say. "You and Gillian."

"Oh, that," he says. He gets up and pulls on his jacket. "That was nothing. I love telling people they're wrong about their entire life view. Makes me feel all warm and mushy inside."

I smile. "Yeah, well, thank you," I say. "I needed to hear it."

"Anytime, Sanderson. I'm glad you're doing this tarot thing," he says as I gather up the cards. "You're good at it."

"Thanks," I say. "It makes me really happy."

Simon lets out a mocking laugh.

"Sanderson is *happy*?!"

He looks around as if he needs to share his disbelief with someone, but like most days in November, the store is completely empty besides us and Susan behind the counter.

"Did you hear that?" he calls out to Susan.

"I heard it," Susan says, smiling.

"Goodbye, Simon," I say.

"Oh, yeah, gotta go tell my mom a witch thinks I should go to BU." He walks to the door. "See ya!" It jingles shut behind him.

"He's a character," I say to Susan.

"Evidently," she says.

I look at my phone. Five beating-heart emojis from Pix and it's almost five o'clock.

"You can head out," Susan says. "You don't want to be late to your dinner."

"You sure?" I say.

"Yeah, I'll see you tomorrow at one for our feast."

"Just bring the turkey, Susan," I say, grabbing my coat and bag. "We've got sides and dessert covered."

"Yeah, yeah."

"I'm serious. You bring too much and then we have all these leftovers."

"Thanksgiving is all about the leftovers!" Susan insists.

I give her a hug. She hugs back too hard. This is our new thing.

"Can't . . . breathe . . . ," I joke.

She releases me.

"See you tomorrow, kiddo," she says.

Outside, it's already dark. The Halloween decorations were all down by November third. Now most of the stores have their Christmas decorations up. Salem will get the bump in business that most New England towns get in December from people looking to satisfy an appetite for classic Christmas Americana, but it won't be anything like October. Nothing is like October in Salem.

Collective Witch doesn't have traditional Christmas decorations up, but when I get there, Taryn is lining the windows in silver swirls of paint. Next to her, Ofira is setting up a display of many-colored candles. They both wave when they see me through the window, and I wave back and go inside.

"It's looking great," I say.

"I just hate that we can't go full Yule because it'll look too traditional," Taryn says. "Non-pagans stole all the best parts of our holiday and went mainstream with it."

"What about just some evergreen branches?" Ofira suggests. "Not a full tree."

"Maybe," Taryn says.

"Are you ready to go?" I ask Ofira.

"Yeah, let me grab my stuff."

She goes in the back and I look around the store. It's been newly stocked since the October decimation and there are in fact some new vagina vases proudly displayed next to some equally colorful vagina pillows. There is also now a stack of copies of Ofira's tarot book by the door with a little sign that says, *Free Magic – Please Take One.*

Ofira comes back with her stuff.

"You have to remind me to get one of those vagina vases for Susan for Christmas," I say.

"Does Susan need a vagina vase?"

"She's been asking for one for years," I say, laughing.

"I can get you the employee discount," Ofira says with a smirk.

We say goodbye to Taryn and Liz, and walk to where Ofira has parked her mom's car. She just got her license two weeks ago and she's only allowed to borrow it because we're only driving four miles.

"Does your family always do Thanksgiving dinner the night before?" I ask, getting into the car.

"It's an endless negotiation between my mom and my aunt," she says. "Tonight is our big family dinner, and then Dad does a feast just for us tomorrow."

We arrive at Pix's house in ten minutes. Ofira parks in front.

"You haven't been here before?" she asks.

I shake my head.

"Pix always comes over to my place," I say.

We get out of the car.

"So this is you meeting the in-laws?" Ofira says.

I make a face that I think means "sort of."

"My aunt and uncle are totally fine," she says. "They're just aggressively normal. But luckily we outnumber them."

We walk up to the door and ring the bell. Ofira looks me up and down while we wait for someone to answer. I have put on actual non-jean pants and I'm wearing a gray button-down shirt and a blue sweater.

"What?" I say.

"I just didn't know you owned clothes that aren't black."

"Okay," I say, rolling my eyes.

"And filled with holes."

I am about to punch Ofira in the arm to get her to stop when Pix opens the door. She's wearing the green dress she was wearing the day that we met.

"Hi!" she says.

Ofira kisses her on the cheek and walks into the foyer.

"Is my mother here?" she asks. "Has the drama begun?"

"Got here right before you," Pix says. "You're just in time."

"Wonderful."

Ofira hangs her coat on the coatrack and goes in.

I look at Pix.

"You said not to bring anything," I say, "but now I really feel like I should have brought something."

She smiles and puts her arms around me.

"You brought you," she says.

I can see her family bustling in the other room, setting the table and carrying plates of food.

Then she kisses me. Here where her family can see, where the neighbors can see, where the whole world can see. And the best part about it is that it doesn't feel out of the ordinary at all. It just feels like magic.

# THE WORLD

Well, here we are. After all that. There were times we really didn't think we would make it, weren't there? Times when we thought that our dreams were ridiculous, our desires destined to remain only in our heads. But it's been all about you, World, from the beginning. We are here to reckon with you, to make sense of you and ourselves. And there are so many times when we bump up against the complications and limitations of this concrete existence, of this planet-sized community of people. But each time we must simply take the next step in the journey, and then the next. And then at the end, you are here for us, World, not as a challenge, but as a gift.

Look at how amazing it is, the whole World stretched out in front of us.

You made it.

We made it together.

# ACKNOWLEDGMENTS

Thank you to my wildly supportive feedback-givers and sweet friends Annie McNamara and Lindsay Hockaday; to romance consultant and book doula Laura von Holt; to my tarot teachers, Bakara Wintner, Jeff Hinshaw, and all the Brooklyn Fools; and to my mental/emotional/spiritual witch guides, Aja Daashuur and Heidi Smith.

All the gratitude to my superstar agent, Brianne Johnson, and to my endlessly patient editor, Alessandra Balzer. At HarperCollins: huge thanks to Caitlin Johnson, Caitlin Lonning, Shannon Cox, Jackie Burke, Patty Rosati, Mimi Rankin, Katie Dutton, Andrea Pappenheimer, Kathy Faber, and Kerry Moynagh; to Sarah Nichole Kaufman and Jenna Stempel-Lobell for their gorgeous design work; and to Cynthia Paul for the beautiful cover illustration. And at HG Literary: a big thank-you to Soumeya Bendimerad Roberts and Ellen Goff.

To the Witch Ones for being the best band of witches anyone could ask for.

To my wife Amanda, to Mom and Dad, to Mike and Aaron—thank you for all the homes we have made together. It has made everything possible.